MW01688551

The Battered Man

For [illegible] +
[illegible]
with never
ending affection
M. [illegible]
Sep. 8. 96

The Battered Man

A Novel

Marion Andre

Mosaic Press
Oakville, ON. - Buffalo, N.Y.

Canadian Cataloguing in Publication Data

Andre, Marion
The battered man

ISBN 0-88962-596-4

I. Title

PS8551.N3595B3 1996 C813'.54 C95-933361-4
PR9199.3.A496B3 1996

Published by MOSAIC PRESS, P.O. Box 1032, Oakville, Ontario, L6J 5E9, Canada. Offices and warehouse at 1252 Speers Road, Units #1&2, Oakville, Ontario, L6L 5N9, Canada and Mosaic Press, 85 River Rock Drive, Suite 202, Buffalo, N.Y., 14207, USA.

Mosaic Press acknowledges the assistance of the Canada Council, the Ontario Arts Council and the Dept. of Canadian Heritage, Government of Canada, for their support of our publishing programme.

Cover illustration and book design by Susan Parker
Printed and bound in Canada
ISBN 0-88962-596-4

In Canada:
MOSAIC PRESS, 1252 Speers Road, Units #1&2, Oakville, Ontario, L6L 5N9, Canada. P.O. Box 1032, Oakville, Ontario, L6J 5E9
In the United States:
MOSAIC PRESS, 85 River Rock Drive, Suite 202, Buffalo, N.Y., 14207
In the UK and Western Europe:
DRAKE INTERNATIONAL SERVICES, Market House, Market Place, Deddington, Oxford. OX15 OSF

In Memory of My Beloved Family that was vanquished by the sentence of the holocaust.

Dedicated to my wife, Ina, whose love subdues my despair and allows me to capture the sunshine of joy.

The author gratefully
acknowledges the editorial work of
Neil MacVicar

Despair, despair
A river of menace
Despair, despair
the bitter ache of my
heart!

A joyous joy
Where is it? In
Heaven?

Despair, despair
My daily curse!
My life's most cruel
Bard!

CHAPTER ONE

It was Wednesday, August 13, 1991, when the cab carrying Anton Thomas, a university professor of theatre history, now retired, came to a halt on a corner a hundred meters or so away from the entrance gate of the Varsunian Institute of Psychiatry.

Varsunian was a Russian immigrant to Canada who made millions as a manufacturer of artillery and ammunition in the late twenties and early thirties. He died in a car accident and to the angry surprise of his family, his will made them citizens of minor financial importance. Seventy-five per cent of his fortune, including a huge piece of land in the centre of the city, was destined for the health needs of the local inhabitants. Upon the considered advice of the medical community, the Varsunian Institute of Psychiatry was born. Anton Thomas was on his way to see a specialist in psychotherapy, recommended to him by Herbert Hopkins, his family physician.

The driver, his foot on the brake and anxious to get clear of this place, was saying to his passenger: "I can't stop over there...." He pointed at the gate.

"The walk doesn't bother me." Anton didn't let him finish the sentence. "How much?"

The driver said: "Eight fifty." Anton took out ten dollars from the wallet which he kept in the inner pocket of his leather jacket, handed it to the man, waved off the change and stepped out. The first thing that struck him was a large graffiti on the white painted brick wall surrounding the lot where the Institute was situated. It read: "Nitwits paradise! You're welcome!" In response to what he saw, Anton murmured to himself softly in a singing fashion:

"Nitwit, pitwit, who gives a baloney!
As long as I'm well treated!
And my doctor's not a loony!"

In the last few months, for a reason he couldn't grasp, he was addicted to silly rhymes. He would speak to Henrietta, his wife, or to his adult children and suddenly, out of the blue, he would make a few dancing steps and blurt out a sentence or two in rhyme. Though people who heard it would often be amused and laugh, Anton was embarrassed by it. 'What the hell are you doing,' he would silently reprimand himself. 'Why are you behaving like a moron? Like a dimwitted child?'

Now he blasted himself out loud: "You're bullshitting again! You're to see a psychiatrist! You vowed to be rational! In control of your mind!"

He continued walking, avoiding the eyes of people who were passing by. He walked through the open, black iron gate, then stopped in the lane impressed by the sight of a guard, a heavy, swag-bellied fellow who was leaning against the wall beside the entrance door, puffing a cigarette.

'My God! That man is big,' Anton thought, snickering. 'I bet I would fit into his belly. Will my shrink look like him? So bloated? So dictatorial? Yes, that's how those who hold the chains to keep us subdued often look. And shrinks who want the truth, nothing but the truth have such a propensity. To remodel you, they coerce you to be a slave to their dictum. No matter how sloppy their view, they beat you to it. They make you swallow their fiction.'

Anton – his name when he arrived in Canada almost forty years ago but now called Tony by most people, including his wife – had a visceral resentment toward psychiatrists. It took a long while for his family doctor to convince him that such a 'hearing' would be useful.

"You're not tied to him forever," Dr. Hopkins was saying. "You can stop seeing him at your will. And he is a bright man. A world traveller. He is familiar with pre-war, post-war Europe as well as you are. He will listen."

But Anton had his own view about the situation. 'Whoever he is, I don't care. I'll go to see him but I will leave if I see that he nurtures a notion that he is a mental giant and I am a pygmy. I won't let him embarrass me. Or put me on my knees while he's trying to trick me.'

Anton, an impetuous man, was well read and well acquainted with the work of Freud and Jung. Their analytical output, published letters and the literature about them was neatly stacked in his study on a shelf of a bookcase behind his desk. There was a period of time in his life when he was strongly impressed by Freud's discoveries, their impact on medical science and of all things, on theatrical activity. Many stage directors he read about or knew were coaching their actors to examine the deeply embedded subconscious needs and desires of the characters they portrayed. Then Anton changed his mind and was hesitant to accept the total validity of psychoanalysis and its applicability to the conditions of the present day.

"The pressures of life we experience, the terror, the horror of some of our days on Earth must have an indelible effect on our psyche. It must shape it, transform it beyond what its shape was when we were babies. When we were formed by our mothers and fathers who took care of us when we were little children." That was his belief and favorite statement to his students.

Now, still standing in the lane and facing the building which sprawled widely just a few steps away, he thought: 'I hope that the doctor I'm going to see is not one of those who will try to entice me to dredge up illuminating incidents from my early life. My experiences as a child. They're buried, forgotten. The sack of my memory doesn't carry them anymore. It only holds the gravel of later days. The stones that I stumbled on when I was an adolescent. The rocks that hit me a while later breaking so many bones in my body. Marring my life!'

His left ear was ringing loudly. Familiar chills were going through his body.

He cursed himself. 'Damn it. You are in the clutches of that shake-up again. Your ear tells you you're ill. Your body tells you you're scared. Put yourself together. Get rid of this shit!'

He seemed gone for a moment, struck emotionally by the discomfort that penetrated his being. Then he regained his composure and suddenly questioned himself. 'What's his name? The doctor. What's his name?'

He shoved his hand into the pocket of his leather jacket where, he thought, he had tucked the note from Hopkins with the date of the appointment and the name of the psychiatrist he was to see. But that piece of paper wasn't there. Neither was it in the wallet which he pulled out from his inner pocket and hastily flipped through it.

"Damn it, I lost it!" He was whispering to himself, now in a frenzy. "I lost it! I lost it! I don't know who I'm going to see! What do I do now?"

He turned his head toward the man at the wall who was stomping out the remainder of his cigarette.

"I'm to see a doctor, but I forgot his name. It's my first visit here. I have an appointment but I lost the card with his name on it, and I don't know what to do. Could you help me to..."

The guardian at the entrance door, who was just about to go inside, responded with a giggle. "You want to be examined by a psycho. I mean a shrink, but you don't know his name? You must be really, eh, tired." He circled his index finger at his temples. Then, as if realizing his gesture was offensive, he swiftly changed gears. "It happens to all of us. It happens to me! Take the elevator to the ninth floor. The doctors up there, usually you start with them before other hands take care of you. They're friendly guys. They wipe your tears. But they make you talk. Oh, they surely make you talk. And you might have to wait in the hall for bruised souls as they call it, the waiting room, before the girl up there, she's hot, will let you see your man."

The guard glanced at his wrist watch, "it's 12 o'clock, lunch time. Our doctors need to fill their stomachs. And gossip. That is what they do while they have their lunches. They tell each other the funny parts of the secrets revealed to them by their patients. Share the dirt."

Following the prattling man's directions, Anton crossed the lobby and took the elevator to the ninth floor. Stepping out, he was now in the brightly lit, tightly enclosed hall for bruised souls. Chairs were next to two square, low tables littered by magazines – MacLean's, The New Yorker, Toronto Life – most of them in a messy state. Some were half opened and hanging over the edge, some badly stained by grease, some torn or scribbled upon. The receptionist was working in a cubby hole opposite the elevators.

Her area was enclosed by walls covered with gray broadloom, and a sliding, frosted glass window. The waiting room, contrary to what the guard said, was empty. Anton was alone in the room.

Before making his presence known to the woman behind the opened window – she didn't bother to lift her head when the door of the elevator slid open then closed with a clamor – Anton looked around. What struck him was the closeness of the space. The waiting room area was not only small but shut tightly. What lay behind seemed impenetrable. Two doors on the opposite side of the waiting room led to the doctors' offices. They were locked as he quickly noted when a skinny woman wearing silvery tight pants, a loose yellow blouse and high heeled shoes, a key in her hand, entered into the space from one side. She gave Anton a sharp, examining glance, then sped by, unlocked the other door and slid into the corridor behind it.

Anton thought, 'Who was that woman dressed up so seductively? A doctor? And was she scared of me? She flew by as if worried by my solitary presence. And why doesn't the receptionist lift her head to see what's happening in the waiting room. She keeps her head buried under the stack of papers. Isn't she paid to keep track of the motion in this place?'

Then there was a low hum in the air as if the air-conditioner was out of order. The overhead lights flickered and the elevator door slid open.

A weird looking man, tall in white overalls, his face pale white and encased by locks of long red hair, stepped into the room. His head slightly bent, he stared at Anton, then grinned and avoiding bumping into him, moved forward toward the door on the right. While unlocking it, he once again gave what seemed like a flirtatious smile to Anton, then disappeared.

Anton, immobile, his heart palpitating, his ear ringing, a shiver of anxiety tracking through his body, thought, 'What's all this? Those strange looking people whistling through and assessing me? This place, it's so filled with mystery. With suspicion. Do I want to be a part of it? Do I want...?'

Now, the crisp voice of the receptionist reverberated in the air. "Can I help you?" she said.

She was on her feet now, Anton could see her young, attractive face and the upper part of her body covered by a tight, slightly unbuttoned blouse, offering to his eyes a glimpse of the shape and the suntanned color of her breasts.

Anton approached the window and replied, "I'm to see a psychiatrist. I'm not certain of his name. I was recommended by..."

The receptionist interrupted: "Your name?"

"Anthony Thomas."

"The name of your doctor?" She was barely able to conceal her bored contempt.

"I just said," Anton stummered, "I forgot his name. I had it written on a card, but..."

"I was asking for the name of your family doctor," was her terse rebuttal. "The one who recommended that you pay us a visit."

Anton answered with a touch of smile this time. "Oh, I know what you mean. The name of my physician is Hopkins. Herbert Hopkins."

She leafed through some papers. "You're to see Dr. Gabriel Wright. He received the letter from Dr. Hopkins. And you called a few days ago." She waved the stack of papers that were in her hand.

"It's all here. Sit down. Dr. Wright will see you in a few minutes."

Anton, bowing his head, thanked her then he sat down on the closest chair, beside the wall of her office. Not really conscious of it, he took out a comb from the pocket of his jacket, passed it through his hair a few times, put it back where it belonged, then lifted his head, feeling that his action was observed. His alertness was justified. The receptionist's eyes were glued to his face.

She spoke, rather gently this time. "You look better now. Your hair's not tousled."

Anton smiled.

"May I ask you a question?"

"Go ahead," Anton answered, his eyes trying to read her face. She's spicy, that's for sure, he thought. But what does she want to know about me? What will she try to discover through her question?

"When you called for the appointment," she said, leaning over through the window, "you didn't give me your real name, and your voice was so gruff. You said," now she imitated him, "I'm a battered man."

"Did I?" Anton was surprised. "I surely didn't realize what I was saying. But there was a reason for it. My mind was elsewhere."

"Meaning?"

"I'm a writer," said Anton reluctantly, sitting straight, his hands wrapped together in the fashion of a preacher. "I was writing a short story. About a man whose life was battered."

"You're a writer," the young woman exclaimed. "Oh, how nice! Is your work published?"

"Yes, my works have been published. Or produced on stage."

How wonderful," she responded happily. "What about the story you were writing? The battered man. Who was he?"

"He was a friend of mine," Anton replied, more at ease now. "When I was young, the closest I ever had. When he was twenty-one, like me, he died. So when I was writing about him and at the same time, it crossed my mind that I should call to make an appointment with Dr. Wright, I wasn't here. I was far away talking to the man whose body was crushed by beating. And whose grave..."

He lifted his head, put his hands on his thighs and added softly: "I'm sorry for being a nuisance. But that is one of the reasons for my being here. Whether I like it or not, I too am a battered man. Alive but battered."

"That's so depressing," observed the receptionist. She was clearly affected by Anton's words. "Are all your stories so gloomy? I hope not. I was going to ask what library would have your works. I'd read them but not if I were frightened by them. Not if they make me cry. Life's hard as it is. In my free time, I want to laugh not cry."

"My stories are gloomy, yes," Anton replied. "They are all a reflection of atrocities that I witnessed in my life."

"Come on," the receptionist cried out. "Get rid of your burden. Spill it out. Once you do that, you will be fine. And the stuff you write will be funny. Not heart breaking. The way you look, I would never have thought..."

The ring of the telephone broke the conversation. The receptionist withdrew from the window and answered the phone with "Greta speaking." While she was talking, the man Anton had seen before, red curly haired, in white overalls appeared in the waiting room on his way to the elevator. Seeing Anton lingering in his chair, the man winked at him, offered him a grin which exposed missing teeth, and disappeared on his way down. By that time, the receptionist was done with her telephone call, and Anton, somewhat uneasy to reveal to her what was on his mind, said to her:

"Miss, would you be kind enough to tell me who that man is? The one who just stepped into the elevator. He waved to me, or rather winked. Showing me his missing teeth," he giggled a bit, "when smiling."

"I saw that," said the receptionist. "He's one of our specialists. Dr. Rolf Hoy."

A smile wrinkled her cheeks. Lowering her voice, she added: "His colleagues call him Dr. Hoipolloi. He stands for the common man. Hates the establishment. And he instinctively recognizes those who suffer."

At that moment, someone was tinkering with the locked door, trying to open it. The receptionist turned, stretched her neck to see what was happening in the corridor, instantly turned back and mumbled very softly:

"Dr. Wright. He always has trouble with the door. Good luck!"

She quickly withdrew into her cubby hole and shut the sliding window.

Anton hunched, the tension in his body rising, waited for the psychiatrist to make his entrance. Finally it happened. A man – medium sized, gray haired and paunchy – swung the door open with one hand. In his other was a large paper cup filled with coffee. He addressed Anton with a friendly smile "Mr. Battered Man?"

Anton replied: "Anthony Thomas. The Battered Man was a slip of my tongue. I apologize for it."

Dr. Wright answered with a tinge of humor. "We'll soon see whether there was any hidden meaning to that slip." Then beckoning with his finger, "Now, follow me."

Anton, his ear ringing badly now, crossed the threshold squeezing past his therapist who, once the patient was beside him, pulled the door shut. He did it awkwardly, standing sideways and making the motion too swiftly. His other arm trembled, a few drips of coffee landed on his jacket.

"Damn!" He took a handkerchief from a pocket of his pants, wiped out the wet spot with barely concealed annoyance. Then, regaining his composure, he addressed Anton, again jokingly, "I'm a coffee addict. I carry it with me all the time." Pointing at his jacket he added "This is the price I pay."

They walked silently down a long, narrow corridor with fluorescent lights in the ceiling. Many offices on both sides of the lane were open. The men and women who were sitting there were chatting, munching sandwiches or making phone calls. Clearly, as Anton decided, this was their off-duty period, the sacred lunch time.

But he could barely hear them. His ear was hissing badly. He was a bit wobbly on his feet and needed all the attention he could muster to stay in control of his body.

And he thought, 'These doctors, here, they're like us. They are made of the same weak stuff. Of the same shoddy material. They're prone to be bitten by the same diseases. How can they then handle the horror and pain that's in the hearts of their patients? How can they be neutral? Unaffected? How can they remain objective, capable of giving sound medical advice when, while examining us, they could be torn by their own tensions, their own log-jam of problems? And how can we, the patients, be open with them? How can we reveal to them, describe to them the turbulence of emotions that thunder within us? The swiftly passing images from the distant past that seem to be filled with mystery, with incoherence, and yet are capable of shaking up our brains, our bodies? How can we make them comprehend the experiences we go through? The so often occurring need to shatter the link that binds us to Earth? The need to be gone, to be free of hardship. Free of pain.'

Then he heard the voice of his doctor. "The last door on the right. Sit down. I'll be with you in a minute."

Anton, anxious now, entered into a medium-sized office cluttered with a large desk, two chairs, wooden shelves filled with medical books, cardboard boxes sitting on the floor brimming with files, and several clay pots each holding a sizeable, tough-looking and prickly cactus.

Seeing the cacti, Anton uttered a sigh of happy surprise. Those green, dangerous-looking dancing figures were his most favorite plants. At home, in his study, he had two. They were his precious possessions. He stepped closer to the half-opened window and once again was overtaken with excitement. The view ahead of him was simply magnificent. The sunny, blue sky with a few fluffy clouds on it was embracing a large part of the city with its high-rise towers like huge, sculpted candles rising up from the ground. At a distance, the lake was shining as if covered with sparkling metalic paint. The joy of absorbing this landscape was overwhelming.

Anton, the tremor in his body gone completely, the ringing in his ear abated to a low hum, sat down in a chair beside his doctor's desk, stretched out his legs, closed his eyes and was almost ready to have a snooze, when Dr. Wright barged into his office shutting, the door with a bang. His face was purple with anger, so it seemed to Anton who jumped up.

Dr. Wright rattled out: "Sorry, sorry, sorry! One of my patients was delivered to the hospital with severe psychotic symptoms. I had to see him. To hold his hand while he was given an injection..."

He stopped without finishing the sentence, and questioned himself: "Why am I saying all this? I'm getting run over."

He looked at his hands. "Where's my coffee?" Then he burst out laughing. "I forgot it. I left it in the ward. God Almighty, I'm getting addled."

He walked quickly away from his desk to a long, narrow table against the wall beside the entrance. The table was laden with old newspapers, empty cups and two electric coffee makers. One was one empty, the other was half full. The psychiatrist looked for a clean cup, filled it and turned to Anton. "Shall I fill one for you?"

When Anton declined the offer, Dr. Wright returned to his desk. The cup in his hand was filled to the brim. He took a sip, placed the cup at some distance from himself, sat down at his chair, wiped his mouth with his hand, and addressed Anton, seriously this time.

"Once again, I apologize for the delay. My work here has some low moments."

He opened a file on the desk and, for a moment, became lost in it. Only now did Anton glance at the desk. It held two telephones, a clock, some photographs, and notebooks. Then he noticed the sheet of white paper his psychiatrist was studying. He leaned forward and read what was heavily printed at the top: THE BATTERED MAN. A small question mark was just beside it. The rest of the page carried a tightly typed text. What it said was beyond Anton's reach. After a brief moment of silence, Dr. Wright said: "We may begin. Your name?"

"Anton Thomas."

"Hmm..," uttered Dr. Wright, looking at the file. "Dr. Hopkins calls you Tony."

"Anton is my original name." Irritation was tightening his stomach. "For some people though, I'm Tony."

Dr. Wright chuckled, "Tony Thomas. Sounds very British." He was mimicking the accent. "But British you're not. That's for sure. Where are you from? Russia, Hungary, Poland? And when did you come to Canada?"

"From Poland, yes. I arrived here in 1957. My mother came first, a few months earlier. We were invited to visit my mother's brother, a doctor in Montreal. His name was Isidor Liebling. He survived incarceration in a German concentration camp and was lucky enough to be granted permission to start a new life in Canada. Soon after we arrived, we applied for immigrant status and became citizens of this country," Anton answered with rapidly growing annoyance.

"But why are you asking me those questions? Dr. Hopkins knew all that. I have asked him to give you a short version of my life. I prepared it for him. I'm certain he passed it on to you."

"I'm checking. I'm checking" was Dr. Wright's defensive reply. "Secretaries who type those letters," he pointed to the sheet lying on his desk, "make errors. Mix up things. I want to be certain that the information I have is correct." Wringing his hands, he continued. "Would you mind if I called you Tony?"

"It's fine with me," said Anton cooly. "May I call you Gabriel or Gaby?"

"Well...," Dr. Wright hesitated.

"Don't worry. I won't," Anton responded, getting the message. "That would put our tete a tete out of balance," he smiled. "Am I right? So, I am Tony. And you are Dr. Wright."

"When we know each other better," the doctor said with a grin. "God willing, comfortable with each other, and the name Anton is well set in my mind..."

"God willing?" Anton cut him off, tersely. "There's a religious tinge to it and I am bothered by it. The way I see it, psychiatry has been formulated, developed by human minds and has nothing to do with celestial power. If in your view the outcome of your treatment depends on the will of the Almighty, whoever it is, then, from the very beginning, to put it mildly, we are blocked. No, alienated from each other! To be of help to me, you must instill me with a strong belief that you possess the necessary skills to deal effectively with my troubled self. You must convince me that you rely on your own wisdom and sensitivity, without expecting to be hopefully guided by the voice from the outerspace. To be effective, you must have faith in yourself. To be secure, I must have faith in you. I read enough about what you practice. I'm not a nitwit who's empty-headed about your profession."

He was getting even more tense now. Light vibrations intruded into his brain. Shivers, like butterflies, were tickling his groin. And he was thinking, 'Why am I barking at the man who is to help me? Who didn't say anything harmful to invite such a response? Do I want to block off his friendly invasion of me? Am I afraid he will squeeze out of me the causes of the turbulence that's operating within me? The juices of my pain? The rotten secrets of my existence?'

He was brought back into reality by Dr. Wright's words that breached the silence. He said lightly: "Tony, a short temper, is this your trait? Was that always an ingredient of your personality? No, don't answer. We will talk about it some other time. When your mood is better, and," he pointed at the clock on his desk, "we'll be less pressed. But let me say, though you sounded irritable, what you have stated is not irrelevant. I didn't expect you would so strongly react to my manner of speaking. God willing is a phrase I use quite often but, if I confused you, I apologize for it. What struck me though was how well your brain works. It is not dulled by your discomforts. It works. And when you stopped speaking, you were inside yourself, puzzled by your irritability. Right? Your mind is questioning your emotions. Good sign! Good sign! What's your profession?"

"Is or was? Before I retired, no, before I quit my job, I taught European Theatre History with particular emphasis on how it developed and progressed in the Slavic countries like Russia or Poland. I taught at York University. I was also a playwright. I wrote plays, documentaries for the CBC. I had my literary work published."

"And now? "Do you still write?"

"Yes, I do. Or rather I did," Anton said. "My novel was published recently. And I was writing quite a bit before I fell ill. That's one of the reasons I am here. I..."

Dr. Wright interrupted him: "We will discuss that subject later. Are you married?"

"Yes, I am."

"Her name is Henrietta." The therapist was reading from the note.

"Yes."

"Have you been together for a long time?"

"Yes," Anton nodded with a smile. "For twenty years. Even more than that. We met in Montreal where I worked at McGill University. Henrietta and I bumped into each other at a reception relating to the construction of the Jewish Cultural Centre. A few years later we decided to leave the city and moved to Toronto."

"Do you always call her that? Henrietta?" He enunciated the name carefully.

"When I'm cool with her. No, when the talk is prosaic." Anton stumbled a bit, "I call her Henrietta."

"And when the talk is poetic?"

"I call her Henriushka. Or sometimes...babushka."

"What does it mean?"

"It means granny in Russian. Henrietta's grandparents on her father's side came to Canada from Russia. After the First World War. From Odessa. Her grandmother used to call her Henriushka. In response, Henrietta, she was a small child then, called her Babushka."

"Why would you then..." Dr. Wright started the sentence with puzzlement in his voice.

Anton cut him off with a smile. "Make her feel aged? It has nothing to do with Henrietta's age. When I call her that, the sound of it is so soft. So caressing. Incidentally," he quickly added, "her mother's family immigrated from Poland to England before the First World War. They lived in London, in a low income district. Henrietta's grandfather was a tailor. Then, after his sudden death – he was a sick man for a long while– his wife and her young daughter, Noreen, immigrated to Montreal. This is where Noreen met Lou Dobin, her husband to be and eventually conceived Henrietta. And her sister Carole. And Peter, her brother. And moved from poverty to riches becoming, with her husband, a revered member of the Jewish Community. They are both deceased now and I often think that I should examine their past and write about them. But that's another story."

After making some notes, Dr. Wright asked, "How would you describe your spouse?"

"She is a very attractive woman in her late fifties. In her younger days, she was a dancer. Now she studies history. She is a weaver. And attends to the needs of impoverished people."

"In what way?"

"Some years ago, I was still teaching and in good health, she and a female friend were co-founders of an organization that supported a group of volunteers who collected and delivered perishable foods to the hungry. Who in fact were on the road to starvation. And still are. The early days of A Slice of Bread is Not Enough, that's what that service is called, were very hard. Most of the proprietors of stores they approached, vehemently denied that there was such a thing as a surplus of food. They shamelessly concealed the fact that on a weekly basis, the unsold, still edible items were dumped in landfill sites. But now A Slice of Bread is Not Enough is a solidly established charitable organization, strongly supported by the municipal and Metro governments and hands out 100,000 pounds of food each month. Not bad, don't you think?"

Dr. Wright nodded his approval. "Is your wife still participating in that work? Is she involved on a daily basis?"

"No," Anton replied. "After more than three years of hard, purely volunteer labor, she and her friend stepped down. They were exhausted and," he paused, "I was hit by my disease. But now, she is busy with something else," he quickly added. "She works as a counsellor at a shelter for abused women. She spends three or four days a week trying to help those women recover from emotional collapse. And to learn how to re-enter the normal world. Whatever that means," Anton sneered. "The way I see it, the air of normalcy does not flow around us any more. What we inhale is the stench of challenge, bombast, competition, unhappiness and fury. What we miss is softness. Tranquility. Or to put it less dramatically, the road that we walk on, for one reason or another, is disastrously damaged. We have pumped big holes in it and we slide into them with brutal consistence. We...."

"Do our best to cover those holes," Dr. Wright interrupted. "But this task is not easily attainable. And that is why people like your wife deserve a lot of respect."

Anton cut him off. "That's for sure. In our society they are unique. The law of the land is care for yourself. It's up to you to stand on your feet or fall on your face. Which way you will go? It is your choice. That rotten philosophy blindly dismisses the fact that human life is influenced by many factors, many of them controlled, manipulated by other people. One person's choice is often in conflict with other people's choice! To be a loser for a variety of reasons is a part of human existence. So knowing that, and facing the loser, we must suppress, diminish their suffering. By helping them whoever they are. That's my view. I have stuck to it all my life and I'm happy to say that Henrietta is on that side too. Though her youth is gone, she rejects the state of passivity. She is compelled to be active..."

"Good for her," Dr. Wright interrupted, clapping his hands. "To stay on top of life, one needs to be occupied. Particularly when one is over fifty. And what better activity than the one she pursues. Do you get along?"

"Better than most married people I know," Anton answered spontaneously. "But occasionally we have our differences."

"Isn't that a natural condition in all human relations?" Dr. Wright smiled slightly. "Those differences, how serious are they? Do they affect the daily routine of your life?"

Anton was hesitant. "Yes, and no. Sometimes her demands are unreasonable. I mean, she has serious difficulty coping with the state I am in. She would like me to be as I used to be. Inflated with energy. Having the physical and emotional strengths to be busy throughout the day and late into the night. She craves to be engaged in a variety of activities; meeting with people, going to the theatre, movies, restaurants. Unfortunately that type of life which I used to love has no meaning for me now. Or to put it more clearly, I'm unable to absorb it. And this is what Henrietta cannot comprehend. That going out at night, darkness .... it lowers my spirit. It turns me into a..."

He stopped talking as if troubled by what he was going to utter. After a few seconds of silence, Dr. Wright encouraged him to continue.

"Please finish your sentence. Let your thoughts flow. Freely."

"When the sun vanishes, I feel morose. Dark inside. Vociferously aware of my shaky state. And that condition is increased by Henrietta's need to handle everything on her terms. Anton, do this! Anton, do that! And when I do not comply with her wish she is incensed. Why don't you vacuum your room? Why don't you get rid of the dust on your desk? On your bookshelves? Why don't you take your dirty shirts and pants to the cleaners? For God's sake, do something! Instead of staring at the tree through the window! Wake up! Wake up! Those constant reprimands overwhelm me. And with her new charitable work, she's so busy. She leaves the house in the morning and she's gone for most of the day. She..."

While he was expelling his dissatisfaction relating to his wife, his inner voice was contesting his vocally expressed grievances. With his eyes diverted to his lap he chided himself.

'Everything on her terms? When you want to go downtown, to your barber, you could take the subway. It would surely make her life easier. What happens? She stops her weaving and drives you there. And waits for you until you're done. So that you do not choke with fear when you ride in a subway car. Anxious that you'll have an attack of nausea and that you will be at the mercy of strangers. Or that you will faint on the sidewalk and somebody will rob you, then another somebody will pull you by your feet to the side so that you don't muck up the traffic of the pedestrians. When Henrietta asks you to make a decision about something, are you prepared to accept the challenge? No. Even if she pleads with you to step in, what's your reply? Do what you want. My brain is not working too well. So you make the decision. And good or bad I'll go along with it. So it is you who is mushy. It is you who is making her pushy. So why are you speaking of her so fiercely? Straying from the truth? Yes, Henrietta harasses you. But not because she enjoys it. She is the way she is because she is scared. Emotionally squeezed by your lame condition. Blame yourself, not her. Stand straight ...'

Dr. Wright was observing Anton closely and was aware that his patient was going through severe inner turmoil. To stop it, he intervened.

"I'd like to hear more about the tension between you and your wife. But not now. Think about it so that when the subject comes up, you're prepared to focus on what bothers you most. Let us not skid on the edges of those differences. You have children, right?

"Yes".

"How many?"

"Four. Two are from Henrietta's previous marriage. Two are..."

"From yours." Dr. Wright finished Anton's sentence. He turned the page of the papers beside him and continued. "You were married before, twice. And those children are from your previous spouses. Correct?"

"Yes," Anton responded curtly.

"Who were they, those previous wives of yours?"

For a moment Anton was silent. Turbulence entered into his head and the image of his first wife appeared to him. She was spread out on a sandy beach, slim, dark haired, tanned, with a happy smile on her face, facing the sun. Then another face and figure appeared, blotting out the other. That female stood on a street, beside an oak tree. She was also quite tall, slim, her dark hair tightly trimmed, a quizzical, unfriendly expression was imprinted on her face. This image also dissolved rapidly.

Then Anton replied. "The first one was a Dutch woman. Her name was Tina. I married her in 1949. I lived in Holland then. I was the Second Secretary of the Polish Legation in charge of public affairs. The youngest diplomat in Europe at that time," he added with a sarcastic grin. "We took our marital vows just before I was recalled. This change in my career happened most unexpectedly so, for a few years, she lived with me in Warsaw. But our marriage, happy as it was for a while, didn't last long. For political reasons, I lost my job at the Ministry. Earning a living was a complicated matter. My mother who lived with us and worked in a pharmacy supplied us with our food. I was shaken by it all and..."

He stopped speaking, took a deep breath, then continued. "A while later, she left me for another man. We had a son."

"Sad story," said Dr. Wright. He made a note on his pad then queried, "And your next spouse?"

"Her name was Catherine. I married her here. In Canada. That marriage also didn't last long. She," he paused, "was as cold as ice. Couldn't respond to the stream of passion that was the governing substance of my body. And my heart. We parted company a few years after we married. We had a son. She let me take care of him. I brought him up. With Henrietta. I wedded her," he smiled, "a few years after the dissolution of my previous marriage. But we had known one another longer than that. We were lovers before we made our vows. In fact, it was she who was a real mother to Catherine's son. And mine."

"But you and Henrietta did not produce an offspring. Was there a reason for that?"

"Yes," Anton responded hesitantly, "there was. When Henrietta and I got together, our children were quite small. Taking care of them wasn't easy. For her daughter and her son, I was a stranger who took over their lives. The same applied to my boys. They were quite shaken up by Henrietta's entry into their lives. The weight of that burden was quite heavy. We didn't want to increase it by having another child."

"Their names? No, here they are," said Dr. Wright, checking the typewritten page. "Greg, Adrian, your boys. Nina, Paul, Henrietta's crop," he smiled. "I can imagine how hard it was for you both to create a new household for the kids. To balance the differences..." Then he added: "Nina. A Russian name."

"Yes. As I told you my wife's family came to Canada from Russia. At the end of the First World War. At that time, I'm sure you know, quite a number of Eastern European immigrants arrived on this continent. They were hard working mechanicals," he chuckled, "not laymen. Shrewd businessmen. They busted, no, boosted that's what I want to say, boosted the entrepreneurial spirit in Canada."

"Indeed," nodded Dr. Wright. "Tell me about them. No, not about your wife's family but about your children. About all of them. About those who," he smiled, "belong to you and about those who are your wife's offspring."

"Oh, my God," Anton exclaimed. "It will take hours for me to sketch their picture. They are young adults and very complex human beings. They..."

"What I need now," Dr. Wright interrupted his patient, "is a brief synopsis of their lives. How old they are? Where do they live? What do they do to earn their living?."

"I see," Anton replied. "Though the subject is voluminous I'll do my best to be brief. My children, as I have told you, there are four of them. Gregory, the oldest, I call him Greg, is forty. No, forty-one. Divorced twice and the father of two children. He lives in Quebec with a French Canadian woman whose name is France. A charming lady. He is entranced with her."

"What does he do for a living?"

"He heads a department of a public relations company that does promotional campaigns on a national level. He's completely bilingual and is doing well. Right now. For a reason I don't quite follow, companies that he worked for before, collapsed. One of them was his own. It went bankrupt. So, from time to time, he's in trouble and needs my financial help to stay afloat. Nevertheless he is very busy. I don't see him very often. But he talks to me over the phone frequently. He cares for me and it helps a lot. Though there were days..." he paused, then said, "so, that's Greg.

Adrian is younger. The son of my second spouse. He's thirty, a very bright young man. A scholar. He received his B.A. at the University of Toronto then went to the United States to continue his studies, and to get his Ph.D. which he did at Yale. He teaches there now and he is highly regarded by his students and his colleagues. He also travels a lot. Spends many months in Europe. Most of it in Paris. Since he left Canada to study in the U.S., I see him rarely. For two, three days a year. No more than that. In other words, he is very self absorbed and quite absent from my life. There is emotional tightness about him that is puzzling."

He paused, concentrating on what he was saying, then continued, "That is puzzling and strangulating. And as I have very special feelings for him, when in pain, I question myself. Was the split between me and his mother the cause of the distance between him and me? Or is he the victim of his intellectual prowess that rewards him well but also seems to negate the need for common emotional bonds?

There is no scent of emotionality in his approach to life. So it seems. Rationality, cold-blooded rationality governs him. So I think am I the culprit of his mental process that is," he smiled lightly, "sharp but not winsome?

Whatever the reason, it makes me...suffer. Yes, this matter haunts me."

Anton paused again then added: "Henrietta shares my feelings. As I mentioned before, she cared for him since he was eight years old. In fact, she brought him up. So we are bewildered that our relationship with him is so lopsided. And a cause of a lot of pain."

He stopped talking. His eyes were rivetted to the desk of the psychiatrist. There was an ache-filled expression on his face. Dr. Wright broke the silence.

"I'd like to hear more about that at a later date. About your relationship with your sons, particularly with Adrian. Now," a smile appeared on his lips, "please give me a brief resume of Nina and ..."

"Paul." Anton was at ease again. The discomfort had gone.

"Nina," he said, "is thirty-four years old. Single. A hard working young woman and very much on her own. I mean, alone. To my understanding unable to establish a long-term relationship with a man. Why? I don't know. She surely is attractive but does not have much confidence in herself. She is suspicious of people, of men, in particular. She...sort of expects to be humiliated. And she's fearful of it. So when she assumes that she's under attack she bites back! And sustains the animosity for quite awhile. She's now unemployed. She was the administrator of a dance company that travelled across the country. Now the company is in financial trouble, is about to go bust and Nina was let go. She's on the lookout for new employment. To be without work increases her self doubt. I'm fond of her. I understand her discomfort. I so much wish she wasn't under such stress."

Dr. Wright made a note on the pad that was beside Anton's file and said "And Paul?"

Anton's face brightened instantly. "That's another story," he said. "He's thirty, bright, brassy and very busy. Doing his CBC propaganda. That's what he does. Promotes the various programs of the CBC. Radio, TV, and visits bars. His life is a happy combination of hard work and...stars."

"Stars? I'm not sure I understand..."

"The women he meets. As he describes them, they're all tall, long-legged, long-haired and bright. He has a lot of fun with them as long as there's no light."

"Meaning?"

Anton answered, pretending to be serious. "In the morning, for Paul, those women...fade. He's too keen to rush to work, and not keen enough to be entangled with a maid."

He burst out laughing but Dr. Wright only slightly shared his amusement. Again he wrote something on his pad, then said "One more question." His head now was on an angle, somewhat turned down, yet his eyes were tightly focused on his patient's face "What's your religious affiliation?"

Anton, startled by the question, shook his head. Then replied: "I have none."

"You have none?" Dr. Wright repeated Anton's words. There was a tinge of surprise in his voice.

"Yes," Anton replied smiling lightly. "After what I saw and experienced...but perhaps I do pay a penalty for that. My Meniere's disease. ."

Dr. Wright cut him off. "You're a Jew, aren't you?"

"Yes, I am."

"A Jew and an atheist. An unusual configuration. I thought..."

"Not unusual for people who lived where I was during the war," Anton interrupted him. "Who experienced what I did. Persecution on a scale that is beyond the comprehension of people who didn't go through it. The loss of almost all members of the family. Brutal material deprivation. But I'm not an atheist. I'm an agnostic. I happen to believe that the human mind is too weak, incompetent to comprehend with certainty the mystery of the creation of the Universe. To state with definitiveness that the Ultimate Power exists. And has the final say about our lives. I have my doubts about it. But, I admit that, as bright as I am," he said this with a self-depreciating smile, "I'm not bright enough to be certain about my view. Also as Johannine Gospel states, 'The Jews cannot know God, since God is only known through Christ', and therefore..."

"When were you born? And where?" Dr. Wright now seemed somewhat curt. There was a frown on his forehead and perceptible coldness in his eyes.

"I was born in 1921. But where..." - Anton answered clenching his fingers, "that is one of my problems. I don't know where I was born. For a long time, I thought..."

"You don't know where you were born?" There was a hint of puzzlement in the psychiatrist's voice. "What's the meaning of that? The date and the place of your birth are surely stated on your birth certificate. How is it..."

What reached Anton was the quizzical tone of the doctor's statement, but not the gist of the query. He was feeling dizzy. The face of his interrogator while he was looking at him was making slow, then speeding circulatory rounds. So was the framed document on the wall when Anton turned his head to it; it was Dr. Wright's award for his twenty-five years of service to the Institute. And then an image burst out in his mind. He saw a large garden enclosed by fir trees and high bushes, filled with flowers in late summer bloom, red roses, begonias, gladioli, petunias, all rising to the sunny, blue sky, opened up, shining and making an ineluctable statement through their shapes and their colours.

His mother, a young, casually dressed woman, medium height, slim, dark haired, dark eyed, a gentle smile on her rouged lips, was there watching two female servants in peasant clothes. One was on her knees cleaning the flower bed filled with pansies, the other was trimming some rose bushes.

Then he heard his mother's voice: "Don't worry, son" – she was whispering – "we will get our visas. It will be easier than you think. The Canadian consul told me so, because you were born in France. Yes, son, you were born in France. Not in Poland. For a reason hard to explain, your father didn't want you to know that you came to life outside of the Polish borders. He and I made love in Vienna where we lived and studied as you know, before we were married. And when my belly started to get paunchy" – Anton in his dream saw her smiling – "we departed to France. Where a few months later you left my body. Then we returned to Poland where your father started to practice his profession. And I was taking care of you. Until..."

He waved his hand in front of his face, thinking 'How could I combine those two things? The garden, the servants, the touchstones of my childhood and then the talk with my mother which happened after the war ended, soon after we learned which camp was the last refuge for my father. Is my memory playing a trick on me? Is it so muddled? So...untrustworthy?'

The image, as suddenly as it appeared, was gone. So was the vibration in Anton's head. Now he could clearly see Dr. Wright's face.

The doctor's eyes concentrated on him and unmistakably carried a message of concern, of anxiety. Recognizing that Anton was with him again, he asked "Are you alright? Should I worry?"

His expression of concern was sincere, there was no doubt about it. Anton instantly felt relieved. And grateful. 'Compassion is a part of that man's character,' he thought. 'A most helpful trait. Maybe what will develop between him and me is a special kind of linkage. A trust, an evolving relationship leading to my recovery. Some kind of friendship.'

He replied: "No, no, don't worry. I'm fine. I had an attack of dizziness. It comes and goes all the time. Dr. Hopkins must have written to you about it. Meniere's disease. One of the reasons for my battered state.

"I'm in good company," he added, his voice had a bitterness to it. "Van Gogh. There was quite a bit written about it recently."

"Yes, I did read it," the therapist nodded. "It seems he had gone through real hell. But don't follow his example," he grinned. "Don't cut off your ear! If you need to imitate him, buy yourself a paint brush. And paint."

They both chuckled then Dr. Wright, became serious again. "The question I asked you, we will come back to it some other time. Henrietta, is she Jewish?"

"Yes, she is."

"So are her children, right?"

The doctor received a silent answer from Anton who only nodded his head affirmatively. Then Dr. Wright came up with a statement.

"Your own children, I assume that they're Jewish. Were they brought up in the Jewish tradition?"

Anton felt anger rising in his chest. He wanted to bark. 'What business is it of yours to ask me that question? What does it have to do with me? With my emotional disease!' But he didn't. He forced himself to give a calm reply.

"No they were not. The two women I was married to in my previous life," he grinned lightly, "before I found Henrietta, were Christian. I'm a Jew but as I've told you, I am an agnostic. My ex-wives knew that and they accepted that our sons would be brought up without religious affiliation. They're neither Jewish, nor Catholic. They are..."

"I see. I see," Dr. Wright stopped him. "My question was off the track and I apologize for it. I presumed that your previous spouses were of Semitic descent and, for that reason, I assumed your sons were Jewish. But are they aware of your descent? Do they know that you are Jewish?"

"Of course they know," Anton's replied. "And they're neither shaken or shocked by it. On social terms, they are inclined to lean toward friendliness and compassion, instead of flexing the muscles of narrow, arbitrary judgements. Insensitive perceptions. They are..."

"I see. I see." Dr. Wright interrupted him again but most gently this time. "The subject you raised, no, I raised, is temporarily out of order. Out of our tangle," he smiled.

"We'll get back to it one day – providing you'll be disposed to do so. But now I would like to hear more about your past. It would help," he smiled, "if I knew you better.

"Your parents." He looked at the file. "Milo and Rosa, right? Born in Poland? What did your father do for a living?"

"Those were their first names, yes," Anton replied. "Or to be exact, my father's name was Emil. But my mother and his friends called him Milo. They were born in Poland. In the part of Poland that, at the time they came to life, belonged to the Austro-

Hungarian Empire. I'm sure you have heard of it," he smiled. "It seems like a joke now, but there were days, when..."

"When what?" queried Dr. Wright.

"When emperors ruled the world. Dissected it into their domains My fadre used to say, 'During those days we were pawns on a checkerboard. The bearded kings were the players of the game.'"

Dr. Wright intervened. "Did you say fadre?"

"My mother often called him Fadre," Anton replied. "And he called her Madre. They travelled a lot. Spent some time in Italy. And had fondness for Latins. So once they returned from their trip, some Latin words," he smiled, "entered into their language. My fadre loved to do that. He loved playing with words. Reshaping them. So..."

Dr. Wright cut Anton off. "Could we go back to the roots of your family? Tell me more about your father. About his family."

"My father's father was a landowner. His father was a rabbi. So I think. I knew him very briefly. I must have been two or three years old when he died."

"So you think? What does that mean? Are you suggesting that the members of your family never chatted about your great grandfather?"

"Not as I recall," Anton replied cautiously, as if treading on ground filled with explosives. "My father was quite impatient with religious rituals. He did not approve of religious orthodoxy that showed contempt for Jewish people who were not prone to follow the religious precepts of the Chosen People," he smiled, sharing his father's derision for that notion.

Which created a thick wall of isolation from non-Jewish people who were not antisemitic but deeply religious. He stood for assimilation. Not for a chosen separation. A position that I think was the mode of living of Mayer Melenbaum. My great grandfather. And of his predecessor, my great, great grandfather who supposedly was also a rabbi. And of all those who were before him. My ancestors, so I was told, came to Poland at the end of the 15th century – after the Inquisition expelled them from Spain. For more than 400 years, they lived in the same corner of the country, trading and working with the local population. Yet on every other level, they were separated from it completely. Mostly of their own volition. As my father used to say, 'because of their superiority complex'." Anton smiled ironically, "'instilled in them by their religious phantasmagoria'. My father detested those who cultivated the idea of the chosen people. And therefore..."

He shrugged his shoulders and stopped speaking.

"I see. I see," said Dr. Wright when he realized that it was all Anton was prepared to say on that subject. He made some notes on his pad, slurped his coffee, coughed as if the liquid went down the wrong way, apologized, and asked Anton to release more information about his family.

"Let's concentrate on your father," he said. "And your mother. I would like to have some understanding of your life when you were a child. Your parents, how did they meet? How did they get together?"

"By good luck," Anton answered. He was silent for a moment, then repeated, "By real good luck. As I've said before, my grandfather was a landowner. Rich enough to send his son to study medicine in Vienna. That is where my father and my mother found each other. They met in a cafeteria lining up for lunch. She was at the same university. In the first year of her pharmaceutical studies. A few days later, they met again and they fell in love. The funny thing was, she was born and lived in a city that was a short distance away from the town where my father lived as a youngster. He knew that city – it was called Tarnopol . He occasionally visited it, accompanying his father on business trips to see various merchants, among them Chaim Liebling, my mother's father. He was a wholesale trader of agricultural products; grain and poppy seeds were the main sources of his good income. His warehouse was next to the house where he lived with his wife and two children, but my father never bumped into Rosa." Anton paused. "The name fitted her well. When she looked at you and smiled, she seemed like a delicate flower. A blooming rose."

"You were fond of your mother," Dr. Wright said softly. "You speak of her with such gentle affection."

"I loved her very much," Anton replied. "The good things that are in me I inherited from her. She was the gentlest person I have ever known. And caring. Not only for my sister and me, but for all those who tasted misery. She taught me that there's nothing more important than compassion. She showed me what she meant by it. And I try to live according to that principle."

"Are you saying that the good things that are in you came only from your mother? None of them were the offerings," Dr. Wright smiled lightly, "of your father?"

After a prolonged pause Anton replied, "I wish I could answer that question. But I can't. My father...my memory of him is covered by such a heavy mist that I can't be objective about him. He rarely appears in my mind. And when he does," he paused, tears welling in his eyes, "it's a memory of how harshly he treated me. When I was a little boy, he often used his belt to teach me the rules of obedience. Naughty as I was, I don't think I deserved to be treated," his lips curved now by a bitter smile, "so roughly. I was afraid of him. But I loved him nevertheless. And there was nothing I missed more than his absence from my life. I would have better understood many things had he stayed alive. I was only twenty-one years old when I saw him for the last time. Too early in my life to be without a father. The emptiness his death has left me with..." Anton stopped for a moment, clenched his hands, bowed his head, then slowly raised it and continued. "There were days when I thought, I won't survive it! I wanted to," he chortled bitterly, "sink. Sink!"

Dr. Wright again made a note on his pad. This time what he wrote was much longer than what he had penned before. Then he addressed Anton.

"You were another man when you talked about your mother. What you have said, moved me. I don't often say that to my patients. But in this case, I think you should know. I certainly would like to hear more about how she had molded your character. But now let's go back to Vienna. You said that your father studied medicine. But," he pointed to the file, "it says here, in the short version of your life, as you call it, a document that you prepared yourself, that your father was a pharmacist. Not a doctor. What's correct?"

"When he met my mother," Anton replied with some tension in his voice, "he abandoned his medical training and switched to courses my mother was taking. To be able to leave the University at the same time as she did. To become a doctor, he would have been obliged to stay at school for another two or three years beyond the time she needed to complete her studies. If he continued his medical training and she was done with hers, they would have been separated. She would have left Vienna. Returned to her family. He didn't want that to happen. He wanted to marry her. And start a family."

"When did that all take place? The Austro-Hungarian Empire collapsed at the end of the First World War. So..."

"While the war was still on, my parents were enrolled at Vienna University," said Anton. "Two years after the war ended, they had their diplomas in their hands. My mother's rating was quite good. My father's was superb. It was typical of him. Where sharp intellect was required, he was superior to very many people. Where..."

He stopped speaking. The expression on his face was stern. His eyes, wide open, were fixed on the wall at the corner of the room. He seemed suddenly disengaged from the surrounding world, alert only to what he saw, captured by an image visible only to him.

Dr. Wright, somewhat puzzled, watched him for a few moments, then said: "Are you tied to something I can't see? A spurt from your memory?"

"Nothing! Nothing!" Anton was awakened now, back in the psychiatrist's office, and noticeably shaken by his withdrawal from reality. He blurted out. "I saw something moving on the wall. A spider! It drew my attention. It crawled! But I was wrong. It was nothing!"

He giggled. "I mean a scratch on the wall but not a spider. See...," he pointed to a narrow empty space between the two walls, "that's where I saw it! A scratch by a pencil or something like that but not a spider! My mind went astray. I'm sorry for it. I'm sorry! Sorry!"

He lied. What he stared at before was not a crawling spider but an image of his parents. He saw them standing by a fir tree, his father leaning against it, his mother somewhat behind it but her face clearly visible. Two very young, charming looking people, offering each other a flirtatious smile, yet tinged with quizzicality. They seemed to be testing each other, asking an unsaid question: 'Are we right for each other? Will we make it if we stay together?'

The image was not a creation of Anton's mind. In the drawer of the cabinet where he kept his memorabilia that had direct connection with his parents, there was a silver box filled with photographs and one of them was the source of Anton's vision. He had first seen it years ago, after his mother died and when he was going through his inheritance – a few pieces of post-war glass and metal crafted jewellery, some letters from her friends, and a stack of small photographs that pictured primarily the members of her husband's family.

What he saw had a long life. Some photographs showed faces and bodies of his ancestors from the early years of the twentieth century, then gradually closer and closer to the days that exploded with the outburst of the Second World War and brought to an end the existence of that family. Most of them died as the victims of the Yellow Star, shot and killed or burned into ashes by the Nazis. The picture that materialized before Anton's eyes was taken in the very early days of his parents' marriage. He was not sure of the background. The tree they stood by loomed so large. Was it rooted on a Viennese street or in Skalat, the Polish town where his grandfather and his parents lived after they had said goodbye to Vienna?

Since his initial connection with the photographs, he examined them a few more times, spreading them out on the dining room table. "Just to have fun by looking at the clothes my uncles and cousins were wearing," as he once said to Greg who caught him studying the images.

In fact, he was trying to discern who these people were. Most of the faces seemed foreign to him. His grandfather had brothers and sisters, that he knew. The people who he stared at must have been their sons and daughters, his cousins, but he didn't recognize them. He couldn't ascertain how they were related to him and to his deceased family. Eventually, Anton abandoned this pursuit. The box with the photographs, locked in the drawer of his filing cabinet, ceased to occupy his mind.

But he didn't want to reveal to Dr. Wright what had distorted his attention a few moments ago so, to cover it up, he kept on with agitation.

"Where were we? Ah, in Vienna. While the First World War was on, they were at the University. Two years after the war ended, they were done with their studies. They got married, took a trip to France, returned to the town where my grandfather lived, did I tell you the name of the town? It was Skalat. And the village that was surrounded by his estate was called Nowosiolka Skalacka. So they went to Skalat, then left quickly to a small town called Zydaczow where my mother's brother lived – a doctor, the local G.P.– and where a pharmacy was for sale. So they went to Zydaczow..."

"You're saying 'they' as if you were not a part of that trip," said Dr. Wright. "Weren't you travelling with them? As small as you were..."

"I'm focusing on my parents, not on myself," Anton replied sternly. He seemed somewhat troubled by the question. "So they arrived in Zydaczow, liked the place, my father was impressed by the pharmacy's monetary potential. It served not only the town but the whole district, so he asked his father to give him the money to buy it, and..."

Dr. Wright interrupted. "Asked his father to buy the pharmacy? It must have cost a lot of money. Was he that rich?"

"You bet he was," Anton replied. "He owned thousands of acres of agricultural land. He farmed wheat and corn. The demand for those products in those days was enormous. He also owned a distillery. Yes, he was a very rich man. And very supportive of his son. My father. He had given him a lot of money. Saved him from bankruptcies. My father was a bright man, not only a pharmacist but also a publisher. And a writer. But a lousy businessman. Without easy access to the pocket of my grandfather..."

"You said that he was a publisher," said Dr. Wright after a moment of silence. What did he publish? Pharmacological..."

"No! No!" It was Anton's turn to cut in. "Science couldn't have been further from his mind. He published and edited a bimonthly magazine the aim of which was to fight anti-semitism. It was called *Counter Attack*. *Kontratak* in Polish. He also wrote articles that spoke of the danger that Hitler's theories and quest for power posed for the world. The magazine started to come out in the early thirties. My father saw ahead of many people what devastations National Socialism would cause, not only to the

Jewish people but to the world outside of Germany and he wrote about it.

"He also wrote a novel and a play that dealt with racism. And was a theatre producer. On an amateur scale. He formed a company in Zydaczow. My mother was often on stage. With other local men and women who wanted the town to be influenced by theatre. They did only good plays. The first play I saw was by Ibsen, *The Enemy of the People*. And," Anton smiled, "he was an accomplished violinist. He played often, in the evening hours, accompanied by my sister who played the piano. They were a fine team, my father and my sister."

"He must have been an unusual man. Loaded with talent and energy," said Dr. Wright, impressed by what he had heard. "A surplus of energy. Is that your inheritance?"

"I guess so," Anton replied. "One of the few good things that my body extracted from the genes of my father."

"I see. I see," said the psychiatrist. "He must have been quite a man, your father. Now let's concentrate on you. During the war, where were you?"

"In Poland".

"How did you survive?"

"I survived the Holocaust by escaping from a ghetto in the city where I lived with my family. I concealed my identity and existed as a non-Jew. A Christian. So did my mother." He paused, then added, "I wrote about it a lot. My literary work, most of it was based on that experience."

"I would like to read what you have written. It would allow me to know you better," Dr. Wright said with a gentle smile. "But now, please give me a hint of your 'concealed identity.' What does that mean? Precisely. That you lived under an assumed name? You weren't Thomas?"

"No, I was not," replied Anton with a sarcastic smile. "Thomas was a name I adopted here. In Canada. The name of my family was Melenbaum. When I escaped from the ghetto, the false document I received with the help of a school mate carried the name Lubecki. Anton Tom Lubecki. It was my name during my existence outside the barbed wire fence of the ghetto and after the war. As a matter of fact, when I came to Canada and for a long while afterwards that was my name. Then I changed it."

"Why?"

"It's a long story," Anton replied. His hands were again clenched tightly, a stressful expression on his face.

"You see..." He was unable to continue. And he thought:

'How am I going to tell him about one of the most bitter events of my life? That collided with my foothold on this Earth? Pushed upward the height of my depression?'

But Dr. Wright stopped Anton's struggle. "You will tell me about it later on. I don't want to be confused by too many stories. I need to put them in separate boxes. So that I correctly position the inner meaning of them. And don't be misled by the surge of your pain. When you are up to it, put it on paper and mail it to me. And next time when you are here..."

Anton didn't let him finish the sentence. "Yes, I will make you aware of what happened. How it affected me. This act of anti-semitic insanity."

The doctor made some notes on the sheet beside him then said, "So you and your mother Rosa survived the war. And your father?"

"My father, was taken to Bergen Belsen during the 'clean-up' of the ghetto. With thousands of other people. To the concentration camp. He died there. Gassed. Turned into ashes."

"How old were you when he died? And how did you take it, once you knew he was gone?"

"I have mentioned this to you before. I was twenty-one. And to answer your second question, " Anton continued with rising bitterness, "like anyone else would in a similar situation. With horror. With pain. With fury. But what happened to him was not unexpected. He should have done the same as I did. And my mother. Run out of the ghetto. There were ways to do it. But he couldn't. He feared that the way he looked – his features were very Jewish – he could not make it on the other side. He also felt that he should share the fate of all those who had no means to arrange escape. You had to be quite well off," an ironic smile curved his mouth, "to pay those who were the organizers of your trip to freedom, and those who kept you hidden in their attic room. Or in their basement. We had the resources. A leather pouch full of gold coins. Quite a bit of jewelery. Before the war started, he was well-to-do. No. As I have told you before, his father was. My grandfather. He passed on a lot of wealth to my family."

"I'm not certain I get the gist of your remark," said Dr. Wright after a moment of silence. "Are you saying that..."

"He chose to stay in the ghetto. Though his wife and his son – me – were outside. And though we tried to induce him to join us. But the way he looked...that was not the only reason for his decision. He was a pharmacist. Partly responsible for the health service within the ghetto. Medication was hard to find. The Nazis refused to supply it. So, my father established an illegal contact with a Christian colleague of his who owned a pharmacy on the other side. For an exorbitant price, the man smuggled in what was required. My father often paid for it with his own money. His need to care for men and women who were 'less fortunate than we were,' as he used to say – for the poor, disabled – was greater than his need to survive. So he didn't. To our heart-breaking regret, he didn't."

"You mentioned that you had a sister. Were you and she the only children your parents had? And what happened to her? Is she...."

"I had only one sister," Anton answered. "Hanka. She was five years younger than me. She died in the same camp as my father. She was taken off the street in the ghetto by German policemen – accused of having a false work pass. Which was not true. She was 16. She worked with me outside of the ghetto, collecting trash for a German firm. Bottles, empty cans, used metal to be transported to factories that worked for the German Army. She was sent to the same camp where my father lost his life, but before him. We were together when she was taken. I saw it. It all happened just in front of me. I ran away soon afterwards."

"When did it happen?" Dr. Wright was shaken by the story, Anton could see that.

"She was gone in 1942. My father one year later," he answered. Anton's face grew suddenly pale. He was trembling.

"Do you mind if we don't talk about it anymore? Right now, I mean. I'm not up to it. I..."

"Of course. Of course," interjected Dr. Wright. "If it shatters you so much..."

Anton breathed hard. "Sometimes it does, sometimes it doesn't. I don't know what causes it but I experience it every day."

After a few seconds of silence, he continued, "On my desk, there are enlarged photographs of Hanka and my father. By some miracle, those pictures survived. I look at their faces every day and ask why were they chosen for that fate. With millions of others! Why? Why?"

"I wish I could give you an answer," said Dr. Wright, avoiding Anton's eyes. "But that's beyond my scope. Beyond the scope of all human beings, I guess. Let's tackle another subject, if you don't mind. The one that has to do with the present. Describe to me, if you can, the effects of your ear problem. Is it ringing now?"

"Yes, it is," Anton answered. "Not too loudly, but constantly. The moment I'm awake, I'm followed by the hum."

"When does it increase? When you are upset? Or angry?"

"No," Anton replied, shaking his head. "Or, at least I'm not aware of it. It has a life of its own. It comes and goes, the level, I mean."

"And the attacks of nausea?"

"They too come and go," said Anton. "They take place when I'm hit by vertigo. When the world around me," he circled his finger in the air, "spins rapidly. It's like a bomb exploding in my head. I have to lie down. And vomit. Then it passes. Slowly. But it eats every ounce of my strength. After it happens, I need to stay in bed for hours. I'm weak. Desperate and weak."

"How can you be desperate and weak at the same time? I would have thought that to be desperate, " Dr. Wright emphasized the word, "one needs to have some strength. Weakness brings about passivity. Desperation gives birth..."

"It's true," Anton interrupted. "I've been in too much of a rush combining those two forces. My despair takes over when my body is less strained."

He smiled sadly. "When I feel better. When I'm able to walk to my desk, sit down in my chair, look at the street – the window is just beside my desk – and think, my body has a separate life. My mind is keen to do some creative work, to be engaged in an activity that is absorbing, demanding, but my body doesn't listen. It is not prepared to be a companion to such plans. It has it's own agenda.

I have a shower. I get dizzy. I put my clothes on. I feel fatigued. And there's a trickle of pain in my chest. I go for a walk. It aches." he touched the upper left part of his body. "And I think – do I have a heart problem? Will I have an attack? I sit at my desk staring through the window and I think, why am I so morose? So surly. Is it my age? Am I going to go soon? I'm in bed at night and I recapture some long forgotten incidents from my past and I think, why am I drawn to those old days? Because I was young then and I'm rapidly aging now? I cannot accept that I'm aging. No! That I'm quite old. Old age is a blot on the human heart. And the human mind. Because of it..."

"You will not receive the Nobel prize for that discovery," Dr. Wright interrupted in an amused tone. He wanted to say more but Anton responded with vehemence.

"I don't care about an award! I want to improve! Be able to write! Instead of working I need to rest. But that's not all. Other thoughts oppress me. Why am I going through this hell? What did I do to deserve such suffering? Is this a punishment for....."

He leaned toward the doctor and cried out. "I want you to help me find an answer to those questions. They eat me alive. I'm sinking into a world I dread. That is what brought me here. The scorching fire of my depression. I'm suffering! I don't know what to do! There's a black hole in my brain! Why? I don't have a clue!"

"Are you on medication?"

"Yes, I am. I mean, I was," Anton answered. "It's called Antivert. I took a pill once a day. Before I went to sleep. It was supposed to control my vertigo. Make me less prone to throwing up. And it did help a bit. I think. But it exhausted me beyond description. While I was taking it, I couldn't move my legs. My daily walk to the corner ... I couldn't manage it. I couldn't go to the store for groceries or to the bookstore to buy a magazine or a book. To fill up the emptiness of my life, I need to read," he smiled bitterly.

"So I stopped using the drug prescribed to me by Dr. Hopkins. It helped me to recover some of my strength. But it didn't diminish my emotional upheaval. Perhaps even increased it. As I said before, I'm in a dark state. I long to be rescued from it."

Doctor Wright shifted in his chair. He was now a greater distance from Anton than before. "Do you ever look at yourself in the mirror?"

'When I shave. Why do you ask?"

The doctor questioned further, dismissing Anton's query. "And what do you see?"

"A piece of shit," Anton wanted to say. But he replied "I see a grim man. Wrinkled. Gray. Someone I can't recognize. I find it hard to believe that the man I once was could have changed so much. So rapidly and so much."

"In what way? Could you be more specific?"

"In so many ways," Anton began. "In so many ways that I can't define it," he said after a moment of tension-loaded silence.

"It is all so tied together. Mixed up. It's like a dirty bag of snake-like creatures each tangled up with the other. But I'm sure we will get to the bottom of it one day. That's your specialty", he grinned lightly. "You're here to help people to get rid of those snakes."

He spoke more and more exuberantly, as if tickled by his words. "There should be a museum or a zoo, yes, a zoo, where they would be displayed after they don't inhabit human minds anymore. And their bodies. I bet people would go in droves to look at them. They would quickly learn how those reptiles are shaped, how they skip around and function. Then they would know how to avoid them!"

"Brilliant idea," said Dr. Wright, a glimmer of a smile stretching his lips. He quickly made another notation on his pad. "Snakes. So they creep into you. And possibly you weren't aware of it. Well, we will talk about that quite a bit. Until you squeeze them out." He pointed to his pad "And I lock them in the zoo."

There was a moment of tense silence in the room before Dr. Wright spoke. "Those snakes, the larger ones. I would like to know what they are. Could you catch them and hand them to me? Now?"

"My hatred of getting old," Anton said with contained vehemence. " My fear of being dumped one day in a hospital ward or in an old people's home. My fear and hatred of being a heavy burden on my wife. Of being alone. Henrietta, my wife, is a wonderful, caring woman and yet I feel I'm alone. People I see on the street. I think, who are they? Do I have anything in common with them? Outside of breathing the same air or stomping the same ground?

As I have told you, I'm sitting at my desk, beside the window and watching the street, looking at people who march by on the sidewalk, staring at cars that pass or slip between two parked vehicles to take hold of an empty space, or watching young women in short skirts, tight blouses, their long legs... you know what I'm trying to say!

I'm doing nothing else but watching. I'm incompetent to act. The narrowness of my life is suffocating. So I think," he put his index finger to his temple, "that's the solution."

Seeing that Dr. Wright's eyes were focussed on him with stern attention, he chortled slightly. "Please don't be concerned. I don't own a gun. But I have a knife. Don't look so worried, that was a pun."

After a moment of silence Anton added: "I take mild tranquilizers day after day..."

His eyes filled with tears. Clenching his teeth, he managed to release a burst of his despair. Then like a child facing a trusted adult, he said softly: "Will you rescue me? I need your help so badly. I can't go on with what's crippling my brain. Squeezing out humaneness from my heart. I can't go on with what I'm going through. I'd rather die, than..."

"I will do the best I can," replied Dr. Wright softly. "But to achieve positive results, I need your help. You will have to open your heart to me. Your mind and your heart. You will have to bring to the surface all those facts that cause your hatred of what is happening to you now. Depression is the surrendering to the force of that hatred. Instead of fighting what one detests," he said the last words slowly, "one abandons the resistance. One surrenders to suffering, to pain. In the expectation of what is inevitable."

"I think I know what you mean," Anton replied. "I'm ready to speak with you as openly as I can. But my memory is in shambles. I will do my best to answer your questions as...as..."

He stopped, pressed his head with the palms of his hands, and continued, his voice quivering a bit. "You see, I've lost the word! I wanted to say that I will fulfill your demands. No! A wrong phrase! But you know what I mean!"

He was tense now, shivering a bit, and beads of sweat appeared on his forehead. Yet he kept on. "You see, this is one of my problems. Both filing cabinets that sit in my brain, you would call them auditory and visual cortexes," he said this with a surly grin, "are almost empty. Somebody snitched the piles of documentaries, audio and video tapes, that kept track not only of my long bygone experiences but also of what was taking place after. Many fragments of my existence that were captured by my ears and eyes and stuck on the shelves of those cabinets are gone!

To put it bluntly, I do not recall what my father looked like. If I didn't have his photograph on my desk I couldn't recall his face. The same applies to my grandfather and my sister. They live inside of me but their features are covered by a heavy mist. The same applies to many people that I have known here, in Canada. Somebody greets me on the street and I wonder nervously who is this person? Or I think – I am familiar with that face but what's his or her name?

And some words elude me. I wait to make a cogent remark to my wife: 'Your tenacity is exemplary.' But all of a sudden this last word is out of my grasp. So I stumble: 'Your tenacity is.... is....' This bloody nonsense happens often and it scares me beyond imagination. I'm a writer, the control of words is my profession. But..."

Dr. Wright offered him a reassuring smile. "I know what you mean. It's a symptom of getting older. I'm a bit younger than you are, not much, and let me tell you," he winked, "in secret. My mind from time to time plays the same dirty trick on me. I talk to my wife, I'm telling her a story and suddenly the sense of it is gone. It doesn't happen too often, but..."

The doctor shrugged, then exclaimed with excessive energy: "Don't worry about it! Forget it! You're not alone in what you go through. There are thousands of people who feel diminished by the process of aging. Learn to live with it.. Don't let it crush you. Knock you down."

"Is there anything more mindless and brutal than aging," said Anton with a smirk. "Whoever invented it, had no notion of what it implied. Which is the best proof that He exists," he pointed at the ceiling, "and is eternal. He surely never experiences the harassment of aging. Charitable as He's supposed to be, He..."

"Your judgement does not coincide with mine," Dr. Wright interrupted him somewhat coldly: "I believe that He knew what He was doing. I do not question His wisdom. You do, I suspect. We'll talk about that."

He paused then added, "As far as your life stories are concerned, tell me whatever comes to your mind. And let me think about them. Interpret them – as you would say. That is what I'm here for." He gave Anton a wink. "That is a part of our game."

"As you wish. As you wish," Anton replied. Then the phone rang. Dr. Wright lifted the receiver. "Dr. Wright speaking." He listened for a moment. "Just a minute."

He put down the receiver and glanced at Anton. "I'll be with you in a minute." Then he walked quickly out of the room.

Anton muttered to himself. "How can he be so hopping around. How can he pay attention to so many things at the same time? Can he really be of help to me? Remove the terror that crushes my mind?"

He looked up at the ceiling. At that moment, he was overwhelmed by the fear that it was going to crash down. It was crashing down. In his mind, the bricks were falling, smashing his head. He cringed, uttered a soft cry, covered the top of his head with his hands, but nothing happened.

Absorbing the innocence of the reality, he took a big breath, wiped his eyes, and ridiculing his imaginary experience, he again whispered to himself. "Bad luck! I would have been safe and sound had it happened."

He was tired now. The conversation with Dr. Wright was more taxing than he anticipated. He looked at his wrist watch. It read 1:45 p.m. "I've been here for almost two hours." He was startled. "I don't know if I can stay here much longer."

He stood up, once again drawn to the sight of the sky, the lake and the city blistering within the frame of the window. Then he was caught by the voice of his doctor who had just returned, quickly walked to his desk, hung up the receiver and pointed to the ceiling with his thumb. "The Top Man needed some information instantly."

He sighed. "I apologize." Then, as if noticing some discomfort on Anton's face, he asked, "Are you O.K.? Not dizzy, I hope."

"No, I'm not," Anton replied. "But if you wouldn't mind, I would like to leave now. I'm quite beat. This is my first visit to a psychiatrist. I never thought it would shake me up so. What I need now is some rest. Some sleep."

"Sure, sure," replied Dr. Wright. "We have talked," he glanced at his clock, "interruptions excluded, roughly for an hour. Our meeting would have ended by now, anyway."

Reflecting for a moment, he asked "How will you get home? You don't drive. Am I right?"

"I don't drive. But my wife is to pick me up. In fact, she must have been waiting for me for quite a while. We assumed that the appointment would start at twelve. And last no longer than an hour."

While saying it, Anton was thinking 'Why am I lying? Henrietta was busy today. Had her history class to attend to. Her latest preoccupation,' he sneered internally. 'The blood-bathed history of the world. I came here by taxi.'

He shook his head as if bewildered by the fluctuation of his mind. "May I go now?"

His heart was pounding again. So was his ear. It was sending a message as Anton understood it: 'Go home! Spread out on your bed! If you don't, you will pay dearly for it!'

"Before you go," said the doctor, "when will I see you again?".

"It's up to you," Anton replied. "You're the man who's busy. I have many free hours."

Dr. Wright glanced quickly at his calendar. "Next Tuesday, at eleven. Will that do?"

Then, taking Anton's silence for a positive answer, he wrote the date and the hour of the appointment on a small note pad which had the doctor's name at the top and a piano keyboard printed at the bottom. He gave it to his patient. They shook hands and Anton walked away, thinking 'In a few days I will see him again. Do I want to? Yes, I do! This crazy house, it's a new experience for me. When I'm better, I will write about it. William Styron did it. Why shouldn't I?'

Before pressing the elevator button he looked around. The waiting room now held a number of patients, all males. Some were weird looking, their eyes glued to the wall or to the floor, others were no different from ordinary people who you see everywhere – in working places, bars, cafes.

Anton thought of the second group. 'They are like me. Would any of my pals assume that I'm a sick man? A psychiatric patient?'

He looked into the receptionist's cubbyhole, he wanted to say goodbye to her. But she wasn't there. Another woman, fat and morose looking, had taken her place. 'Pity I can't see her,' a touch of regret rang in Anton's mind. 'It would have improved my spirit. Would have put me in a jiggly mood. Perhaps would have made me feel hunky.' He shook his head. 'Jiggly mood? Hunky? What kind of language is this? What made me come up with it?'

He didn't have the time to search for an answer. The elevator door slid open, Anton stepped in and, a few moments later, he was riding down, squashed by people. When the elevator reached the ground floor, he crossed the entry hall and was quickly on the sidewalk in front of the Institute.

CHAPTER TWO

The traffic was horrendous. Cars were speeding in both directions, their drivers honking with impatience when impeded by daring pedestrians who, risking their lives, were swooshing from one side of the street to the other. The sidewalks were packed with men and women of all creeds and races, many of them young, in their bright summer clothes. They were all racing to their destinations, chattering and laughing when bumping into each other. The sun was shining, a breeze was caressing faces, there was a busy, joyous feeling in the air.

Anton, looking at the crowd, commented to himself, 'There were days I belonged to that traffic. I too raced in all directions to fulfill my aims. To grab hold of the enjoyment that was the crucial need of my life. But for me, all of that is gone. Evaporated into thin air. Why? Why? Why?'

A taxi was passing. Anton lifted his hand and the car came to a screeching halt. He slid into it, gave the black driver his address and, a few moments later, was on his way home.

'Soon I will be back in my ghetto.' The thought filled his mind and he was instantly transported to the ghetto where he had lived many years ago. He stood on a narrow street at night – small, dilapidated houses, a few dying trees, all lit by a round, golden shield of the moon.

'That's when I decided to get out,' he thought. 'When I made up my mind to leave my parents, my friends and to get out. It was the moon that yanked me in that direction. And my mother!' Instantly, in his mind, he saw her standing beside him and whispering: 'Go! Go! It will make us happy. Your father and I want you to stay alive. Here you will perish. There you will survive. And as your dad would say: the moon tells you the same. It shines so brightly to let you to see all the obstacles that may lie hidden on the road you'll be taking. Have courage and go! Don't worry about us. I know that this concern floods your mind. I know! I know!'

He shook his head, the image was gone. Now he chastised himself 'Where you have been living for many years is not a ghetto. This is a free, happy part of the city that offered you so much attention. So much joy. Yes, you tasted some defeats, but joy was the call of the day. Exuberant joy that came from having a loving, caring wife, from seeing your children growing up beside you, from establishing a name for yourself, making your work a success You're crazy to say that you're living in a ghetto. But if you want to stick to that notion, what about your home? Shouldn't you call it a jail?'

For a moment, a smile stretched his lips and he ridiculed that absurd idea. 'My house filled with books, antiques, works of art – a jail?'

Then he was hit by a bomb that exploded in his head. A voice, similar to his own was screaming: 'Yes, a jail! A walled-in space where everything seems to be closeted in semi-darkness. A place where comfort is ostensibly in your hands but the strain of being closed in most of the time – lost in trips to the past – chokes you! A home where one hears voices mostly from outside, or at night from the TV set with your wife beside it. Where the phone rings rarely, mostly for Henrietta who is engrossed in her creative work; where visitors appear rarely and do not stay too long, overcome by the moribund tension that vibrates around them. Where silence, intertwined with the hum in your ear, is the rigour of existence. So jail it is. And you're the prisoner!'

His head was buzzing. For a moment, he thought he'd throw up. The driver who for the last few minutes was watching him through the rear view mirror, steered the car close to the pavement, brought it to a stop. "Are you sick or something? I've been watching you. Your cheeks are purple. And you were making all kinds of faces."

Anton took a deep breath, exhaled, repeated the action, then replied, "I'm fine. I had an attack of nausea. It happens to me sometimes. But it's gone."

He inhaled and exhaled, then asked, "Where are we? I have lost the sense of it. I'm not sure I recognize the area. Is it Bloor and...?"

The driver interrupted. "It's the corner of Spadina and St. Clair. We're very close to where we're going. Are you ok?"

"Yes, I am. And I thank you for your attention. You're a nice man."

"Thanks," said the driver with a smile, maneuvering the car into the traffic.

He took a turn to the right, the car was on its way east. Anton, feeling much better, observing the street, chanted softly to himself:

"Nice or not nice, who gives a turkey!
As long as I stay alive!
As long as I'm not murky!

Again!" He caught himself, laughing. "I'm on my stupid track again!" He lifted his fist and punched himself lightly on the chin. "Enough of this malarky! Put it back where it belongs! In a hole in the ground! Together with..."

"Are you talking to me?" Before Anton could answer, the driver braked rapidly, avoiding a collision with a silver Mercedes driven by a young man in a white shirt who unexpectedly swerved to the left to reach the outside lane.

"Fucking bastard," screamed the taxi driver. "I thought that guy was going to kill us! He didn't even look! Crazy man!. Rich fucker!"

But Anton, though startled, paid no attention to the incident. The words 'together with' were still racing through his mind. "Together...together with...the darky!" He triumphantly finished his rhyming cadenza. "Yes! With the darky!"

"What?" The driver glanced at him suspiciously.

"No! No! I wasn't referring to you. I was playing my game. Binding together words that rhyme." Anton burst out laughing. "You know what I mean. You give me a dime, I'll give you a rhyme!"

The driver wasn't amused and he was speeding now.

Anton noticed it, leaned forward and pleaded with him. "Please, don't rush. It makes me nervous."

The black man pointed with his thumb to the street. "I don't rush! I follow the pace of the traffic. That's the way we must go! If we don't we're asking for a ..... blow!" He giggled and Anton exclaimed, "Bravo! Now you know what blurs my mind! You and I are of the same kind!"

They both burst out laughing then the driver concentrated on his task of staying in his lane or swinging right and left to avoid being crushed by zooming cars. The cab was now passing houses, churches and office buildings that Anton knew. The driver took a sharp turn to the right and came to a stop in front of Anton's house.

"We made it," the man blurted out. "Now get out, go in, throw up. And go to bed!"

They both laughed again. Anton paid for the fare and, a few moments later, entered his home. He called out. "I'm in! Henrietta, I'm in!"

There was no answer. The paintings on the walls, the old fashioned, precious furniture were dusted by silence. Anton, a frown on his forehead, took off his jacket, hung it on a wooden clothes rack in the hall, and walked through the living room and dining room to the kitchen. On the pine country table, where he and his wife had their meals, was a note: Hi, lovely, I'm gone to do the groceries. I'll be back soon. No phone calls. If you're tired, take a nap. I love you. That's how I croon!

It was signed: Henrietta busybody. No! Henrietta on the bustle. Whose beloved crony is Sir Cheese Anton Thomas! Bye, my love! I need to...hustle!

Seeing the words Sir/cheese puzzled Anton for a moment then he howled with laughter. The origin of that configuration echoed in his mind. Henrietta was often in the habit of addressing Anton: "Yes, Sir. No Sir. It's up to you, Sir." She was imitating her mother who in a similar fashion used to underline her unwilling subservience to Henrietta's father.

One day Anton said to his wife, "Do you know what the word 'Sir' means in Polish? Cheese. Cottage cheese. The spelling is different but the sound is familiar. So when you address me so ... politely, what rings in my ear has a different meaning. It says to me that I am cheesy! Of inferior quality! That's why I don't like it. It makes me feel sleazy!"

And Henrietta replied, "I don't agree! When 'I Sir' you, I'm expressing my reverence, not scorn. So 'Sir Cheese' you will be. It's a call to me from my mom and I don't intend to have it erased. But I assure you, it's filled with warmth. Respect. And glee."

Recalling the incident and staring at the note Anton said to himself, "My wife's poking fun at me! No! She's trying to make me laugh! To de-morose me," he chortled as if relieved of his sadness.

He opened the fridge, took out a carton of orange juice, poured it into his favorite Mexican blue glass, sipped it slowly, enjoying the taste. When the glass was empty, he took it to the sink, rubbed it under hot water and placed it where it belonged, on the shelf of an open, white cabinet attached to the wall beside the pine table. The cabinet was crammed with tea cups, wine glasses and old Fiestaware dishes, Henrietta's precious possessions. This whole action lasted no more than five minutes. Then he left the kitchen taking the note with him. He was on his way upstairs to his study, his asylum; he would spend most of his time in that room.

When he reached it – a spacious area divided by a large archway, one section his working space, the other housing Henrietta's word processor and a handsome red leather couch where he had his naps – he was again despondent.

As if compelled by an inner force, he stopped by the edge of his desk and looked around. His eyes lingered on all the objects that dominated the area. Several book cases leaned against the walls, packed with volumes of books. There were two photographs of his wife when she was still young, paintings, sculptures by renowned Canadian artists, Eskimo carvings, sea shells and corals of all shapes and colors displayed on glass shelves attached to the windows – his collection from Florida beaches – and his own works of art. These were curiously shaped tree barks and driftwood in vertical positions reminiscent of human figures, lacquered with liquid plastic to preserve their jagged structure, adorned and embellished with tiny oyster shells attached to their outstretched arms or heads, surrounded by sea shells and dried, thorny blow fish, all glued to cork-covered wood.

He was taking in all of it, thinking, 'Is this a jail? This basket of riches. Why did I call it a jail? Why not a paradise?'

Then another thought swooshed through his mind. 'When my passage to the underworld takes place, will I leave from here? Will this be the setting of my last scene on Earth?'

He turned his head once again toward his own artwork. It was sitting on an old cedar chest, between a Mexican clay sculpture depicting Jesus hanging on a cross and an African wood carving of a half-naked huntsman or warrior with a sharp spear in his hand. On the wall behind the chest was a large, strange painting of a simian human creature gazing through grey stripes resembling jail bars. To the right of it, on a pedestal, was a wooden sculpture of a kneeling, naked woman, her face turned downward, her eyes and lips revealing a mischievous grin. To the left of the chest was a narrow, wooden filing cabinet. On its top was a whalebone Eskimo carving: a flat, mask-like male face. His eyebrows, eyes, lips and ears expressed silly amazement, the bewilderment of facing the perplexity, treachery, cruelty, the inherent factors of his existence.

'The symbolic miniature of the world the way I see it,' he commented to himself ironically.

'The world that is populated by struggling, frightened specimens,' he once again focussed his eyes on the painting, 'who are confronted by the abysmal horror that accompanies their lives, softened somewhat by the beauty created by nature.' He was smiling gently. His eyes lingered for a moment on the female body. 'And by the mind-shutting joy of sexual encounters.' Now his eyes are on the figure of the African huntsman. 'In chains of grotesque violence that began with the human need or craving to devour the flesh of animals then rose to the next level of detesting and killing with spears or hatchets other human beings who, enticed by the same corporal necessity or greed, dared to scour other men's territory. With the compulsion to murder.' He continued, now looking at the figure of Christ. 'All those who preached love instead of hatred who, God sent or not, became the guiding spirits of our existence.'

'How is it,' he mused, 'that I didn't realize before, what message that part of the room was sending? I structured it so unconsciously, yet it so expressively reflects my feelings.' Then shrugging his shoulders, he pondered sarcastically: 'In a world like this, what's the point of struggling to stay alive? Of battling one's illness? Or of staying sick, yet surviving?'

He sat on the reclining chair behind his desk, rocked backward and forward a few times, his fingers crossed, his eyes drawn to the modest houses on the other side of the street. He saw them through the open window and his gaze went to the trees that grew on their lawns. The breeze was soft and the heavy branches were steady. But the smaller ones – red or yellow dotting their green leaves – were trembling as if possessed by a demon.

He wondered, 'Do they sense their days are about to end? Is this why they shiver so desperately? The way I do?'

Then he asked himself another question. 'Why is it that every time I keep staring at the tree beside the house, the leaves, whatever their color, in some places turn into a grotesque human face? A bushy head of a malevolent, middle-aged male with a protruding nose, narrow eyes and lips; the light cutting through the leaves underlining the shapes? When I asked Henrietta whether she could see that image, she giggled. "No, I can't! Only a dreamer like you could transform a bunch of leaves into a human face. But take a picture of it. Or even better, turn it into a painting. I bet it would sell. And it would give you the jolt you need. It would make you live in the present. Not in the past. It would help you to regain some of your self-esteem."

'What a naughty remark it was,' he thought. 'She knew I had zero talent in that sphere. Had I been hunky, she wouldn't have said it. It's because I don't jiggle her...' They were the same words that had come to his mind when he was leaving the Institute. But this time he recognized their origin. They had an old and odd connection. Henrietta's son, Paul, a teenager then, once addressed Greg, Anton's son in that manner. By then the two boys had been under the same roof for many years. Paul seemed to love and hate his one-year-older half-brother, competing with him fiercely for parental and public attention. The two boys were in their bedroom, arguing loudly. Anton, who was on the stairs on his way to the study, overheard the argument.

Greg was shouting: "You're not ready for it! Look at you! Skin and bones! That's all that you are! No muscle! No..."

Paul cut him off, screaming angrily: "Don't give me that shit! I'm as much a hunk as you are! If you want me to prove it,

I'll screw your girlfriend! She won't mind! Then let's ask her who was better, you or me. I bet she'll..."

At that moment, Anton barged into their room, caught them in a fighting stance, gave them hell for their 'scummy talk' and, for punishment, withdrew their allowance for two weeks. The boys were shocked by his action; the thin stack of two dollar bills that they received on a weekly basis was all they had to pay for movies, jazz concerts, McDonald's hamburgers. They left their bedroom in a fury, spent some time on the street, then returned, humbly apologizing for their "dumb behavior." Then they thanked Anton for his silence – the concealment of the fracas from Henrietta who was out of the house when it happened but returned soon afterwards – and that was that. An issue of that sort had never again troubled Anton's relationship with his boys.

Now struck by it, he was amused by the upsurge of the incident, from the archival glaciers to the front line of his memory. And he mused, 'Sexual urge was the cause of their upheaval. It made an impact on them no less strongly than it did on me when I was their age. I too was in those clutches. I too did all kinds of crazy, naughty things, not only when I was young and innocent but later on, when I was a mature man and, yes, subservient to that craving. Had I not met Henrietta, who knows what mark it would have left on me? She was as sex-crazy as I was. She tempted me endlessly to satisfy her craving.'

A series of slow-flowing images from his past emerged in his mind. It was a hot, starlit summer night. He was in his car, on the highway, on his way back from the University – his summer assignment demanded, unexpectedly, that he'd be in school that evening longer than usual – rushing to Henrietta who he was to meet in a Mexican restaurant to celebrate the tenth anniversary of their marriage. Initially, it was to be a family party at home with the kids and some friends. Then the project was abandoned. Their offspring were too busy to participate; they were all working in restaurants or at summer camps to earn spending money. The choice of the Mexican restaurant was not incidental. It was the "munching grove," as Henrietta called it, they both cherished. It was where they had their first meal outside of their living quarters after they moved to Toronto.

Anton, weaving through the heavy traffic, was cursing himself. 'You're late! As usual! And you didn't buy her a present! How will you explain it? By telling her the truth that you put it in the back of your mind and didn't find the time to do it today? Or by telling her a lie that you tried but couldn't find the right thing. A piece of something that would carry the right message. That would pinpoint the ten years of the bumpy ride you had together, yet honeyed by love. On a mattress of sex. That was crude,' he corrected himself. 'But she wouldn't mind hearing it. There's truth and humor to it. And the explanation is only half a lie. When you thought about it, you didn't have a clue what to give her. So that is what she'll hear. And she will accept it graciously, knowing how constipated you are. Sometimes. When you have a bright idea but not the knowledge to implement it. How to turn what flickers in your mind into marble. Or at least into stone.'

He was in the city now, parked the car, then raced to the restaurant that – a neon sign hanging over it – was nearby. Entering it, he saw Henrietta instantly. She was sitting at a table by the window, looking grim. Noticing him navigating the crowded tables to reach her, she uttered a sight of relief. "Thank God! I was so worried. I thought you had an accident."

They kissed each other and sat down. Anton apologized for being late and for being empty-handed.

"What I was looking for," he said with a touch of a smile in anticipation of her response, and leaning toward her to avoid being overheard, "was an object that would reflect our happy life together. A mattress of sex! A blanket of love! Do you know what I mean?"

Henrietta giggled. "That's exactly what you should have bought. A new mattress. And a new blanket. We badly need both."

Then she unzipped her bag and took out her present for Anton. It was a small Eskimo carving of a fear-ridden bear that was standing on his hind legs, holding one front paw on his cheek, and with the other paw covering his crotch. She handed it to her husband.

"This bear is Jewish. And he cries 'I'm a worried bear! I must earn a living! Support my family! Like professor Thomas! Oi vay!'"

Anton roared with laughter. Then, suppressing it, they were in a public place after all, he thanked Henrietta for her precious gift. They toasted each other with champagne, followed by a few rounds of tequila, supported by their favorite meal; tacos de pollo, guacomole del norte and refried beans.

From then on, they didn't talk very much. They were both very hungry, Anton especially so. Bent over his plate and munching the spicy food quickly, he was not paying much attention to the surroundings and to the commotion developing at the table a few steps away.

An immaculately dressed young man sat with a young woman, she too was wearing the most fashionable clothes, a tight silk blouse accentuating her breasts, a short leather skirt revealing her slim legs and thighs covered by black panty hose. He was berating her in a tense whisper, "Can't you sit still? You're shifting in your chair as if a needle was in your ass! You're making a spectacle of your legs! You're showing your panties to everybody! Is it the hot food that makes you so jumpy? What the hell has come over you?"

His companion grabbed his hand and whispered back. "Don't be so grumpy. When we get home, I'll show you how hot I am! You'll have to work hard! And if you don't..."

They noticed that their talk had become a source of amusement for those who sat nearby. They instantly paid their bill and were gone.

After they left, Henrietta, who was a bit soused by then and had absorbed the prankish conversation with concealed enjoyment, whispered to Anton, "Did you hear what they were saying?"

"A pile of crap," he snapped.

"No," Henrietta retorted. "It was fun listening to them. They were so busy with each other. So focused on one thing..." Then, placing her hand on his and expressing herself most softly, she added "You too have eaten that spicy stuff. Is your...musician hot enough to fiddle my organ?"

"What?"

She repeated the question, almost only through the motion of her lips. "Will you fiddle my organ? Will your fiddler play my viola? When it does, I have music in my ear. I need it now. You're my Horgan. I'm your Lolita.. But if you can't, don't worry. You're still my Horgan. And I'm your Perdita."

Anton giggled sadly, then frowning, asked himself 'Why did she call me Horgan?' The answer came to him right away. Horgan was the name of his school associate, a waspy right-winger whom he detested. Whenever he spoke of him, he would start with "that fucking dick..." Henrietta in her racy moments would often coax him "now I want your dick!" but one night she changed it to "now I want your Horgan!" From then on, it stayed that way. The nickname for his fiddler was Horgan.

He giggled, amused by the recollection. Then he wondered, 'Is this the cause of my problem? The source of the creeping tension between me and my wife? That my Horgan works no more? That the fiddler hears no more the tempting voice of Lolita?'

When the symptoms began to pester him and were the cause of friction between them, he pondered it a lot but dismissed it as if there was no sense to it.

'It's not my fault, but hers! If she'd coax me more, if she were inducive, persistent, I would respond. When I have a hot bath I have an erection. What I need is an injection of crude passion. A massage of my flick. If only she'd try. But no. That wouldn't do. For her, I'm the pusher and she's the receiver. All she can do is lie still. So in the end who's the victim? Me! It's Anton Melenbaum, Lubecki, Thomas who pays the bill.'

He also lambasted himself often for those plastic observations.

'You were no less sex-dry than she was. You have seen her naked body more often than she had seen yours. She had seen to that. She often invited you to take a bath with her. She played with you when you least expected it. In the movies. While you were watching the screen, she'd place her raincoat on your knees, slide her hand underneath, unzip your pants and massage your Horgan. So why are you complaining that it's her fault not yours? So you'd better think it over, or lock yourself in a caboose!'

He toyed with the subject frequently, yet dismissed it as if there was no sense to it.

But now he was less sure than ever. 'What if that's what makes me so torn to pieces? So unhappy? I'd better discuss it with Dr. Wright. He surely has faced many people like me. Senior citizens,' he chortled bitterly, 'boring and bored sexual non-performers.'

He turned away from the window, walked to the closet in the other part of the room, took out a pillow that was stored there, placed it on the couch, kicked off his shoes and lay down.

'What I need is sleep,' he thought. 'No dreams. I dream enough while I'm awake. I need to block it out. By untormented sleep.'

At this moment, Dr. Wright's words relating to his name rang in his mind. 'Why does he want to know what made me switch? Does he think I was playing some game? No! That's not what he is after. He read in my face the inner horror that was part of this transformation. Why did I go down on my knees instead of fighting back the monstrous lie and the blackmail? Was it because I was ill, in the first clutches of my disease? I had better write him a note and tell him the story. And maybe he is right. Maybe once I spill it out, I will have less disdain for myself. So Anton, go to work! And hope that this honest explanation will make you less jerky! Less murky! '

He giggled, sauntered back to the chair behind his desk, sat down turned on the light and quickly scribbled the note to Dr. Wright. It said:

Dear Dr. Wright,

This is the confession you want to hear. Mellenbaum was my family's name. My ancestors – as I was told by my father – lived in Spain. When the Inquisition took its course, some were annihilated but others escaped and after a long journey and a lengthy stopover in Germany, found their safe haven in eastern Poland. After one generation, they lived there in peace for close to half a millennium. Then when the Aryan masters, murderers, occupied that territory, almost all of my family – twenty-four human beings – were beaten to death, hung on trees, shot or gassed in concentration camps. Four Mellenbaums outlived the Holocaust; my mother, my father's sister, my distant cousin and myself. Those other three are now dead. I am the only Mellenbaum still alive. But instead of being thankful, I am, as you know ... adrift. I believe this is the main source of my inner combustion. I am deprived of the linkage with all those people who were the elemental part of my grassroots, of my upbringing, and who served as a safety net for those members of the family who, for whatever reason, were in need of such protection. This cruel happening had the most devastating impact on my life. The older I grew the more painful and heartbreaking it was. The eradication of my family. Why did it happen? What force imposed on us this sadistic torture? As I have said before, this is the cause of my inner unstoppable conflagration. And of my inevitably shrinking duration. Enough on this subject. Lubecki. This was the name I acquired when I decided to escape from the ghetto. My high school buddy, Ignacy Szer, was a Christian Pole, the son of a high-ranking officer in the Polish army. To save my life, he supplied me with the birth certificate of his deceased younger nephew. His name was Anton Lubecki. Once in possession of this document, I applied for and received an identity card – every Pole was obliged by the German occupiers to be in possession of this at all time – and from then on, until the collapse of Nazi rule, this name was my shield. Once the Polish state was reinstated, I validated through legal procedure the ownership of this name. Eventually, as Mr. Lubecki, I arrived in Canada.

Then one day, I was hit by a brutal revelation. I received a letter from a Polish man, a resident of Warsaw. His name was Piotr Lubecki. He informed me that he had learned of my whereabouts from an article about me that was published in Toronto, in a book that focused on Polish Canadian Identities. In other words, on emigrants from Poland who had made an impact on the social, political or cultural life in Canada. The sender of the letter expressed his positive thoughts about what he had read about me but he also said that it was he who had delivered his brother's birth certificate to me. And because of this, he not only deserved to be mentioned in the "story of your dash to life instead of death in a concentration camp," but was "due financial remuneration for his deed. I risked my life giving you my brother's birth certificate, the Nazi police would have killed me had they discovered what I had done. Saving the neck of a Jew. And for this reason, you owe me a reward. Money I could use to keep my life in order."

I was shocked and shaken by the letter. I had never met the man, had never heard of him. I answered gently that he must have been involved with another Jewish person, not I, and that it was my very close school friend who had supplied me with the document and that he could be contacted to prove my statement. The two-page response I received a month later was wicked. On the first page, Piotr Lubecki accused me in the most deleterious manner. He called me an ogre, a swine, a beastly liar, a crafty prick and a cold-blooded hooligan who "would rather destroy the person instead of paying his debts." Then, on the second page, he announced how he would handle this case. He wrote: "I could be bashing you again and again until you surrender but I am too old and tired to stay on this track. Therefore I am informing you that unless you rub out the name Lubecki from your documents, I will bring this to the attention of the Canadian Ambassador here and to the press telling them what a swindler you are and how you have mistreated me. I will give them your address so that they can reach you, examine your inhumane stand and bring to the attention of the public what a dishonoured man you are. Keep this in mind, should you decide not to accept my demand your teaching career will be at risk. Those who employ you at the University, once they know what kind of man you are, will not want you around. That's all I have to say. I am expecting your response soon. Signed, Piotr Lubecki."

Anton added this to his note 'the spooky gook'. And he continued:

My initial response to this ugly ploy was to disregard his demand. Yet I was very perturbed by his vicious diatribe. I tried to reach Ignacy Szer whom I had not had any connection with for many years but who, I thought, still lived in Poland. A woman in Warsaw – she had kept my mother in hiding during the Nazi days – knew him well. So I phoned her. She greeted me most warmly and I explained the reason for my call. I said that I badly needed to be in touch with Ignacy and that I hoped that she knew his whereabouts. Her reply was that Ig, whose father and mother had been dead a long time, had divorced his wife and left the country. His present residence was somewhere in Latin America but she hadn't a clue where.

Once again in a state of shock, I tried to convince myself that I should see a lawyer and ask him to deal with this case. But then, because of the real explosion of the symptoms of my illness, frequent attacks of nausea, vomiting, pressure in my head that seemed to cause complete loss of balance, I realized I was unable to cope with legal proceeding. For this reason, I dropped the name

Lubecki into the garbage and legally assumed the new appellation, Thomas. I informed my enemy what I had done and that was the end of the story. I never heard from this madman again. I assume that, shaken by the act of cruelty he had committed, he lost his life. That's it! I also want you to know that during the period of this trial, Henrietta couldn't have been more helpful. She stood behind me all the time, she held my hand, she was the Goddess of Love. She was, and is, above all other people who I am acquainted with. Yes, way above!

That's all that I wanted you to know. I hope what I have told you is not too rough. But that's what my life is. Tough! Rough!

Sincerely yours,

Anton Thomas.

He placed the pages in an envelope, addressed it, put a stamp on it and left it on his desk, planning to mail it the next day. Then he turned off the light, spread out on the couch and a few moments later he was asleep, unperturbed by nightmares or sudden tremors in his body.

When he woke up, it was dark. As he lifted himself up, he saw his wife sitting on a leather stool, just beside him. He didn't see her face clearly; the street light barely penetrated into the room. He muttered, "Henrietta!"

She replied softly, "That's who I am." Then, after a moment of silence, she added, "I've been sitting here for a couple of hours. I came home, called, but you didn't hear me. So I came upstairs and there you were. Asleep on your couch. Breathing so softly that it made me anxious. But then you murmured something, as you often do when you have a dream, and though I didn't catch what you were saying, I knew," she smiled, "that you were having a conversation with somebody. I wondered who it was? And what were you and your guest mulling over? I'm used to watching you when you're hearing voices so I calmed down. I relaxed. What about you? Are you ok?"

"Yes, I am."

"How was the meeting?"

"Time will tell," he replied. "But my hope is not at the highest, I mean lowest, level. And as long as you're beside me..."

He lifted himself from the couch, leaned toward her, kissed her cheeks, her mouth. "I don't know how I would manage without you. Remember that."

She kissed his hands. "Thank you for that. Our feelings are mutual. Remember that."

They were holding each other, facing the window. A sliver of the moon was hanging on the sky. It shone in their direction. Then a small cloud whisked by, embracing the moon, extinguishing the light. The room was filled with darkness. Anton and Henrietta could barely see each other. They cautiously moved to the lamp on Anton's desk. But before they reached it, the cloud that blanketed the moon disappeared and the silvery sliver was again free.

Henrietta whispered, "It shines for you. It sparkles on your face. A good omen, as your mother would have said." Then stroking his hand, she added, "If you want supper, I'll prepare it for you. But I won't eat. I must get to work. I'm late with my delivery to the Guild. I haven't done much weaving in the last few days. I've been so busy at the shelter ... and in a fog because of your sickness."

After a moment of silence, Anton responded with growing intensity in his voice. "I hate that fog too. But I'm not the producer of it. It is a design of a force that I have no access to. That I do not control. Surely you're aware of it. Surely..."
He didn't finish the sentence. Suddenly a pang of fear hit his body. 'I'm going to die,' he thought. 'Soon I'm going to die.'

Shaken, he stepped back to the couch, collapsed on it, closed his eyes and unconsciously, as if to push out the stress, he pressed his chest with both hands.

Henrietta grew anxious and whispered, "What's the matter? What's the matter?"

"Nothing," Anton whispered back after a few seconds of silence. "Nothing. I'm ok. Don't worry." But his eyes were still shut. He was breathing slowly and his fingers were still on his chest.

More nervous now than before, Henrietta asked again "How ok? Tell me? I need to know. Please, tell me!"

"I'm fine," Anton replied somewhat more at ease now, yet still in a horizontal position, his head resting on the back pillow of the couch. "I have told you, don't worry. I'm fine."

Henrietta persisted. "How fine? Your voice denies what you're saying. You speak in such a troubled manner. And your hands ... do you have a pain in your chest?"

"I'm fine," Anton answered with a surge of annoyance this time. "How many times must I repeat that I'm fine?! I am fine!" He stretched his words out to emphasize the point.

The discomfort he felt before was almost gone. He lifted himself up, wanted to walk to the chair behind his desk, but the quick motion brought back the unease and the signal of it was clearly etched on his face. He instantly knew how his wife would respond, wanted to mollify her agitation but, before he managed to utter a word, she had the first say.

She jumped off the couch and, trembling with anxiety, shrieked. "You're fine? Don't play that game with me! I want to know how you are! I'm entitled to know! I take care of you! I suffer enough pain..."

Anton interrupted her in a matter-of-fact manner. "A while ago, we had a similar discussion. The situation was similar too. I was in pain. And you asked me not to tell you about my small discomforts. It was too great a burden on you to hear day after day, hour after hour, how I feel. The rotten part of it, I mean. That's what you said and I promised not to put that weight on you anymore. I was going to make you privy to my hardship when it was really rotten. Minor symptoms, they were my problem. Not worth sharing them with you. Not important enough to bring about the kind of turmoil you have gone through right now. So what I felt, I tried to make nothing of it. As you wanted. I'd rather protect you..."

He heard her gasp then utter a soft cry. He made an effort to control himself and spoke very gently. "I didn't mean to slam you. You know how emotional I am. When I am upset."

He put his arms around her, his grip was tight, and continued, "Henriushka, I'm sorry. Please believe me. That's all I can say. I am so sorry."

Not only her grandparents, but also her mother, all deceased now, called her Henriushka. Whenever Anton used that name, she knew it signified his deep concern for her, his compassionate, caring feeling toward her. The warmth of his embrace penetrated her body. She didn't have any doubt that what he said was genuine. And she responded in kind, kissing his lips, putting her head on his shoulder and hugging him. Then, turning on the lamp, he chortled. "Do you want to hear my latest poem? It just swooshed through my mind."

Without waiting for her approval, he stood up straight and recited:

"Foggy, shmogy, who gives a hoot!
As long as I'm the king!
As long as I wear the...boot!"

Coming up with the last word, he stomped on the floor with his heel. It instilled the phrase with an oppressive, dominant quality.

Henrietta instantly followed. Stepping away from him, then immediately changing her position, her arms outspread, her hips wiggling to the rhythm of the chant, she sang:

"Foggy, schmogy, I don't give a pea!
As long as I'm the queen!
As long as I have... thee!"

"Bravo! Bravo!" Anton roared with laughter. "Where the hell does it come from? This compulsion? The need to rhyme? By the way, don't take personally my sing song about the 'boot.' It had to do with the world, not you. You're too cute..."

"Great! Now let's go down and eat!" They hugged each other again, walked down to the kitchen, had their supper together – pea soup, sausages, bread and cheese, a glass of wine – then they split company.

Henrietta went to the basement – her weaving loom, balls of wool and other equipment were there – to work on an autumn-colored throw that was to be delivered to the Guild shop the next day.

Anton returned to his study and tried to write. He was working simultaneously on a novel that dealt with a comically turbulent incident which occurred to a Jewish-Canadian couple torn by the husband's illicit sexual pursuits. He had started working on it while still teaching at the University, encouraged by his publisher. His name was Harold Topper.

He was excited by the comic tilt of Anton's novel. "This is what we need. When writers produce stories about marriages, what they most often come up with is so dreary. They describe the lives of some country folk a century ago who bitch and bitch and bitch about nothing. Who are good church-goers and bad sleepers and who are so sacrosanct. I want to publish books that talk about now. I want stories that are funny. So if you finish yours..."

Anton was halfway through the novel but, dissatisfied, had dropped it. For a reason he couldn't fathom, he chose to continue working on this work of fiction, as he called it, which was a carbon copy of a scene involving his father that had rotted in his memory for many years.

He was on his way home from second grade in elementary school. Crossing the garden, it was early fall, he approached the back entrance of the house. Then he stopped by the open window of the breakfast room, next to the solarium. He saw his father standing beside the country table, leaning on its surface. His shining blue eyes were focussed on Helena, a young servant who stood on the other side of the table, her blouse torn open, showing her naked breasts. For a tense moment, they watched each other then they raced around the table, Anton's father trying to grab hold of the woman who, laughing hilariously, was doing her best to avoid being captured. Or to tease the man.

The story didn't go any further. It had appeared in his mind for the first time when he was a teenager and it flickered in and out in his young days, particularly when there was tension between him and his father. He was emotionally divided about his parent. He admired him for his quick wit, intellectual dexterity, passionate belief in social justice, compassionate concern for the poor. Human suffering was the most frequent subject of their dinner conversations. And yet, at the same time, Anton saw him as a short-fused slave to an abrasive temperament, and he rebelled against his credo that children's obedience was the law of the family. The older Anton became, the less accommodating he was and at a larger distance from his father. Their stressful relationship was an irreversible part of their home life and, eventually, a subject of Anton's literary output.

One of his early short stories in the particular, The Foe of Chastity a portrayal of an rambunctious intellectual who lived in Lima and whose name was Miliano, was infused with the shortcomings that Anton saw as characteristic of his father. The introductory page offered the following information to the reader.

"Miliano, outside of his professional work as a dentist which he found exceedingly uninspiring, was constantly preoccupied with a number of soul-rectifying activities. He regularly practiced playing the violin accompanied by his daughter Anneta who showed a great deal of talent as a pianist, published and regularly wrote biting articles for Counter Attack, a weekly Spanish magazine devoted to the combat of racism in Peru, directed amateur theatre shows (his wife Rosita was often a leading actress in them), and steadfastly worked on his plays and his novel. With such a heavy load on his mind, that also bristled with disdain for weakness, short-fused temper, self-aggrandizement and Supreme Court Judge-like severity, he did not have much time for Antonio, his son. For incalculable reasons, he was not too fond of him, paid little attention to him, except when his tough-fisted interference was required by the boy's mother."

In fact, the way Anton recalled it, the upbringing of the children was his mother's responsibility. They grew up under her tutelage, supported only occasionally by their watchful father. The warmth she exuded and her uncanny insight into their children's emotional needs was the protective shield that Anton used to a larger degree than his sister. As bright as he was, he was frequently an underachiever in school. According to his father, he didn't work hard enough. Yet the cause of it had nothing to do with insufficient brain power but with the low respect he had for himself and the fear that resided in his heart. He often thought that, in comparison to his taller, strongly muscled and mostly Christian school mates, he was an unattractive, unappealing creature, and that his brain had only a modest capacity to handle the school curriculum.

"I'm not a math wiz," he often complained to his mother, coming home from school. "Nor a physics wiz. I stumble like a fool when I'm told to read a poem out loud. In the gym, I'm at the bottom of my class. My skill at making people laugh is nil. My intelligence is that of a street bum. Of a cretin!"

In response his mother would hug him, caress him, and would say "Your history teacher told me that you're a brilliant student. Your teacher of literature made me believe that no one at your level reads as much as you do. More than he. And you received the highest marks in the class. You're like me. I was never very good at algebra. A clunkhead when making jokes. A klutz in the gym. Now have a glass of milk and a pastry. Then have a bath and rest. I love you, my son. My pet. As your father would say, you're the best!"

In Anton's view, the last observation was wrong. His father would have never said that. One time, he remembered it vividly, his father entered the fray. Standing unnoticed in the narrow corridor connecting the kitchen and the hallway, he overheard the conversation and said bitingly:

"You're different because you're a Jew. You were made that way. By us," he pointed at Rosa and himself, "your mother and I..."

"You were made by whoever was responsible for it," interjected Anton's mother, the index finger of her left hand pointing at the sky. "We were only..."

"You were made by us!" Anton's father cut her off. "In accordance with the Laws of Nature. Your ancestors lived in a desert. The scorching heat, the food they ate shaped their bodies, their features. The way you look, you inherited from them. So be proud of it and don't piss me off by complaining how poorly you're built. The girls don't mind your looks! So clear your mind! And make a better effort to improve at school! You're soft willed! Lazy! Look at me..."

Anton's mother cut him off crisply. "Here's your tea. That's why you left your study. So take it and let me have my chat with Anton. I know how to soothe him. You and I..."

The way Anton understood it, she wanted to say: "We differ about how to handle our son".

But he couldn't have been certain of it. His mother did not finish the sentence. Anton's father grabbed the tea cup and walked away without saying a word. That was the image that was deeply stuck in Anton's memory.

The source of tension between his mother and his father became clear to him when the "spirit of sexual desire' entered into his body— his father's phrase relating to an erection – and when he overheard a heated exchange between his parents who were locked in their bedroom. He woke up, late at night with the need to go to the bathroom, and on his way back to his room, he was struck by his mother's harsh whisper:

"You're a dirty rascal! A serf to sex! Each business trip you take, you bounce with a madame whore! Your female colleagues who travel with you! I have a list of your affairs! Your lawyer friend gave it to me! In the last four years..."

She was interrupted by the trembling voice of her husband. "My lawyer friend? I will break his neck for meddling in my affairs! He wants to fuck you so he meddles with me! Bastard! Now, listen to this! What you're accusing me of is only partly true. I did it once, maybe twice, when I was away from you. When I was lonely and drunk. In need of an embrace. But I love only you. I swear it on the lives of our children. What more can I say? It's true. It's true!"

Anton tiptoed to his room, cried in his bed and was scared by what the next day would bring. But the early morning breakfast was as swift and plentiful as usual. His sister was in a radiant mood, oblivious to what had transpired last night.

His parents seemed also brimming with joy, cracking jokes about the "daily torture" the kids had to suffer "slurping hot oatmeal with milk and raisins. The food of peasants! And of Jewish crazies!" They exuded nothing but love for each other.

Anton was perplexed by their serenity and, many times during his young days, he questioned the veracity of the images that so often occupied his mind.

'What lives inside of me is it a figment of my imagination? Established to pester me for some secret reason? Am I punishing my father that way for his coolness toward me? Am I turning him into a monster and my mother into a martyr?'

He once revealed his troubling thoughts to a close high school buddy, a bright and caring Christian boy whom he trusted. After hearing the confession, his friend laughed.

"It seems to me more like a dream than a true story. The first one in particular. But if what you saw or heard is true so what?

My dad also goes fucking. He too likes to spend time with sluts. That is how we're made. Victims of bad construction. So forget it. And do what you need to receive the gift of sexual satisfaction."

For a while Anton was able to convince himself that what lingered in his mind was a dream, a product of his own sickly imagination. And he stopped thinking about it. He was free of the torment. Then after the war, soon after he learned how his father had died, the images again persistently infiltrated his mind.

He was infuriated by them and blamed himself for keeping them alive. 'The man was tortured, murdered. Why would you cling to remembering him as a philanderer? Not as a human being who, though burdered with faults like anybody else, was a decent, compassionate creature.' To clear that particular reminiscence from his mind, one day he approached his mother – they were still in Poland, a year before they had migrated to Canada – telling her more or less directly what reverberated in his head. He asked her if there was any truth to it. "That my father was a sex maniac who cheated on you."

Her response was evasive but he had never seen her so angry. "What he was is in the past," she yelled. "I loved him and he loved me. He took good care of us all. For you to ask me that question now is vicious. If you were younger, I would slap your face. But as you're old enough to understand what it means, I will spit at you. Taste it if you will. My bitter spit!"

She spat at him and ran, sobbing, to her bedroom. Anton followed her, tried desperately to appease her but the door to her room was locked. For two days, she refused to see him, rejecting his efforts to explain to her the inner battle he was going through. And his pain. Eventually, the tension subsided. She allowed him to express his remorse, asked him to "Forgive and forget the wicked flare up. My doing." But she begged him to never again confront her with the subject.

From then on, for many years, the acrid memories of his father evaporated almost completely. The exigencies of the daily existence were too demanding, particularly after he landed in Canada. He was so deeply involved in the tough business of settling in the new land, possessed and enthralled by the challenges that he sucessfully resisted the painful entries into his childhood.

The intricacies of achieving status within the theatre community were the strongest components of this blessed self-defence.

After years of struggle, underscored by relentless persistence, Anton managed to become a sort of celebrity. His literary output was well praised as was his work at the University.

He once lectured his students: "Canoeing through the turbulent waters of the cultural sea is difficult. One must be rivetted only to that task, be free of other compulsions. Otherwise, the inevitable happens: one is faced with an explosive encounter. A disastrous collision!"

During those busy, mind-taxing days, Anton lived only in the present. The emotional consequences of the past seemed invisible. But when he retired, though he was devoting hours to writing, step-by-step memories of the old days started to re-occur.

"They creep up on me again," he once mentioned to Henrietta. But what he remembered seemed colorless; the images were two-dimensional and distant, as if disengaged from his personal life. What flashed in his mind would disappear quickly, without damaging his emotional balance. Then their number increased and their effect on him became more and more visible. He was much more aware that the novel he was now rewriting was, in disguised form, a reproduction on paper of the rough side of the life of his parents. As if prodded by his mother, he questioned the fairness of revealing, even in the most oblique fashion, the addiction to illicit love affairs, the human weakness that had an upper hand in the life of his father.

Yet he couldn't resist writing about it. The assuring voice of his self-defence said the subject matter was too common for anyone to make the connection .

So he kept on working on the novel, was halfway through it, but the recent days of his physical and emotional discomfort created a new impediment. His mind, so nimble in normal circumstances, now functioned with infuriating slowness. Words and phrases he wanted were lost in a maze or, if he found them, had a mundane quality.

He scribbled a few sentences, didn't like what he wrote, pushed the pad aside, turned off the light and, in his usual manner, stared at the street through the window. A few cars were parked beside the sidewalk, the street lights were on, so were the lights in the houses that he faced. But there were no people about. The street was motionless, silent. He lifted his eyes to the sky, his hands resting on the edge of his desk, locked together as if in prayer, and then it happened. An image appeared, fairly close, between two heavy, long, slightly curved branches of the tree on his lawn. He saw himself in a luscious garden, sitting on a swing. He was five or six years old, with his young, sharp-faced father pushing him forward and chanting, baritoning in a rhyming fashion:

"Balama, Talama, Balama, Talama
Balama too too too!
Balama, Talama, Balama, Talama
Balama, moo, moo, moo!"

His mother was also present. She was standing a few steps away, licking an ice cream cone. Anton, his sturdy, little legs swinging in the air, was turning his head toward his father as if wanting to say something but each upward shove made him switch in the opposite direction. "Balama, Talama.." was ringing lightheartedly in the air. Then this image dissolved abruptly and another took its place. Anton, still the same little boy, was standing beside his mother sobbing and shouting.

"Daddy slapped me! I wanted to ask him what Balama, Talama means! And he slapped my head! When I was on the swing! Why?! Why?! He's mean! Mean!"

His mother hugged him lovingly. "Daddy didn't hit you. He tousled your hair. He didn't want you to fall off the swing. And the words he sings mean nothing. They are sounds he makes to tell you how he enjoys playing with you. How he loves you. It helps him to get rid of his worries that sit in his heart. Your daddy worries a lot. He's under such duress. Do you know the word duress?"

She dried his cheeks and handed him the ice cream cone which he grabbed quickly. Then the image was gone.

What Anton saw now was the starlit sky with a sliver of the moon imprinted on it. There were tears in his eyes. And he said to himself smiling with bitter sadness:

"Thank you, mum, for the ice cream. And for solving one of my puzzles. Duress is what I am under. Did I inherit it from my daddy? I don't know, but I think so. Had I known him longer, I would have known for sure. But he was gone so early in my life. So I can only guess and blabber the way he did. To clam up my bitter thoughts. To rise above my distress."

He was once again very tired. His ear was buzzing, light tremors were criss-crossing his body. He went to the bedroom, the bed was already made, Henrietta saw to that, took off his clothes, slipped into his pyjamas, walked slowly to the bathroom, peed, brushed his teeth, went down into the basement, kissed his wife good night, returned to the bedroom, slid under the blanket and his head sideways on the pillow, whispered to himself: "I wish my wife was more like St. Joan than like Desdemona."

Why that sentiment crossed his mind he didn't know. And he chided himself. "Your mind works as if it were hit by a sarcoma! Go to sleep. And wake up clear headed. With a grin. The way you did when you were a little boy."

Then he thought that it would be useful to share the mystery of the discovery with the psychiatrist. "That's what his role is," he was convincing himself. "To assist in making what's incoherent, coherent. To cleanse my psyche of the rot that has piled up on it for so many years. Dumped by ...who was it," he pondered, "who loaded me with that crap? How did it happen that I'm so besotted by it? Subservient to it. Who am I? What am I? Why am I?"

He fell asleep. He was snoring lightly but again no nightmares, no disturbing dreams interrupted his rest. He didn't even hear Henrietta, a few hours later, joining him in bed. He was sleeping soundly.

And the moon was still in the sky, shedding the light of hope, faint as it was, on the slice of Earth that was Anton's.

CHAPTER THREE

The next four weeks were exceptionally difficult for Anton. He suffered a number of violent attacks of vertigo, had some chest pain, was bed-ridden for many days and so physically and emotionally exhausted that he was unable to concentrate on the 'life stories' that he would have to come up with for the next session with Dr. Wright. The scheduled appointment with the psychiatrist was cancelled, Henrietta took care of that, then it was renewed and erased again. Dr. Wright made a couple of phone calls inquiring about Anton's health, the last time at 10 p.m. during the third week of his illness. Henrietta was touched by Dr. Wright's attention to her husband, so was he. But when another call came, this time in the mid-morning and one week after the previous one, Anton, though he felt much better, refused to talk to the therapist.

"Tell him," he spluttered to Henrietta who covered the receiver of the bed-side telephone, "that I can't talk! That I have been chased by demons. That they flogged my body. That they tormented me because I refused to be their toady."

Henrietta did not repeat to the psychiatrist what she had just heard. She thanked him for his "patient interest" in her husband then explained to him that Anton was still in a rocky state, still too weak and stressed to pick up the phone.

"But I will see to it," she said, "that he returns the call, soon. And that he makes an appointment to see you. His first session with you made him feel so much more earth-bound. Awake! You infused him with energy. And courage. I thank you for it. You did us both so much good!"

After she hung up, she sat next to Anton on the bed. She stroked his head and gently pointed out to him that once again he came up with "rhyming drivel" and asked him to explain the meaning of what he had said. She couldn't grasp the sense of it. Its implication.

Anton was no less bewildered. The moment he had blurted out that sentence, he was shocked by it. So, without responding heatedly to her punishing term "drivel," he rested his head on her lap and whispered, "I'm in a state of sickly delusion. What I need is...eh.. a closet to be locked into. It would be better if I lived alone, don't you think? In seclusion!"

"You're blabbering again," Henrietta responded softly, tears welling in her eyes. "You need to listen to your inner self and reveal it to your psychiatrist. If you don't, you will sink deeper and deeper into your quagmire. You must fight the demons that rip your brain. You must..."

With those last words Anton was hit by an echo of something he had heard before. 'How do I know them so well?' Then an image captured his mind. It was a cold, wintry day. He was fifteen years old, standing by a huge tree on a snow covered street of a Polish city, close to the hockey field beside the gymnasium he attended. He was a part of the school's hockey team; they had played a game with a team of another school and they had lost. Anton, the goalie, was blamed for it. A few metres away was a bunch of his teammates who pounded him with snowballs, screaming: "Kike! Kike! You made us lose! We'll rip your brain! Turn you into beef! Heil to those who hate you! We claim the same!"

At that moment, a gym instructor saw the skirmish. He lifted the hockey stick that he was carrying and hurled himself towards the boys. "Get away," he roared. "You are the guilty ones. He played well. You played like sleepy dogs. You crawled like turtles! Leave Anton alone or you'll end up in jail! Get out of here!"

The gang dispersed instantly. Then the teacher addressed Anton, "Don't take that shit lying down, my boy! When they call you kike, call them monsters! Swines! Fight back! Don't cringe! When I saw you clinging to that tree, I thought there is a lemming whose wish is to die! Life is hard! There are always enemies to be faced! Be prepared and fight back! Be tough! Not scared! Break your fear! Break it!"

Saying the last words, he shook Anton's shoulders. Anton practically felt the grip, now. Then, that memory dissolved and another took its place.

The same day, in the evening, Anton was in his father's study telling him about that "rotten kafaffel" and about the Christian teacher who had "saved my life."

Emil listened attentively then said, "You were lucky, my son. That gym instructor is a decent human being. I would like to meet him and interview him. Our community would breathe easier reading about a man like him. But..."

He got up from the chair behind his desk, pointed his finger at his son, and stated sternly, "Don't you ever fight back! With words, yes. On the pages of a book or a newspaper, but not with your fists. That gang just waits for it. They want nothing better than a chance to break your bones. You must protect your body, remember that. That's all you have. Your brain, your heart and your flesh. And one more thing," he chortled, lowering his voice, "your prick! You're old enough for me to tell you this. Take care of it. It will give you a lot of fun. Of all things in our lives, there's nothing that can match it. The pleasure that you will derive from your penis by putting it to good use. But remember, prior to the prowl, no booze!. Well, a glass or two of vodka would do you no harm but more might liquidate your charm. Your organ might not get stiff when you need it most. Believe you me, without liquor, your sperm machine will be your music maker. Your merchant of joy. Don't let it be harmed! "

The image was gone but Anton was still in the thrall of what he saw. His eyes shut, a happy grin on his lips, he stayed silent, unresponsive to what Henrietta had said to him a few moments ago. Then opening his eyes and sliding his hand under her robe to stroke her knee, he whispered. "I'm so happy. I just finished talking to my father."

Henrietta was accustomed to these phantom conversations. She asked sweetly, "And what did he say?"

"That I should never forget the value of my Horgan. That I should always remember the joy it gave me. Though it is about useless now," he chortled, "for a long time it stood up well to its task. Henrietta, do you feel as I do? Are your memories as bouncy as mine?"

"They are, my love," she said. "Where your hand is now sends a message I miss so much. But I'm an invalid too. Just like you. What you're touching now is closed up. So we must find something else..."

Anton stopped her. "We have. When we are hugging each other, there's magic to it. I so much wish we did it more often. We seem to..."

Henrietta interuppted, "Sh! This is the wrong time to start a discussion. Not now. The moment is so idyllic. What else did you hear from your father?"

She had hoped to hear something like: "Your wife is a charming, strong creature just like your mother. Tell her that. Be gracious. Don't play the boss!"

But Anton, sitting up, answered with a touch of derision in his voice. "How he regretted slapping me so often and so hard when I was a little boy. Making my bum so blue!"

Then he corrected himself. "No! He didn't say that. I am telling a lie. He would never have apologized for smacking my ass. He was too sure of himself. Too certain that whatever he did was right."

"He was just like my father," Henrietta commented lightly. "I've told you before that I was his punching bag. Always in the basement. Where he played billiards. That was the style of the time. You had to show your children how strong you were. And that you were the boss. Dad was the whip. Mom was..."

"The floss," Anton finished for her. They both laughed and Henrietta said, "I thought your rhyme would deal with 'billiard.' Dad was the whip," she repeated Anton's words. "Mom was the vineyard!"

They burst out laughing again and Henrietta said to Anton, "You feel better today, don't you? It's such fun to see you in an upbeat mood. Your illness is behind you, am I right?"

"I think so," Anton replied. "My ear doesn't ring. I am not dizzy. So if it stays that way, tonight let's go out for dinner. McDonald's precious food. Hamburger and potato chips. And French champagne! To soften up what's...crude!"

Once again the sound of their laughter filled the room. Then Henrietta grew serious.

"What you have told about your father, I've heard before. A long time ago. You were soused, we were chatting about our youth and you told me that he beat you, hard. That he not only bruised your bum but did lasting damage to your heart. He made you a shadow of yourself – that is how you worded it. A coward fearful of darkness. Of hard-fisted men."

She paused for a moment then continued with a pleading note in her voice. "Will you tell Dr. Wright about your latest contact with your father? It would be so useful. He would learn how close the two of your were. How he influenced your life. For good and bad. How what he did still torments you. Or lifts you up. The early days with your father linger so strangely in your memory. They have formed and deformed your life."

"Something like that," Anton said. "The way he treated me, much of it gave me strength. And much of it made me little."

"By the way," he continued with strange animation, "when I was young and strong I was not frightened of tight-fisted men. Once we were on equal footing, I could stand up to them. Equal footing! I guess you know what I mean. A condition that allowed me to think that I am not a persecuted Jewish monster but like anybody else. A God-created human being," he snickered.

"During my days with the Polish Underground movement and during the Warsaw Uprising, I stood up against those who tried to turn us into serfs. I did my share of shooting them down. I faced the bloody Germans, no, the bloody SS men, the bloody Nazis, with a rifle. They were a hundred meters away from me; we were behind a sandbag barrier, they were on the other side of the street hiding behind armoured vehicles. I saw their heads covered by helmets, their pistols, their guns, but I was not afraid. On the contrary, I was buoyant with pride that I was facing them on equal ground! I was not a haunted man but a hunter! Not a rabbit to be slaughtered. I was ready to jump over the sandbags, cross the street and the piece of grassy land that separated us..."

"I know, I know," Henrietta interrupted him, softly. "I have read it. In your first novel. We both know it is filled with your experiences. There is such a strong personal tinge to it. And it characterizes most of your writing. Your plays and short stories are so much the reflection of your life. Young men so often think and speak the way you do. And go through the fire of hell that torched you. And still does. In a different way now, not in the form of naked aggression. But it burns you nonetheless. The pain you suffer is devastating. And yet there is a desire in you to keep that fire alive. That inferno is the source of your creativity. So what you're faced with is a dilemma: should you let it die or keep it going and going and going. Why don't you write about the world that surrounds us now? Like the story you once wrote about the rebels in Latin America. When I read it, I couldn't believe it was you who wrote the piece. You were so cool about it yet so convincing. Their struggle was so sharply etched and the portrait of the doomed hero was gripping and filled with pain. Yes, *The American Boots* had a strong impact on me and I often wondered why you have distanced yourself from such works. You start writing about something that does not connect with the Holocaust, then you drop it. Like the novel you have been working on for the last six months. A marital comedy as you called it. How far have you pushed it? Nowhere! And didn't you tell me you made a mistake? That you should have set it in war-ravaged Poland, not in Canada today? That their antics would have better fitted the rugged landscape of a ghetto? You're encased by that image. Inflamed by it. Though it burns you, you longing for it is steady. But no matter how you crave it, you must find a way to extinguish it. Or at least to diminish its intensity. Otherwise..."

She was too tense to finish. She stood up, walked to the window – it was wide, there were four casements – and opened the Venetian blind. A burst of bright light entered the room. She opened one window, looked outside at the garden and exclaimed, "Anton, look! The sun is blazing. There's not one cloud in the sky. It's fall, but the grass, the bushes are still green. Come and look! And write about us! A short story! Like the long poem that you wrote for me several years ago when you were tanning yourself in Barbados. A letter to my wife you called it. Remember?"

She rushed to the night table on her side of the bed, pulled out the top drawer, took out sheets of paper with text printed on them. She faced her husband. Her pale cheeks and the silvery streaks in her dark, curly hair were sparkling, touched by the rays of sunshine. In the pose of a dancing nymph, she read:

The beach is white, semi-circular and wide,
somewhat like a stage.
For the backdrop, there're palms on the sloping hills.
At the sides, steep and craggy boulders, arching forward
like watchtowers.
Would one want to, curtain could be drawn between
  them,
so symetrically placed they are.
Behind the hills and on a tiles covered land, a curious
transplant from the Roman past – pillars, arches, flying
nymphs – the hotel.
Above the beach,   the canopy of the sky,
                below the sea.
That's where I'm heading, the second day
in a row, its Sunday,
                and very early in the morning.
The sun, a glowing disc,
                just woke me up.
Down on the beach, the sole intruder, the human
world is still asleep, I bow my head, and with
solemnity I didn't know I possess
I pay homage to the force that made this Paradise.
That's the beach I'm sitting on.
                Without you.
Alone.
                But for myself – devoid of people.
Yes, there're are no people at all, but palms on the hills,
like Spanish dancers, costumed green, with fans swaying
in the wind,
no people
        but the sun bleached twigs – driftwood in our
vocabulary – like thin gymnasts' legs,
                erect, and piercing the space.
I must say,
                strange feeling this,
To be here,
                without you,
                alone,
without people,

only with the translucent blueness of the sea that smacks
my back,
with the palms that whirl and sway in obedience to
the wind, with white crested waves that, rising and
falling,
thump the sky poised cliffs, which like
charcoaled remnants of an ancient
fort
stand guard between the land
and the sea.
Paradise? No doubt.
A feast to the eye. A music to the ear. A caress to
the body.
And yet......
strange feeling this,
to be the sole recipient of this beauty,
to be grateful, embraceful, yet alone, unable
to sing the praise,
together with you.
Strange feeling this,
to have you within me
but not without,
to conjure your face
but feel not the touch,
to repeat your name
yet hear no response,
to clasp...a red speckled stone
but not your hand.
Why is it that I need you so badly?
With these thoughts,
unnoticed,
a rain-soaked tarpaulin
invades the sky.
The sun switches off.
The white expanse shrinks,
the green-clad palms shrivel,
the smell of rotting fish, like
dirty vapour rises from the sea.

Paradise crumbles.
There's only wind, that roars and howls,
waves that pound the cliffs – and with
what venom! And darkness, and rain
that comes down with ferocious speed,
and as if armed with nails, pierces the
boulders, the sea and the sand.

With this, I run, surrounded
by havoc, my head under my arms,
my back pummelled by water.
And when I climb the steps -
I hear a shriek,
no, a bellow expelled from the
darkest pit of the sea:

"Paradise not shared, is Paradise lost"
You of all people should know that!
You dink! You loony loon!
You cooky nut! You fool!"
Phantasy? Perhaps...

But that blast which reached me from the
bottom of the sea, has not left my ear.
When I hear it,
I laugh, but the message is so simple,
So potent, and sound, that I can't refute it,
but must pay heed to it, nay, bow to it with
reverence and joy, and in turn send the message
to you:
Paradise not shared is Paradise lost.
You, of all people should know that!
You.......
And filled with two soft boiled eggs and buoyed by
champagne, my breakfast, I want you to know
that I made a vow – as solemnly conceived
as I know how

that you and I will never
disunite,
but will share the space that
is given to us,
empty or crowded
tiny or big,
silent or loud.

And that we will not be alone, but always together.
And that you and I will forever inhabit our
Paradise.

When Henrietta, somewhat breathless, finished her recitation, Anton raced towards her, clapping his hands and calling, "Bravo! Bravo! You delivered the poem with the flair of a top-notch actress. It sounded so melodious. So revealing. I didn't know that it was imbedded in your mind. You must have studied it recently. You couldn't have delivered it so well if you didn't. It's an old poem. When did I give it to you. Ah! When I returned from Barbados ... In the early winter of 1982."

"Yes, I read it many times," Henrietta replied softly. "To reassure myself that our Paradise won't vanish – burned by the fire. You know what I mean. Fight it, my beloved. Fight it! We can still enjoy life. Our years to come don't need to be trampled by grief. "

Anton held her tightly. "There's nothing I want more. I will do all I can to put the past to sleep. If I can. My sessions with Dr. Wright might help."

He pointed at the blue sky, "As long as there's sunshine. As long as it doesn't rain. No rain! No rain!"

He kissed her mouth, pulled down the zipper of her negligee, kissed her between her naked breasts, then turned away as if taken aback by his act.

Henrietta noticed the startled expression on his face and exclaimed with feigned disappointment, "That's all?"

"What more do you want? More disrespect for your front?"

They both huddled with laughter then Anton slapped his cheek and said, "I'm speaking like a fool. Like a love starved adolescent. I'd better go to the bathroom and take a shower. It will make me less...eh..."

"Effervescent," Henrietta finished his sentence mirthfully. "That's for sure. Today you're effervescent. Which makes it easier to talk something over with you. I need to take a trip. A brief one. To Montreal. The manager of the Guild shop wants to see me. She wants to discuss my approach to design. When I spoke to her on the phone, she said she likes my work but that I'm 'too original'. That's how she put it. She would prefer if my blankets were less startling. She called it 'less avant-garde.' More commercial. So next week I'll have to go for two or three days. Business matters aside, the trip will do me good. It will let me refresh 'my stifled mind' as you would call it. I need to change the pattern of my life. Give it freshness. You know what I'm saying. Are you agreeable? Do you feel strong enough to be comfortable without me? Not shaky because you're alone? If you need to you can always call Paul or Nina. They would gladly come. So may I go and feel secure that you'll be ok?"

"Go. Go,' Anton exclaimed lifting himself from his horizontal position. "I'm in good shape. Your departure will do me no harm. As a matter of fact, it will make me feel better. It will remove the guilt that sits in my dish," he was punching his chest on the left side clearly referring to his heart, "that you are a give-it-all woman and I'm a Pinocchio. No," he accentuated the next words, "A piddly fish!"

Henrietta smiled, "Let me tell you, your penchant for rhyming is quite distressing. Though you may find it caressing!"

Anton retorted, "Your penchant for criticism is so flunky. Though you may find it picky. And spunky!"

While he was speaking thoughts raced through his mind. 'She'll be gone! I will be alone! What if there's a storm and I'm hit by lightning? Will I be dead with no one around? God! My fear is a curse! A never-ending blight! Anton, fight it! Fight it! There's nothing else left but a ruthless fight!"

He quickly got to his feet, helped Henrietta to stand up and, to quell his anxiety, kept on: "You will go by train, right? Call the travel agency and make your arrangements. And I'll go to the bathroom and have a shower. And shave my dirty cheeks," he laughed. "Then I will phone Dr. Wright, make the apointment and put my brain to work. My crucial 'life stories'. Pick up those incidents that linger and linger in my mind. God Almighty," he laughed again. "I'll be sinking once more into the dust. But I need to do it. To cleanse my soul, this exercise is a must."

He started to walk away from his wife, took off his pyjamas, dropped them on the floor, then stopped and yelled, "Jesus! I've been rhyming! Have I been doing it all the time?"

Receiving a silent nod from Henrietta, he excoriated himself savagely. "Once I'm aware of it, I want to cut off my tongue. I'm supposedly cloning my father, I know, but it is a duplicity, not an honest reflection. Why am I doing it? Why can't I stay free of that addiction?"

Henrietta offered the answer, "Because it amuses you. Makes you laugh and momentarily removes your depression. That is why I play that game with you. To help you disperse the gloom. But why ask me? Ask Dr. Wright."

Anton exclaimed, "I will! I will! Suffering – I was told – is the wage of sin. So I must find out what I have done to be dumped into that filthy bin!"

Then, as before, he vehemently punched his jaw and screamed, "Oh, my God, another outburst of my rhyming fury! Why do I get so incensed?"

Henrietta who now was barely listening to his verbal bombast – she was entranced by his naked body – said quickly, almost with awe in her voice, "Because you're standing in front of me without your pants! You're still so sharp looking. So munchy. Is your Horgan still for rent? It stands out quite raunchy!"

She hoped she would diffuse the anger that tortured Anton and she achieved what she wanted. Anton replied instantly, in vaudevillian fashion:

"Horgan, Morgan
Who gives a hoot!
As long as you are the mistress!
And you play the flute!"

Henrietta intoned in response: "You're again surrendering to your rhyming disease! Don't get angry! It's a tease! A tease!"

Anton answered, pretending to be in tears:

"This is my last rhyme!
That garbage – no more!
If not, I will attach a label
To the front door!
It will read: here lives a rhino!
No! A rhyming flunky!
So avoid him! Who needs to have
contact with a braying
donkey!"

They both howled with laughter. The stepped toward each other and embraced so strongly that a shot of pain rocketed through their bodies. They broke the hold, looked at each other with intense affection then, as if overwhelmed by it, split apart. Anton went to the bathroom; Henrietta to the kitchen to prepare lunch.

For the moment, they were happy. Very happy.

CHAPTER FOUR

The next day, Anton called Dr. Wright. He arranged for an appointment and three days later – the calendar read Friday, September 21, 1991 – he faced his psychiatrist for the second time. He was brought to the clinic by Henrietta who was going to do some shopping in the area. It was noon. She was to pick him in an hour.

The day was nice; warm and sunny though a few dark clouds were dotting the sky. Anton, alone in front of the building, murmured, 'Those clouds will soon band together. The sun will be gone and it will rain.' That observation made him anxious but he chided himself, 'Henrietta says you're a devoted pessimist. You negate all the bright aspects of life. Why can't you think that those clouds will disappear and the sky will remain sunny?'

The voice of his mother reverberated in his ear. She was repeating the first sentence of the question that appeared in his mind. Then an image hidden in the archives of his memory, unreconstructed until that moment, materialized. He was seventeen years old, a high school student in Lwow, the major city in Eastern Poland, sitting at his desk in his room, writing an essay on the tolerance or intolerance of religion in ancient civilizations, a subject on the agenda of the teacher of world literature. It was a warm, rainy day in early fall. The window in his room was open and if he stretched a bit, he could hear and see his parents who were sitting in a glassed-in porch. They were talking animatedly about a lecture Emil had delivered the day before to the Patrons of Culture, the "well-greased" – as he called them – Jewish doctors, lawyers, merchants and industrialists who lived in the city and who would gather once a month in their club to learn what was going on in the "civilized world." Anton hadn't attended but his mother had and as he now overheard, she was most upset by the speech her husband had delivered to that crowd.

"You couldn't have been more negative," she berated him. "You scared all those people beyond reason. You sounded as if the world was on the verge of collapse. You're a devoted pessimist. You ...."

Anton's father interrupted the trouncing. "Rosa, you're right. I am deeply pessimistic. That is what I had to express to that crowd. Hitler is gaining power. The world is silent about it. When he hits, the blow will be traumatic. I know that. I see it happening. And it brings a suffocating pain to my heart."

"That's a suicidal forecast," Rosa raised her voice. "You see everything so scuttled by doom! Is it because you're an atheist? As your father would say, you are dismissing God as the Super Power. As the final Judge of human life on earth. If you believed in Him and trusted Him, you would not see the world sinking into disaster. You would not surrender to this thrust of doom. That is all that occupies your mind." She grew softer and smiled. "Excluding even the sexual encounters that brighten your day no, your nights. You focus on nothing but gloom. I can't take it anymore. That gloom and doom. That doom and gloom. It makes me crazy!". She paused for a second then added with a pained sigh: "And what you will give me now is a hug. Not a word of retraction, but an embrace that solves nothing. A well-meant yet empty embrace. Therefore out of place. Out of place."

The scene evaporated but Anton was so overwhelmed that he couldn't move. And he thought, 'Again, a visit from the past. My mother was so eloquent, acerbic and pain-ridden while talking to my father. And he took it so well. He was so quiet. So much in shackles. As if unable or unwilling to go deeper into the matter. He looked and sounded as if he was torn by grief.'

Then another thought flashed through his mind. 'How truthful was that scene? Was it really something that I had experienced or was it a figment of my imagination? My mother and my father are so far away from me and have been at such a distance for so many years that I cannot judge the accuracy of such a phantasmagoric event. When I heard them talk, for a moment I thought I was part of this chat. My father played me! And my mother who lambasted him was a carbon copy of Henrietta.'

The notion that he had invented the scene shook him up even more. He turned away from the entrance of the Institute, momentarily forgetting where he was and what had brought him there. Then he came back to his senses. He looked at his watch. It was ten minutes past twelve.

"I'm late," he uttered softly but with vehemence. "Dr. Wright might leave his office to have lunch, thinking that I'm not coming Anton, you're a dumbwitted bum! No! This is a pissnomer!" He often used this word instead of misnomer. "A dumbwitted creep!"

He ran up the stairs; there was a buzz in his ear. He twisted through the crowd of patients who were waiting for the elevator and was the first to enter when the doors opened. He travelled to the fourth floor and, when he exited, the attractive young woman whom he had seen during his first visit exclaimed with a smile:

"Mr. Battered Man, you're late. But I'm glad you made it. Dr. Wright mentioned that you were unwell. I'll open the door and you can walk straight through to his office. He's expecting you."

Anton said, "I'm sorry for the inconvenience." He wanted to continue with another line, 'but I'm a sick man, so I deserve a pocketful of lenience,' but managed to avoid it and was happily surprised by that unexpected achievement. 'I put a brake on my rhyming gift. God almighty, that's a lift. A wondrous lift!'

Realizing what switched through his mind, he exploded with laughter. The receptionist looked at him with apprehension, perhaps even with some disquietude, yet stepped out of her cubby-hole, unlocked the door that separated the waiting room from the doctors' offices and invited Anton to enter. But before letting him go she asked, "Are you still writing?"

Anton replied, "Not much. I'm too busy taking care of myself. Writing wise, I'm a slouch."

The young woman said, "I read your novel, *Sophia...Sophia*. I spotted it in the library. I was very moved by it. My father came here from Poland, but I know so little about what was going on there during the German occupation. You called it fictitious but I'm sure you were writing about yourself. It made me see you in a different light. The man you wrote about, that fictitious character," she smiled, "he went through hell. He was so wrapped in tragedy."

Anton instantly wanted to interject, 'You're right. This is the cause of my mental allergy.' But he managed to supress that need. Instead, he thanked her for her "heart-touching comments" and rushed through the corridor to Dr. Wright's office.

As he entered, the psychiatrist was sitting behind his desk and listening to someone on the phone. Seeing Anton, he gave him a friendly smile. With the palm of his hand he pointed at a chair beside his desk and made a gesture that indicated that he still had to pay attention to the person who was on the line. A few minutes later, observing the signs of irritation that were reshaping Anton's face, he gently addressed his loquacious interlocutor: "I can't talk to you any longer. One of my patients has arrived. Relax and I will talk to you later. Sleep if you can."

After he hung up, Dr. Wright took a deep breath then said, "Sorry for holding you up. I am glad you were able to make it. You look fine. A bit pale but ... would you like a cup of coffee? The pot is full."

Anton replied, "No thank you. You look so tanned. Were you away? Somewhere in the nomads' land?"

Dr. Wright grinned. "Yes. A week before you called, we were in Mexico. On a sandy beach in Acapulco. The sun was blazing. My wife and I had such fun. But the chemistry of the land," he winked, "did some harm. She contracted a stomach flu. When she feels some pain she gives me a call..."

Anton cut him off. "So stomach pains, those are her blues! A touch of diarrhea and she needs to call you at work and talk to you about it for several minutes? This is unfair to your patients. They need your ear, your attention and their time with you is so tight. I too am affected by an organic disorder. I urinate often eight times per day and three times during the night. I walk in to the washroom and I spit venom at this bladder geist. I detest this blight. But do I make an issue of it? Do I ..."

He stopped raging. For a moment he was silent. Then, smacking himself on the cheek, he stood up and erupted again. "Why the hell do I bark? My father would say I am behaving like a dumb-witted animal. Why do I question your wife's access to you? Dr. Wright, for my misdemeanor, I apologize profusely! My mind ....."

"Calm down. And take your seat." Dr. Wright asked with a touch of discomfort, "How frequent are these outbursts? And, in your view, what brings them up? What triggers that rebellion?"

"Rebellion? An astute observation," Anton responded instantly. He was now less tense and eager to deal with the subject. "Rebellion was the motivating force of my life. During my young days, I confronted the authoritarian stand of my father, my neighbors, my school teachers – I am referring to Christian Poles who had contempt for Jewish people – and later on I rebelled against the Nazis, the murderers of our people! I fought them when they invaded Poland. I gunned them down during the Warsaw Uprising. And later on..."

Dr. Wright halted Anton. "Sorry to interrupt you. When I saw you the first time, we barely spoke of your experiences during the Nazi days in Poland. But I would like to know how you handled the brutality of those years. How you survived that terror. Now please continue on the subject of rebellion. Can you define your enemy? What is it?"

"Injustice," Anton replied emotionally. "Search for justice, rebellion against injustice. This is the ruling factor of my life. The condition of existence of people across the globe occupies my mind with unending persistence. I am pained, horrified by the suffering of millions, no, billions of human beings whose lives are torn to bits by the hunger, terrestrial devastation, and by the fierce tribal, I mean ethnic, racial strife. That leads to the torrential bloodshed. The most gruesome human blight. If the flood of blood that flows in all parts of the world, for instance in Africa, by some magic could be turned into water, the Sahara desert would disappear. That dry land would be criss-crossed by rivers, would be overgrown by red-rooted palms. By fluorescent bushes. And hunger in that part of the world would disappear. And..."

He stopped, once again punched himself on the cheek, then whispered, "Once again I apologize for my babble. I so easily get carried away by subjects that," he smiled lightly, "foment and ferment my personality. As my wife would have said, 'You were always on the swing of emotionality.' But now more than ever. Is this because...." He paused, shivered as if gripped by a pang of cold, then changed the subject. "Was I rhyming? I tried not to, but..."

Dr. Wright interrupted him. "Yes, you were. But don't be concerned. I want to study your rhyming skills. So continue in the same manner. And answer quickly what flashes in your brain this minute. Reply!"

Anton blurted out instantly: "Sleet! That is freezing my feet! No! My meat!" he pointed at his crotch. "That subject inhabits my mind. When darkness sets in, it lights up. The question, I mean. Why is it so useless? That's the crucifying gist of my torment. The ruthless part of my grind."

Dr. Wright said, "A moment ago when you mentioned your wife, was this subject already in your mind? How she spoke about your..."

Anton cut him off. "That's for sure. The subject," he pointed again at his crotch, "makes me angry. Silly. And dour. I wish..."

He stopped speaking, grinned bitterly, then finished the sentence. "You surely know what I crave. To express my loving in sexual terms. To be free of those wicked, incapacitating germs!"

"If you are so depressed by this condition, how are you getting along with your spouse?"

"Fine," Anton replied boisterously. "Though often she thinks she is the tigress and I am a mouse."

Dr. Wright asked, "Were you also rhyming in your youth?"

"Not at all. When I was a teenager my obsession was mountain climbing. I wanted to be a leader in this field. But my dad supressed it. He thought I was physically inept for that pursuit. I was not strong enough and emotionally fragile to boot."

"Where do you live?" the doctor asked unexpectedly.

"During the summer in Suntario," Anton answered instantly. "During the winter in Wintario!"

Dr. Wright repeated with intensity,"Where do you live?" -

Anton responded with dazzling velocity. "On a bumpy road. Away from the beach. Where I study day and night how to bitch. And I'm progressing quite well. Nonetheless I'm sick of it. When I bitch I want to end up in a ditch."

"How do you feel when the sun is setting?"

"Sunsets make me shiver. What will it be – I think to myself – heart failure or rupture of the liver? And how long will that process last? An hour or two? I trust I will sink fast."

"To change the subject;" Dr. Wright fired his next query. "Who do you vote for, if I may ask? The Tories or ...?"

"Tories? They're the pits," Anton shot him down. "Their leaders care only for their own eh... posteriors! If I knew how, I would tear them to bits!"

"I see," said the psychiatrist. "And how do you feel after making this statement?"

"Fine! Because I didn't need to conceal my view. And what's more important you didn't bash me. You didn't boo!"

After a tiny pause Anton added: "Can we stop? I'm a bit tired now. I'd rather abandon this test. Otherwise I will be a flop. Or will turn into a pest."

Dr. Wright, an earnest expression on his face, answered quietly. "But of course. I wanted to examine your rhyming skills. They are impressive. And what lies behind them?"

Anton responded with passion. "That's the question that haunts me all the time. Am I aping my father or am I a maelstroming madman who plays this idiotic game to garner some fame? That's why I'm here. To recover my senses. To get back into gear. I want to be in that condition fast. As I have told you before, my life is a bag of misery. No, its a bust! A bust!"

The psychiatrist responded calmly. "You're cruel to yourself. You overplay your condition."

Anton raised his voice. "Then make me stop! If you think I love it, you're wrong. I hate that...music. I don't play this drum of my own volition!"

"Relax," Dr. Wright commanded gently. "No more rhyming. The test is over."

When Anton obeyed, the therapist watched him for a moment, slurped a few drips of coffee, made a lengthy note on his pad, then inquired: "Is your ear ringing?"

"No. The hum is almost gone."

"And how were you in the last few days?"

'As if I were stoned,' Anton was going to answer. But he didn't. "Not too bad. Somewhat in a daze."

"I see," said Dr.Wright. "Let's hope it will stay that way. Now are you ready to come up with one of your life stories? Those that have been haunting you. I assume that you gave some thought to it and made a selection."

"No, I haven't. As you know, I was ill. But this is not the only reason for my dereliction. I couldn't focus on the troubling elements of my past. It all turned out to be so hazy. The early days of my life. My school days. The encounters with my family. I was unable to make any sense of it. So I gave up. Thinking all the time that I may not be able to squeeze out my depression. That I am in a downfall, about to experience a sharp regression."

"No rhyming please," Dr. Wright said again. "You told me you detest it. So why can't you stop?"

"Because I'm infested," Anton replied sharply. "That's why I'm here! You tell me why am I a dunce who rhymes. Who..."

Dr. Wright interrupted. "My turn, please. As I said before, your capability of coming up with words that click is amazing. Where does it come from? Were you born with it," he smiled, "or did you acquire it later? You're a theatre man. Is that the source?"

"No. No," Anton replied with agitation. "This habit, on the scale I'm addicted to it now, grabbed hold of me recently. When I stopped working. When I decided that I'm...nobody. That's when I began playing with words. But why, I don't know. To keep my mind busy, I suppose. To make me less murky!"

Dr. Wright nodded with a grin. "This observation might be quite correct. But where does it come from? This facility for phrasing? Did you know a poet who..."

Anton cut him off. "My father was a writer. And an avid reader. He once said to me: 'There are not too many things in life that you really enjoy. Sex is one of them. Having a loving wife and children is another. So is travelling. But what gives you a special kind of satisfaction is playing with words. When you listen to them, they seduce you. In life, outside of those things that I have mentioned to you, all the rest is for the birds!'"

While saying this, Anton, in his mind was turned into a youngster. He and his father, a young, thinly built fellow, with slightly receding hair, round eye glasses and an ironic smile on his lips, were sitting on the deck of a restaurant facing high mountains.

It was a warm summer day, the sun was blazing and his father was singing:

Balama Talama
Talama Balama
Faloma Saltoma
Oh, Dee Da Doo!
Tompeena Tampoona
Croosspena Talpoona
Estola Damdola
Oh, Bee Ba Boo!

Then the image was gone. Anton chortled with laughter and explained to the psychiatrist.

"I just saw my father. In my screwy imagination." He knocked at his head. "We were vacationing together, in the Tatras mountains. I guess I must have been ten or eleven years old. We were having lunch on the deck of a posh restaurant and he hummed to me like this. Anton raised his head, focussed his eyes on the psychiatrist then recreated the song with the vocal intensity and the rhythm of horses hooves. When he finished, he responded to the doctor's puzzled expression with a giggle. "These strange sounds were my father's invention. He jokingly called them the primitive language of the ancient tribes. When I asked him what it meant, he replied with a smile: 'I am not sure. When they started this linguistic dance, who knows what rambled in their minds. But take note of this. In poetry, rhyme and rhythm are everything. The most basic ingredients. So if you ever decide to be a poet, remember what I've told you. Be cognizant of it.' He raised his finger and repeated sternly: 'Be cognizant!'

"And because he asked me with such severity to be cognizant of his advice, this rhythmic, rhyming blabber stuck with me forever. Often when I go for a walk on an empty street, I intone to myself in the same manner. No real words but..." He sang:

Oh, Boola Toola
Oh, Toola Boola
Oh, Soleetona!
Oh, Tompeetoola
Oh, Deara Tora
Oh, Sonteefona!

Anton ended his performance, laughed again, then asked the psychiatrist, "So what do you think of this tribal fiction? Is there any sense to it?"

"I am not sure," Dr. Wright replied hesitantly. "I would rather hear your assessment of this quandary. When you chant in this manner – how do you feel? Does it lift your spirits, make you happy or..."

Anton cut him off. "It improves my mood, that's for sure. But it also makes me question my mental state. I ask myself why am I so addicted to this musical rambling. Why am I so servile to the input of my father? Why am I so poisoned by his hoopla?"

He stopped, lowered his head, clenched his hands to compose himself, then blurted out: "When he was gone forever I was in deep pain. But to survive I had to use all my energy, all my brain power to keep going, to stay alive and to fight the beasts who were strangling us. So I did not think of my father. And I did not subject myself to his defense. But today, for a reason I cannot comprehend, I follow his habit. I sing that stupid song. And I talk to him. I see him, hear his voice, I ask his advice when I am at a loss to resolve some problem. And...."

Dr. Wright interrupted. "So you are convinced that this musical rambling originated with your father. He was the instigator. The catalyst of your disease. According to your judgment, he was the culprit and you are the victim. Correct?"

"Yes," Anton replied calmly.

"You have mentioned your father was an accomplished writer," Dr. Wright said unexpectedly. "Do you have any copies of his work?"

"Yes, I have. One is a novel called *Landscapes*. My title for it would have been *The Landscape of Distrust*. It embraces the fluctuation of life of a Jewish family in a small town in Poland after the First World War. An accurate and vivid description of the harshness of their existence. And filled with biting humor," he smiled, "that buzzed in their home, easing the tension that haunted them. The other work is a play called *It Started With a Lie!* A scornful, satirical attack on antisemitism. I carried those copies with me when I came to Canada ."

Dr. Wright made a note and asked, "Is there anything in those books that indicate....."

"That my father imbued the characters he created with his personal, nonsensical blabber?" Anton finished Dr. Wright's question. "Not at all. But this fact had nothing to do with what I told you before. That there was some positive motivation for his folly. He wanted to say something that was of importance and that was crushing his mind. So..." After a long pause he continued, "I possess another work of his. The sketch of a letter written by him. It was addressed to my mother. She kept it for years. Then a month or so before she died, she gave it to me as part of my inheritance. It was, of course, written in Polish but I translated as closely as possible and I keep both texts in my safety deposit box which has all kinds of items that I call precious. Next time I come here, I will bring both documents with me to prove that what I am saying to you is true. But now, if you would like to hear it, I will recite what was written on those pages. I know those lines well. They are embedded in my mind. Forever! And what you will hear will tell you what kind of person my father was. How he spoke and and saw and assessed the world we live in."

Without waiting for the doctor's consent, Anton rose, stepped back as if taking the proper position on stage, then, stressing the pertinent words, started to recite.

"My dear, sweet Rosa
When I was teeny-weeny I was an expert
In the language of antiquity!
The words that I heard in my ear and
invented, had to do with the stone ages -
the period far gone!
Those mental gymnastics of mine were in...
ubiquity! When I was alone!
Always when secluded, I engaged myself in this
poppycock!
Only don't mock me! Don't mock!

The stone-age people, once their inner structure attained an upper level – more human, less nimalistic – exalted Mother Earth for this gift. The supremacy over all other species that surrounded them was what they appreciated most! So they thanked her often for this upper lift!

The tribal group, all male, standing on the river bank, naked, facing the rising sun, one arm outstretched, hand upturned toward the sky, was singing a hymn to her, their daily, choral toast! It sounded like this:

Tookamooka, Tookamooka!
Grosevana, Grosevooka!

Which meant:

We bless you! We bless you!
Our Mother! Our holy Mother!
Zodoma! Boloma!
Telatteema! Toeetoma!

It meant:

Stay with us! Don't leave us!
We need you! Don't grieve us!

They continued:

Keepa Leeta! Tolameeta!
Tompeeloma! Rosstopeeta!
Boteelooza! Booteelooza!

The m*essage was:*

We are hungry! We need meat!
Give us a giraffe!
Or a zebra!
We must eat! We must eat!

Then suddenly there were on their knees, bowed and exclaimed happily:

Marulah, Marulah! Tamehr! Tamehr!
And bless you for letting us shove....
You know what! You know where!

This was their daily prayer, their ukukalaka!
Then the whole band would jump up, sing and dance in a slow stamping rhythm:

Somaka, Pollaka, Tomitta, Toutaaka....."

Dr. Wright, his face grim, lifted his right hand. "Enough! I would rather see you sitting on this chair," he pointed to it, "responding to my queries in a less..... theatrical manner. I must be able to comprehend your statements and what you have done just now....."

Anton stopped him with a burst of laughter. "I apologize. Most profusely. I was only trying to make you aware of how I see my father and what influence he had on me. How he...."

He rushed to his chair, collapsed onto it, then froze. His body was half bent and stiff, his face carried a message that he was involved with something or somebody. Then, after a few minutes of silence, he addressed the psychiatrist softly.

"He is with me. Now. He wants me to reveal the rest of his letter. I can't refuse him. That letter had such an impact on me. It made me...."

Now tears were dropping from Anton's eyes. He wiped his cheeks with his handkerchief then whispered, "May I continue? Please let me."

Dr. Wright was shaken. "Go on. Expose what's hidden in your memory."

"Thank you." Anton sighed with relief. "It won't be too much longer. Where was I? When did I stop?" He pondered a moment then said with a smile, "Ah, I know. Somaka, Pollaka, Tomitta, Toutaka. The stone age band was dancing in front of my father and he wrote this to my mother:

'I did not comprehend the meaning of this charade but those words, this is what I muttered to myself when I was a kid. And I was so enticed by those stone-age figures. So intent to grab hold of those early days of human beings. So curious and intent. Often when I was in bed, in the dark, I saw those people and I mused: how tough it must have been for them to stay alive!

Were they cognizant of it, baffled by it and did they search for an answer what was the cause of their pitiful existence? Or were they like all other beasts, grappling only with their most basic needs? Daylight, food, a partner for fucking. Were those items the main ingredients of their subsistence? Then it struck me. Though thousands of years divide the sour, creepy life of those tribesmen and that of our people, what we crave is just the same what they craved. Don't we bow our heads to red/golden dawn? Don't we gorge on steaks and seek sexual satisfaction? In a variety of ways, we have moved forward, that is an undisputed fact. But on the ground level our prime pursuits are just the same. Grotesque! Burlesque! The only thing that makes us different is that they always stayed together, shared the daily/nightly joys and torture of their existence. And we go through life mostly alone. Faced with quandaries beyond our resolve.

Those stone-age humans were a united band, depending on each other, seeking together the solution to their traumas. We are self, self, self-oriented species, abducted by this idea and the most servile servants of it. We stand and preach that to face life, to extort from it success and joy, we must do it all on our own. This is our official creed. And .... foam. We need resources, power to be above all others. We must acquire riches to prove we are better than the hoi polloi. We persist in believing that by possessing more and more we are not only in the fruitful, potent condition but we are also the embodiment of the most glamorous mold. No matter how ruthless we become, fiendishly fighting for the sustainment of this position. No matter how much envy and hatred it evolves in all those who are way below, unable to be a part of that transition. Who are in pits not of their own volition. Who lack the sleaze or the stamina to conform with the process of that action. No matter how much harm it carries, we push and shove the legitimacy of this stance.

'But this kind of travel through life equals disgrace. Self slaughter! I don't approve of it at all. I consider the mind and heart a blotter. In the language of my youthful days the word for it was -- glide. It stood for the achievement of happiness. The blissful plight. So will you swing with me? For better or for worse, will you vow to be forever my bride?'

Anton raised his head, looked at Dr. Wright, and added with a touch of a smirk: "That's the end of that....serenade. The letter had his signature. It said Olim. My father's name was Emil. But those who were close to him called him Milo. And the last words underneath his stone age name were :

Mamabutta! Fillo! Fillo!
Kiss morleepa! Milo! Milo!

What was the meaning of it all I don't know. But I presume...."

"Thank you for this performance," Dr. Wright intervened gently." It tells me a great deal about your father. What puzzles me is that you have managed to memorize all this. You have told me that your memory is in a shambles. So how were you able to retain the text of this letter? Are you absolutely certain the whole thing is not a figment of your imagination? That you have not, subconsciously, invented the whole story to...," he paused for a moment, "smother the guilt and embarrassment created by this addiction? The text you have just presented borders on the absurd. Are you implying that your father was an irrational human being?

"Yes, he was," Anton replied with annoyance in his voice. "Many experiences disappear completely from the human mind. You surely know that. But some are tightly lodged in the mental computer. I press the button and they instantly appear on the screen. And they often visit me on their own. My father... there were two parts to him. One was filled with softness, gentleness. The other had a harsh dictatorial quality. When those two parts collided, he was hard to cope with."

Anton, now curled up in his chair, took a deep breath. "Could we stop talking about my dad? To reveal the truth about him makes me cringe with shame. And very sad."

Dr. Wright instantly replied. "No more questions on this subject. Your well-being matters a great deal to me. And don't hesitate to tell me if you feel uncomfortable." He looked at the clock. It read 12:30. "I am at your disposal for another 25 minutes. Are you up to it?"

"Yes, I am," Anton answered now more relaxed. "What is your next question?"

"I would like to know more about your mood when you're humming. How does you mind react to it?"

Anton swiftly offered his reply. "Often it makes me see faces, bodies of women I was involved with when I was young. I shared my bed with so many attractive women. Not for long though. They were easily replaceable," he shook his head with self-derision. "But that was the sexual rhythm I followed in those days. Do you think that I was obedient to my father's instructions? That it was he who instilled in me this..."

"No rhyming, please!" The psychiatrist raised his finger to make his point . "Your father's influence upon your life. We will try to decipher it but it will take time. We must proceed slowly. Cautiously."

"Yes, you are right," Anton slipped in. "But before we go any further, I want you to know that I inherited my temperament from him. His volatility was legendary. My mother called him an explosive sermonizer. When he talked about the issues that troubled him most – politics, racial upheavals, the meaning and the tragedy of human existence – he would make a point that he shouldn't be interrupted. He demanded that we look at him and listen in silence. He spoke in parables yet with clarity. Lucidity. And with passion. He spoke with intensity. His voice would rise, become gruffer or more stern then it would thunder. When this happened I couldn't listen anymore. I would lose track of his thinking. I would feel fear maiming my heart. I would want to escape and hide in a closet. I..."

He stopped, clenched his teeth as if shocked by what he just said.

After a few seconds of silence, Dr. Wright spoke softly. "The way you describe your father's speaking habit. Is this how you remember it? Was it always imbedded in your memory so precisely, or is this a current recall? Expanded, aggrevated by your present condition?"

"I have no answer," Anton replied tersely. "In the past, no. Since I arrived in Canada, I haven't been thinking very much about my father. My thoughts relating to him had only to do with his death. The cruelty of it. The insanity of those who killed him. When those thoughts occurred, my mind, my body were flooded with pain. They sharply suppressed my energy. And as my struggle here – no, my tough climb upward – demanded that I sustain my energy on the highest level, I forced myself to focus only on my daily life. The past was gone. I was only concerned with the present. I returned to my younger days of my life because I am sick and retired. There is nothing unusual about this kind of pondering, I am sure you agree. People who age, persistently add up what happened in their lives. They examine how they lived when they were kids, how they functioned as adults. They want to refresh their minds how it all went by, the good and bad things. The long, dark days of sorrow. The short nights of happy dreams. How it all transpired so quickly."

Anton paused then blurted with an ironic smile, "Sad note, right? To change the subject, let me report to you what kind of a dream I had two days ago. You might be puzzled by it and amused but it will shed some light on why I need your help. You are interested in dreams, aren't you? You do analyze them?"

"Yes, I do," nodded the psychiatrist. "To dissect dreams, to trace and reveal the subconscious roots of a dream is one of the valuable tools of our profession. Subconscious cravings are often the interwoven elements of visual presentation during our sleep. And that is why..."

"So you are still addicted to this detective work," Anton interrupted with a broad smile. "Good for you! I was always fascinated by that gimmick. Had I followed my father's way of thinking, instead of being a theatre man and a writer, I would have been a psycho. No, a shrink!" He laughed, recalling the words of the guard during his first visit to the Institute.

Then, now serious, he told the doctor why he wanted to describe his dream.

"When I woke up very early in the morning, what I went through...the only way I can describe it is that I was the victim of a most humiliating experience. When you hear it, you might decide that..."

"Go ahead," Dr. Wright said tensely. "After you tell me your story, I'll comment on it."

Anton straightened in his chair and began. "I was sitting behind a desk in an office of the Social Club for Sex Competition. I was the founder of the organization. A tall, bulky man came in and said to me: 'I was coaxed by some of my friends to join the club. But first, I want to know what it stands for?'

'I replied that the club makes the members compete with each other. The one who screws the most women each week is the winner. And he receives a reward. A solid cut in his monthly fee. We call it The Financial Remission.

'Then the man said, 'And how is it determined that...'

"I answered quickly that it is done by a simple method. We all rent a room in one of two hotels. The managers are a part of the game. The next day, they deliver to the judge the room number, the description of the female and the claimant's name. Then I added: 'It works fine. It's a road to a bubbly, blistering fame!'

The man questioned: 'And the judge, who is he?'

I replied: 'He's the priest, sorry, the prince of the congregation. We elect him for half a year. We like the system of regular rotation. It disposes of favoritism. We call it The Members Salvation.'

And the membership, how large is it?' was the next question of the joiner.

'It is small. About fifty. But all the men are, how should I put it...nifty. Before they join the club, we measure their penises. If it is less than three inches long during the erection, we make them go home with a letter of rejection. They can apply again after they have had a surgical operation. It is called penisian amelioration.'

Then the man asked: 'Is there any pre-determination who is entitled to apply?'

"My answer was 'No. We accept males of all races and creeds. But we select them carefully. We want only those who fulfill their and our needs. We want performers who are the best. We want them all to bring glamour to our fest."

Anton finished, inhaled then deeply exhaled, relieved that he had managed to get rid of that burden. "That was all. My dream was gone but it scared me shitless. I was shocked by its obscenity. And by my insanity. I wanted to talk about it with Henrietta, but I couldn't. She would have been shattered by it. She would have wanted me to be carried to a psychiatric ward. So what do you make of it? Where do I belong having such a screwy dream? I wrote it all down the next morning. It is not a writer's invention as you might think. Neither was I drunk that night. So tell me, am I going bonkers? Am I..."

"The strangest story I have heard in years," Dr. Wright interrupted. "As much as I would like to, it would be wrong for me to interpret your dream right now. What are your thoughts on the matter?"

Anton replied as passionately as before. "I was addicted to sex! Intercourse meant so much for me. I valued it not only for the physical ecstasy it gave me but because it gave me an emotional lift. I started to ... co-work with women when I was fairly young, I must have been seventeen when I had my first slide in – that's what my father called it – but my school mates were ahead of me. They started earlier than I did and they were more frequent at it. They were tall, blond and easily attracted female attention. I was dark-haired and rather short. The gymnasium I attended was filled with Christian boys and girls. There were only few Jewish girls. One of them, her name was Zosia, the equivalent of Sophia," he smiled, "chose me for her partner."

He paused, looked into space, then continued. "What happened afterwards was strange. We made love a few times, went to see movies together, then she dropped me. 'You're not lively enough,' she told me. 'For you, love making is an effort unless you are certain that the girl has the warmest feeling for you. You want her to adore you. But I only like you. I tried it before with another boy for whom I couldn't have cared less and, each time he entered me, he gave me a jolt. So our affair ends now. Don't try to lure me anymore.'

I wanted to call her a whore. But I didn't. We parted peacefully. I thought of it a lot in my growing up days. And I learned that what she had said was correct. I needed love more than anything else. I was attracted to women, yes. I slept with many. But the punch of my performance was low when I felt that their emotional need for me had diminished. Then I would start searching for someone else. That was one of the problems of my life. I searched too much. Three wives, many mistresses. I think I didn't trust that I could be loved. That I deserved it. So I changed partners. And wasn't faithful. I always wanted to be at the top. And to achieve that, I was ungraceful," Anton paused. "Did I say anything that clarifies the meaning of my dream?"

"You surely have. Your confession was honest. If we communicate on this level, I think, eventually, I will be able to help you. The main thing in the relationship between a psychiatrist and his patient is honesty. No matter how hard that is. So continue in that way. To break the crust of the past, we need to face it. Grasp it's meaning. Then, what torments you, may disappear. At least for a while. Yes, Anton," he grinned lightly, "try to change gears."

He paused for a moment. "As far as your dream is concerned, I wouldn't pay too much attention to it. Possibly your incapability to be Henrietta's love partner created it. The way you talked to me about it when I saw you last time, this condition riled you hard. It still does. Write about it. With your cleverness, you could turn it into a funny," he smiled, "short story. Maybe that would help you to put that problem aside. Just remember, you're not alone. There are thousands and thousands of people who share your experience. Once we age..."

Anton cut him off, heatedly. "It makes us delirious. I have told you this before. One is involved only with oneself. It makes one beserk. Cringing with fear."

He stood up. Then, a moment later, uttered in a self-deriding tone: "Oh, I'm babbling again. I'm fit to be tied. If I..."

Dr. Wright got up and cut him off, sternly. "Mr. Thomas, please sit down. You're performing. And we need to get to the bottom of this. What makes you so explosive? Shall we continue or would you rather go home? Our session should last," he looked at the clock on his desk, "another ten minutes. The choice is yours."

"I'd rather stay," Anton answered softly. "Sorry for the commotion. Your questions reach me. So does your attention. "

They both sat down. Dr. Wright scribbled something on his pad, then said, "If you don't mind, we'll go back to your father. So it was he who spurred you in the direction of rhyming. Am I correct? Only don't do it now. "

"Yes. That is my connection with him. He was an ironic, insightful intellectual. But so closed up. Like a monk. And not tender. In some way, he was a freak. A pest."

"A pest? What do you mean by that?"

"I don't recall if I've told you during my first visit," Anton responded with some hesitation, "that he molested me when I was a child. Not sexually! Nothing of that kind," he corrected himself. "But he harassed me. I had to be at his beck and call. I couldn't play when I came home from school. I had to sit at my desk and work on my assignments. And when I was guilty of some misdemeanor, he whipped me with his belt. Many times. That was his way of impressing upon me that obedience was the rule of the game. And it went further than that. He preached that obedience is the key quality that allows us human beings to go safely through life. That one must stymie rebellious feelings no matter what the reason. That one could be persuasive, seductive in resisting the imposition of...bad rules," he smiled scornfully, "but never aggressive. To fight with claws is the culture of vultures. My father's words. We must back away from it. We must disentangle ourselves from the need to be destructive."

"And yet he..." Dr. Wright started to speak but Anton went on.

"Yes. He treated me badly. And then I lost track of him. He was destroyed in a concentration camp. I would have done anything to save his life. I loved him!" He paused. "Crazy as it might seem, I loved him madly!"

"Yes, I'm sure of that," said Dr. Wright. "Possibly that's why those images appear to you now. You're angry with yourself because you have given your father a low grading. And what flashes in your mind denies it. Those images are the symptoms of the guilt that haunts you."

"Is that why I'm rhyming? By mimicking him, am I penalizing myself?"

The psychiatrist replied, "Up to a point, yes. But possibly there are some other reasons for it. As you told me, your contact with people is infrequent. And, as you have a need to be impressive," he smiled lightly, "those who you address orally or on paper, you make a special effort to have them on your side. To draw them to yourself. To make them think of you. To impress them and make them laugh. The words you fling with the speed of lightning are often very funny. So that helps you to put a higher value on yourself. When you do it, I suspect it draws away your attention from the tension that overpowers you. It diminishes the depression." He paused, then added, expanding his grin, "And also because when you say something unpleasant, the rhyme that follows softens the blow. Makes your original intention seem less aggressive."

"I buy your observations," said Anton, his face brightening with pleasure. "Though it all boils down to the fact that I'm developing a childlike mentality. Not to be scorched by madness, I rhyme! Unable to graciously accept the impending fatality, I roll in grime!"

"Fine. Fine," said Dr. Wright with impatience. "In my opinion, the latest poetic phrase of yours is not worth a dime! Is there another dream you would like to share with me?"

After a moment of hesitation Anton replied, "I don't think so. No other dream clogs my mind."

Dr. Wright wrote something on his pad, then said, "You seem to be intrigued by madness. Is that what bothers you most?"

"Yes. I think about it most often. Can it be reversed?"

"We'll give it a try," the therapist responded. "But will-power is needed. Without it we won't get too far. What else drains you?"

Anton grinned. "Can I give you the reply in my comical fashion?"

"In rhyme? Go ahead"

Anton quickly took out two folded pieces of paper from the pocket of his jacket, straightened them out, and started to read:

"I am aging and in agony
about walking, chatting or flying.
Whatever I do, I think:
That's it! This is my road toward dying.
I believe that my Day of
Judgment is nearby
That's what makes me bitter
and tense.
Quite often it makes me cry.
Sometimes, to get rid of the pain,
I want to jump off
the roof of a high-rise building.
Or be hit by a car. Instead of staying on Earth
I'd rather live on a star.
What drains me?
For most years of my life
I've been holding onto the
value of living with evanescent
conviction
But now this trust is gone.
What once had a mushy,
sweet surface to it,
today is hard and sharp
as stone!
Yes, what I taste and see,
is not what I used to call
happy, true life!
But a brutal, sordid replica
of it!
Most frosty, stormy sea!
I'm trying to make some sense of it, what is its aim,

its rotting essence,
but I'm unable to capture its meaning!
So each passing day I sit by my window, watch the street
and think, my suffering – it is so reprehensible!
So demeaning!
And filled with irony! It is this quality that makes me steam!
I always wanted to be the pathfinder! The front stage climber! The master!
And look what I am now! A despondent dependant!
A tear-jerker! A living disaster!
So what I would like to see happen now is a simple solution.
I'm prepared to take it, a quite gentle dissolution.
I would like to apply for a permit to leave the Earth!
And fly to Mars.
No! It's brutally cold there! That would be a farce!
I want to be allowed to stay on the Moon!
Yes! Where once I settle down, shedding
the triteness that masters me, wearing
no clothes and transfixed by light,
I will stay happy and silent! And free of
my blight!
So Moon it is! If I can reach it!
Oh, it would be a boon for me!
So I will pitch for it! The idea...
I won't ditch it! I won't ditch it!"

He finished reading and said softly, "That's it. Did you get my message?"

Dr. Wright seemed stunned. He cleared his throat before replying. "Who wouldn't? You mean to say that you prepared this poem for our meeting?"

"Yes," Anton answered. "I wrote it last night. Henrietta was asleep. She snored so gently," he smiled. "And I slipped out of the bedroom, sat at my desk and scribbled that confession." He smirked, "It's yours if you want it. You were my inspiration. I hope what I said will not incite your anger."

"Why should I be angry? Because you're keen to die, consumed by your depression? To think that way is your prerogative. How sensible it is? That's another story. We'll discuss it at length. Be sure of that. I only wish you could curb your emotions. Be more cerebral. In better control."

The doctor paused for a moment then pressed on. "Your work, yes, give it to me. I want it. And I'll treat it as a gift. And you believe that you're a nobody? What nonsense. What a waste of talent. There's still so much you could do. If you were...," he smiled, "in awe of yourself. Instead of being like a ship adrift. You're a legend in this city. I've made some inquiries. Your lectures were highly regarded. Your writing on social issues had many followers."

Anton responded with an ironic grin. "If that's so, why does nobody call me? My phone is dead all day long. Isn't there anybody in this city who would want to talk to a legend? Disrobe the legend," he winked. "Make the legend smile? No, Dr. Wright. That is not the case. I'm on the outskirts of the cultural life in this city. And in this country. In spite of my input for 30 years, I'm one of the vanquished." He paused for a moment. "But you sounded like Henrietta. Which is most touching. Maybe when we talk much more..."

Anton didn't finish the sentence but handed Dr. Wright the poem and remarked lightly, "You might be startled by my handwriting. It is not very legible. But because you have heard it, the words might appear to you less fudgy. That's what my father used to call my scribbling. He would say to me: 'My son, I wish I could read what you write. But the way you put it on paper, it's so fudgy!'"

As he was speaking, Anton was mentally transported to his room in his parent's home. He was fourteen years old. It was Sunday morning and the sun was blazing. His father stood by his bed and was scolding. "It's late and you're still sleeping. Why don't you get up, go to your desk and learn to type?" He pointed to a small uncovered typewriter that was on a narrow table beside the wall where Anton did his schoolwork. "I bought you that machine so that you could avoid the complaints of your teachers that your handwriting is so fudgy. He noticed a piece of paper stuck into the typewriter, made a step towards it, leaned over, pulled out the sheet and read aloud what was printed on it:

> My...you know who...is a dreck! He's a tyrant, a fucking fool, and a wreck! Do I need to say more? You know the rest! He is a bamboo! A pest!

Anton's father, his face torn by rage, roared: "What's this! This inane rhyming?" He turned around, pulled the blanket off his son and yelled again. "You're naked! And you were masturbating!

The image was gone but Anton was still with it. His eyes glued to the space above Dr. Wright's head, he muttered to himself. 'Yes, I was masturbating. To contain my zest. To satisfy my lust If I were to do it now, I'd be pressing a limpy hunk of flesh. A robust machine, way back, that's now ready for scrap. A total bust. So how do I live now? Help me! Or I won't last!'

The psychiatrist understood what had happened. "Did you see your father?"

"What?" Anton was shocked, realizing Dr. Wright had read his mind. "How did you know?" Then he continued more calmly, "Yes, I saw my father. He was complaining about my shoddy handwriting. But he hugged me. That was the first time that I felt his hand on my shoulder. He was cantankerous as usual, but friendly."

When he uttered those words he thought, 'Why did I lie? Am I protecting my father so that my shrink doesn't absorb my ranting against him? Or am I confused? Not certain that what I was saying about him was true. How do I come to grips with that? Was he a pest or was he...?'

Dr. Wright's voice dismantled Anton's self-absorption. "That revelation is quite telling. I trust it will stay with you. It will help you dissolve those negative feelings." He looked at his clock. "There are a few minutes left. And I have an idea for you. But first, are you doing any writing?"

"No," Anton replied. I put aside my new novel for a while. Until.. " He wanted to say 'until my brain works better', but the psychiatrist, a touch of a smile on his lips, didn't allow him to finish the sentence.

"What if I gave you an assignment? Would you be able to put your mind to it?"

Puzzled, Anton asked, "What kind of assignment?"

And at this moment, he was hit by the answer. 'He wants me to give him a story of my life! Shit! I have been recoiling from doing it for years. Though encouraged to do so by my publisher. And some other people who care for me, my wife included. Shit! Shit!'

Dr. Wright who was observing him with sharp attention, responded with a nod. "Yes, you read me correctly. I would like you to sketch the story of your life. Your childhood. Your adolescence. And, eventually, your previous marriages. Pay attention to what led to their breakups. What you will say might shed some light on your current problems. In short, portray the shape of your days before you came to Canada. Also include the story of your early years in this country. Don't write it as a memoir or confession," his face brightened with a smile, "but as if you were writing a story about somebody else. You write about him not about yourself. Do you know what I mean? You let your mind roam. Cry for him if you want to. Bash him if you need to. Exhort him. You..."

"You're joking! You're joking!" Anton jumped from his seat. "You want me to write a novel about myself? That's crazy! I would not only exaggerate the various sentiments but also toy with the truth. I would..."

He paused, clearly thinking about the consequences of such an assignment, and was hit by a discovery. "Just a minute. I know what you're after. My interpretation of me. Which would allow you to decipher how I see myself. Dissect the ambiguities. Discern the consciously or unconsciously shaped lies. Exaggerations! Then you will confront me with those findings. What an idea. You're a wise man. But what about those periods of my life that I cannot recapture? That are gone. Forgotten. Do I...?"

"Do whatever comes to your mind," Dr.Wright interrupted. "Those are your decisions. And if there are loopholes in your story, don't be concerned about it. Let your writer's instinct handle that."

He smiled then he continued, "Lies and exaggerations are the barriers we need to dismantle, to improve the state of the emotional health of our patients. Lies have a protective quality. They govern many actions of human beings. Hide their misconducts, shade their pain. But, at the same time, they haunt them. Not only when they are unravelled and the world tumbles around the liar, but also," he shook his finger to emphasize the seriousness of what he was going to say, "when the lies are retained safely. When they have achieved what they were invented for. Some psychologists call it the positive result of the lying factor. Though they bring the desired gain, at some point, out of fear or shame, they start persecuting the person who devised them with growing, ferocious intensity. Sometimes that emotion blows their minds. So to avoid such an occurance..."

Anton interrupted him. "Those dreary dreams, they scorch me so!" He spoke vehemently as if acting on stage. "They grind me to bits! They blind me! And make me so tired! Bad sleep, filled with lies, that's my diet. To be aroused, then ground to bits, then strengthless – that's my life. My daily triad!" He burst out laughing. "How's that for an answer? I agree with your position."

Dr. Wright was not amused. He shook his head in disbelief. "You're rhyming again. When will you stop?"

Anton responded, "When you make me sane. Or," he pointed with his thumb, "when I go down the drain!"

He punched himself in his jaw and rattled out loudly, "You see, it comes on its own. It's my bane. My fucking bane!"

Dr. Wright's response to Anton's words was stern. "I very much hope that in your story you'll make a special effort to avoid this word play. If you don't, I will find reading it difficult. It will undermine my attention. I also assume that the text will be typed not handwritten." He smiled. "I'm sure that you're accustomed to this requirement."

Anton replied, "That causes a bit of a problem. I do not use a typewriter any more. My handwritten work is copied at home on a word processor by a typist. But I wouldn't want that young woman to be privy to my personal experiences. To my upheavals. So I would have to put the burden of reproducing the text on Henrietta. And I don't know whether her schedule would allow her to do it quickly. When would you like to have that novella in your hands? In three or four weeks? Would that be alright?"

"That would be fine. Incidentally, what made you abandon typing and reinvent handwriting? I thought that's what a computer can offer..."

Anton cut him off. "It's mind-draining! Confusing. I know that many writers do not feel that way but I do. Perhaps it has to do with my age but I cannot fuse what's racing in my mind with the need to carefully watch the screen. When I am writing fiction I must be mentally free. Unencumbered by the necessity to punch the right buttons. To keep my eyes drawn to each line that appears on the screen. I must listen to the phrases that are being born in my brain instead of paying attention to the technical process of operating a machine. The word processor is a clever device but it is hostile territory for an image chaser like me."

"I see. I see," Dr. Wright remarked. "You seem to be quite passionate about the subject. Why?"

Anton, aware now of the belligerence of his response to Dr. Wright's questions, apologized for his "unwarranted, silly outburst" and explained with discomfort the reason for it.

"My refusal to use the word processor for my creative writing was a subject of tense arguments with Henrietta. She believed that once I mastered the skills, I would be most comfortable with it. She can't accept my logic that I cannot waste time studying the function of that machine. I must concentrate on my creativity. When I write, lost in thought, I feel relaxed. I have some ... respect for myself. I know how silly it sounds but that's the fact."

Dr. Wright changed the subject. "When shall we meet again?" He was quite unnerved. He must have felt that the session was a failure. Seemingly unaware, he was tapping the top of the desk with his fingers.

Anton said, "Could we deal with it at a later date? I will call you in a day or two, if you don't mind. And perhaps you would prescribe some medication for me. If my anxiety does not diminish..."

"Yes, I will put you on medication. A tranquilizer called Xenox."

He pulled open the top drawer of his desk, took out a small bottle filled with pills, dropped one on a Kleenex which he also pulled out from the drawer. "Take it now. It'll make you feel better."

Then he added, "Oh, you need water." He quickly left his chair, walked to the table by the wall, poured water from a bottle into a glass and returned with it to his patient.

"Now you can swallow it," he said, pointing at the pill and handing the glass to Anton. "Take a good few sips of water."

Anton followed the instructions, thinking: 'I hope it will not mess up my mind. It's in a big enough turmoil already. I hate medication! But...'

Dr. Wright watched him. "I'm not an advocate of treatment by medication alone. But Xenox will improve your state. I will give you a prescription for twenty pills. Take them when you feel anxious, one or two pills a day. No more. And lie down if you need to. The pill might put you to sleep. Hopefully without bad dreams."

He wrote out the prescription, handed it to Anton and added with a supportive stare, "And if you need to, you can be hospitalized. Shock therapy has good effect on patients who lose control of themselves. I don't think you need it yet, but that's what I would advise if you continue to be so much under the hammer. My last question. When you're at home, are you as acrimonious with your wife as you were with me?"

Anton replied, "I don't know. Maybe you should talk to Henrietta. She wouldn't object. She would do anything to straighten me out."

Anton looked at the clock. "I'm late! Goodbye Dr. Wright. I need to rush to the gate!"

He turned around and was on his way, fast, to the elevator which he caught the moment he left the doctor's area.

The sky was a bit cloudier now, but the sun was still quite hot. The street, as usual, was packed with people but Anton didn't pay the slightest attention. He ran out of the building, spotted the car, raced to it, slid into the seat beside Henrietta and, when he shut the door, uttered a gasp of relief.

Henrietta asked nervously, "Something wrong? Did you have a rough meeting?"

"Nothing! Nothing! He gave me a pill. That's all!"

"A pill? What pill?" Henrietta's nervousness increased.

"A tranquilizer," Anton spilled it out, loudly. "We talked about so many things, I got confused. Out of grasp with what was going on. Please go! I need to be away from this place."

"Why?" Henrietta asked tensely. "You were so keen to come here. I thought..."

"Yes, I was!" Anton cut her off, hit once again by the complexity of the task imposed on him by the doctor. "But when I got inside, I went berserk! Whatever the question that shrink put to me I answered in rhyme. The proper and improper words were gushing out my throat. I didn't know what I was saying. Something flashed in my mind and I blurted it out. And it had the weight of a stone. It crashed my logic. So I gave in to his push to write a story about myself. But not about myself. About the young days of a phantom called Anton. To pinpoint the black holes in his life. He turned me into a detective about myself. Into a snooping ranger. And when my work is done, to make it legible you will have to waste your time to put it on the computer. So you're my partner in that venture. And I hope..."

"Be careful," his wife interrupted him. "The rhyme is about to come!" A thought flashed through her mind. "You know what? I'm going to make an observation. You rhyme when you're embarrassed. That's how you deal with it! Instead of ...."

Anton interrrupted. "Rhyming, embarrassment, good connection! Now I know who's at fault. Those who treat me meanly. As if I were a dolt. So to save my body and soul I say to them, buddy, I'm above you. I've got talent you don't have. So screw yourself. And leave me alone. Or you'll have..."

He stopped for a moment to find the right matching word but Henrietta didn't let him. She raised her voice. "Don't say anything! Be silent! Or you will go home on your own!"

Tears moistened her eyes. She dried them quickly with the palm of her hand, started the car and, a moment later, they were squeezing through the heavy traffic on their way to their house. They didn't talk. Henrietta was too anxious to initiate a conversation. Anton was too distraught to speak. A few times, he looked at her and thought, 'I should talk to her. She loves me so much, but she is at the bottom of her resistance by the grief I have caused. I should beg her forgiveness. I should talk to her.'

Then, another voice reverberated in his mind. 'Stay silent! Whatever you will say, you have said before. You're a rotting companion. An excruciating bore.'
Hearing those words, he jolted in his seat. Yet his action was unnoticed by Henrietta. Cars were whizzing by and intersections were entangled with people. Her attention was focussed on driving.

Half an hour later they entered their house. Anton went to pee, then took off his clothes and slid into his bed. He felt drowsy; he needed to rest. Before he closed his eyes, he asked Henrietta, "Remind me, when I was out of sync in the last few weeks – were there any phone calls? For me?"

"Yes," Henrietta replied. "Ron Dubin called. Wanted to know how you felt. So did Nina and Paul. They called several times. And came to see you.

"And Greg? And Adrian? Did they call?"

"Yes, they did. They wanted to come but I said no. When they rang, you were still quite shaky. They could have unnerved you even more. Your sons are young and strong," she smiled, "you were weak. I thought it would be better to delay their visit. When you want them here, they will come. Adrian, in fact, said that he will see us very soon. Possibly next week. The way he spoke I am ready to bet that he will come without any warning. Out of the blue. He was very concerned. So was Greg."

"How nice of them," Anton whispered. "I hope they're doing alright."

"Yes, they are. Greg is busy as usual. Promoting whatever there is to promote. He loves Montreal. And Adrian..."

Anton finished the sentence for her. "Loves travelling to Paris. Or to Rome. Or Vienna. He's a lucky guy to be able to afford that. Mr. University Professor. In the USA! Rambunctious as he is, he made it on his own. He surely knew how to play."

They shared a soft giggle then Anton asked, "So that was all? No more callers? How strange. I didn't tell you that, but before I got ill, I sent some theatre people, I used to call them friends, copies of *Sophia...Sophia*. I thought that after reading the novel they would contact me. To retie the old ties. But no one did, except for one person. Dougie Jinglatt. He called and told me that he loved the book. That he was shaken by it. I asked him to visit but he said he couldn't. He's in real trouble, as you know. No work. No money. He lives off the skimpy earning of his wife. But he dialed our number and talked to me for awhile. No one else has. God, how deserted I am by those I stood behind when I had some eh...power. That feeling of being dumped crawls inside of me all the time. It makes me so angry. And so sour."

Henrietta said, "Forget it. And sleep, my love. Your state will improve. I'm sure. I'm nearby if you need me. And don't be concerned about the story. You will do it well, I'm sure. And I'll put it on the Mac. Dr. Wright will read a proper version of your tale. So don't worry. I so much hope that you will sleep without a dream. That you will rest. Just rest."

She bent over him, kissed his cheeks, his lips. Then he closed his eyes and was ready to snooze but a thought awakened his mind. "You know, it just struck me. When I was speaking with Dr. Wright I didn't tell anything about my sister. I mentioned to him that she had died, but that was about all. My father and mother are enclosed in my mind. But not her. I see her photograph on my desk. She looks at me so inquisitively, but my recall of her is so...non-existent. No stories about her are imbedded in my mind."

Henrietta asked, "Is there a reason for it?"

"Not that I know of," Anton said softly. "I had a loving relationship with my sister. We were close to each other. We never quarrelled."

Then he contradicted himself, internally: 'You're tinkering with the truth. What you have said is a cliche. When you dig deep enough into your memory, you will come up with another view. Hanka was your father's favorite. You were jealous of her. Only when she was gone did you make a cloying turn about. She was younger than you, but you were humbled by her. She was brilliant in everything she put her mind to. She was first in her class. Her piano playing, she outclassed everyone that you knew. She studied languages with ease. And she rhymed...'

An image from the past rolled before his eyes. His father, his sister and he were in a canoe on a lake, moving towards the shore. The sun was blazing, the quiet water sparkled as if sprinkled with crystals. Anton, in his late teens, was rowing. His father who was sitting behind his son with his daughter beside him was engaged in a verbal duel with her. "Now it's my turn," he said. " I'm going to say a phrase or two, then you make you know what. A rhyming...glue!"

He straightened up. "The sun is shining! Water is in the magician's hand!"

Hanka instantly supplied her line. "He likes to play with people's hearts! That is his stand!"

Emil quickly delivered the next opening. "That magician rules the world! Makes it dance and teeter totter!"

Hanka belted out, raising her eyes to the sky, "Let us cruise safely! Protect us from slaughter!"

Her father continued, "If I had my druthers, I'd be a man in high gear! I'd be dancing and singing all night! I'd be..."

Hanka finished the sentence. "A balladeer!" Then she flounced and sang "and I'd be a dryad! Living in a tree! That would make me..."

Her father stepped in. "A friend of the birds. A solitary bee!"

They chuckled, Emil kissed Hanka on both cheeks, then addressed Anton.

"See how clever she is? When she grows up, the world will be hers It might be yours too if you work harder. You're a good rower and quite a competent diver, but your higher skills need to improve. So keep at it. Do not follow your mushy groove!"

He patted Anton's shoulder as if expecting some reply but his son did not respond. He kept rowing but managed to catch the expression on his sister's face. It seemed that silently and compassionately she was conveying the message: 'Don't pay any attention to what you have heard. Our dad is a loving person but sometimes he behaves like a brat!'

The image faded and Anton muttered to Henrietta as if she knew what he faced a moment ago. "So that's the kind of humiliation I went through when I was a boy. My dad liked her better than me. He always stressed my shortcomings. For him, I was worth no more than a dime!"

His eyes were now shut. He was breathing softly, sliding into sleep. Henrietta watched him for a few minutes and whispered, "No matter what swings in your head, you're still my man. My gift from Heaven."

She left the room, went to the kitchen, had a cup of tea and a few crackers for lunch, then walked down to her basement studio and began to weave.

When she was gone, Anton opened his eyes and whispered to himself. 'Henrietta is a treasure. So gentle. So thoughtful. So much in need to free me from my disease. But will it happen? Will I ever again be at ease? At my age, the chances are so small. Who has the power to make it happen? Who do I call?!"

He tried to shut off this rambling but the notion of impending departure was snaking through his brain. He was torturing himself:

'How many days are still left for me? The clock's ticking; the music of death does not subside. The end is approaching. So where will I be?'

Then he murmured the answer to that question:

'As I said before, I will fly to the Moon!
On a rocket called boon!
And live there for a while!
And to keep in shape, walk each day
at least a mile!
And sing a song about survival!
I'll be free of duress! No more pain!
No more earful of drivel that is tribal!
No more rough spots that are tainted on my mind!
I will not be deaf! Neither will I be blind!
What will spread before me will be a cushion-like sky!
That's why it makes good sense to withdraw
from Earth!
To die! Yes, to die!"

Hearing those words, Anton closed his eyes and soon afterwards was soundly asleep.

When, a couple of hours later, Henrietta looked into the bedroom to check on him, he was snoring loudly and, from time to time, was expelling in an intoning way some silly words.

They sounded like:

bing bing bing bing
tato fink tato fink

Behave yourself! It's safe!
Soup's on the table! Be brave!
Be brave!
Fadre Madre Fadre Madre
Madre Fadre Madre Fadre

CHAPTER FIVE

Anton woke at 5 a.m. after almost fifteen hours of uninterrupted sleep. Still in a bit of a stupor, for a few seconds he was thought he was sharing the bed with his mother. He heard her whimper, "Bring him back to me! Bring him back!"

His mother's voice dislodged the haze that was lingering in Anton's head. 'Why did I think of her? Calling me to bring back her husband? My father?'

An echo of an incident that had taken place in Montreal a short while before her death sounded in his mind. She was living in the Jewish Old People's Home that was under the medical surveillance of her brother and, having a serious heart problem, was hospitalized. Anton visisted her every day. One evening, after returning home from the hospital, Anton received a phone call from a nurse.

She said, "Mr. Lubecki, your mother is in poor shape. She's shaky and mumbles all the time, 'Bring him back! Bring him back!' The doctor said I should call you. That your mother wants you. That's why I'm phoning. To bring you back to her."

Anton rushed to the hospital and tried to soothe her feelings, telling her that he was with her and would come any time, day or night if she wanted him beside her. It took a while before she was able to understand what had made him come. Then, she whispered: "It was nice of you to come. But I didn't want you. I wanted your Dad. I wanted him to come and hold my hand. Before I die, I want him back. Can you do anything to make it happen? You're his son, so call him! Bring him back to me! Bring him back!"

A day later, she was in a coma. A week, later she died. That evening, when Anton was called to see her, was the last time he exchanged a few words with her.

Now his ear pounding – he had been free of this discomfort for a while – he was thinking, 'What a strange occurrence. Before I fell asleep, I reconnected with my sister. And my father. When I woke up, I heard the voice of my mother. Is this a reminder of the oncoming departure?'

There was already some light in the room. It was seeping through the turned-down slats of the window blinds. A thin ray of sun was on Henrietta's face. She was soundly asleep, breathing hard but shifting from one position to another, her eyes twitching, and heavy frowns crossing her forehead.

Anton recognized the symptoms. 'My sweet wife is troubled by a bad dream. I bet she has a nightmare about me. Should I wake her up? No. When she does it on her own, what fluctuated in her mind could give her a lift.

The factual reality of a problem is much more digestible than the rabid spectacle of it in a dream. So, soon after she opens her eyes and transfixed by the sunshine, she will relax. And humorously dismiss that distorted, malodorous scene. Which wouldn't have rocked her brain had our nights together been soothed by sex.'

Realizing a rhyming cadenza was a part of his reflection, he wanted to shout: 'What? Another slip! I thought I'd done with it. I thought this insanity had gone. I'm supposed to rhyme when I'm hit by humiliation. Who did the trespassing this time? What's the correlation?'

He slipped again but this time he didn't scream. He carefully stepped out of bed, put on his robe and tip-toed to the kitchen. Suddenly he realized how hungry he was, his stomach was rumbling. He soft boiled two eggs, put a slice of ham on a piece of dark bread, smudged it with mustard, made a large pot of coffee, then sat down at the kitchen table and, devouring it all, he mused, 'I haven't made this kind of meal for weeks. At least six. Does it mean something? I think it does. It conveys that I'm out of the fix!'

"Again!" He banged the table with his fist. "Again! I must find a way to get rid of this shit! What if I paid a fine for it? Each time I come up with this idiotic addiction, twenty dollars goes to the Humane Society! To help save dogs from this affliction. No!

To the Foundation for Disabled Kids. They surely will benefit from it. That will be the blitz! "

He instantly and internally made a comment: 'A well-sounding rhyme! The wrong word! Anton, you're a nerd!'

He giggled, almost chocked on a mouthful of food, but the idea stayed in his head. 'That's the route I must pursue,' he thought. 'Just to see whether by emptying my wallet I'll become more resistant to rhyming. Whether...'

The clinging word didn't materialize. Anton was quite surprised by this blow, but also thrilled by it. And contemplating it while slurping his coffee, he made the decision that the Foundation for Disabled Children would be the beneficiary of his mental slips.

'I did it five times today already,' he calculated, 'that's 100 bucks! I'll mail the cheque to them. No! I'll ask Henrietta to do it. So that she's aware of my commitment. No! She may argue that this is not the way to get rid of that dreck! So I'll be doing it on my own. Anton, this is a good track!'

He gasped, realizing that he had made another slide. 'That's another 20 bucks! God Almighty, I'll be a beggar in a year or two. I'll...'

This time he managed to avoid a verbal collision. Pleased, he finished eating, washed and dried and put away the dishes, then tip-toed to his study.

Once there, he took a chequebook from his filing cabinet, wrote a cheque for $120, put it into an envelope, addressed it – the location of the Foundation, the postal code and the telephone number were on a card of his Rolodex – put a stamp on it and uttered a sigh of relief.

"I'm not overspending," he said to himself. "This donation will teach me a lesson. And it will offer a touch of ease to the Foundation. And as I do trust my sense of not wasting money..."

Once the business transaction was completed, he relaxed in his chair and looked around. All that he saw, shelves bulging with books, precious paintings, sculpted figures, Eskimo carvings and his own work of art made him buoyant.

'This room,' he observed silently – the pounding in his ear reduced to a low hum – 'carries the imprint of such relevance. It is filled with joy and ease. There's nothing spurious about it. I love this zoo. It is the best place to write my life story. No! That of a dunce called Anton Thomas, Anton Melebaum and Anton Lubecki who was/is the owner of a dreadful past, and a carrier of a disease that... No!' He chortled with laughter. 'That'll cost you 20 bucks! To pay a fine was a brilliant stroke. A lucky fluke. Anton, you're on the mend. Anton, you're on the mend. Anton, you're a Duke!'

"Ouch!" He slapped his mouth. 'Another blasphemy! And $20 out of your pocket! You're a parasite! And what you came up with is so trite! Ouch! Forty bucks! But I am not going to pay it now. I'll wait a week to see...'

He grabbed his pen, made a note on his calendar to pay a rhyming fine for the period of one week, then turned his mind to the issue of writing his life story.

'How do I handle this?' he mused. 'As I have said to Dr. Wright, there are such holes in my memory. How do I plug them? By allowing the writer's instinct to take over and fill the empty cracks with incendiary events that may shed some light on the shape and confusion of my life? Hoping that what I will be saying is the dictate of my subconscious feelings and that the basic elements of truth will emerge? How strange that I'm the only witness to my life. That's what torments me the most. That my family, all those people I loved, are gone. I'm the only survivor of that wicked past. Will I ever see them again? Or are they nothing but ashes? Or dust?'

Caught in the web of bitter Holocaust memories, he didn't notice how he had slipped again, matching past with dust. Lost in thought, he sat at his desk quietly. Then awakened by the stream of sunlight that flooded the sky for the second day in a row, he searched for a pad of paper that was to serve as a cage for fragments of his life and wrote on the first sheet:

Dear Dr. Wright,

This is the story of Anton Thomas, formerly Anton Melenbaum, Anton Lubecki.

When you finish reading it you might be disgruntled by it. Or stupefied. Or offended. You also might be in conniptions!

But don't be concerned by those evaluations too much. Remember, this is a work of fiction!

He turned over the top page. On the second sheet, he tried to write the first few sentences, but was unable to do so. All kinds of images were surfacing in his mind; towns, cities where he had lived as a young boy, all covered by such a heavy mist that he couldn't recognize their specificity.

'I believed,' he shook his head with bewilderment and annoyance, 'that I'd be capable to sketch the landscape where I grew up under the protective umbrella of my family. But I don't know how to make it happen. How do I start this...novel?' He sneered at his helplessness. 'No description of the homes we lived in? No images of our gardens? And my schools! I can't shape them at all. In my mind, they don't exist. How do I treat...'

His quandary was answered by the stern voice of his father: 'In cold blood. Write tersely and to the point. Don't waste your time on descriptive passages. Deal with what troubles you. Concentrate on the enigmas. And speak about them fearlessly even if they are a product of your imagination. Don't be concerned that you might be offending me. And don't rhyme. As I overheard you, it will cost you a large fine.'

The voice that spoke loudly in his brain ceased but a sharp hum again invaded his head and his ear. The sound, very persistent made him anxious and angry. To suppress the discomfort, he clasped his head with his hands, his elbows on the desk and again blurted out to himself:

"This hum has been activated by my father! Why does he buzz me when I want him least? I know why! 'Cause he still rules over me. 'Cause he is a..."

Again the familiar voice reverberated in his brain: "Don't say it! It won't do me any harm but it will cost you money! Climb upward not downward. Climb! Or you'll spend the rest of your life in hell. I have seen it all. I recognize the...

Anton wanted to scream: 'Don't finish! I know what's on your tongue! An invective against me! Though I'm your son!'

But he didn't say a thing. His angry need to respond was overpowered by another thought that hit like lightning in his brain.

'It's not he who buzzes me. It's I who is buzzing him! It is I who procures his appearance! When I'm perplexed or ill at ease, I want him to make the decision. And when the outcome is a heart-searing blow, I want to blame him for it. I want to scream; it is he who made me do it. It was he who instrumented my fall.

But, though I hear his voice and see his face, it is I who speaks. And makes the choices. Under his disguise. Emil Melebaum – he is me!' Now he was on his feet and yelling: "Anton, have the gumption to admit it! And stop playing this shoddy game! You inflame yourself by it! And you will be the victim of of..."

He clamped up hearing Henrietta's voice. She was standing by the door of his study, her concern for him was imprinted on her face. "I heard you scream! Are you ok? You left the bed so early..."

"Early is right," Anton responded, deeply embarrassed. "I followed the sunrise. And you were so restless. Were you infected by one of my dreams?"

"You can say that," Henrietta replied, still anxious and moving towards her husband. "I'll tell you all about it but first I want to know what happened. Who did you talk to? You spoke so angrily but so fast that I couldn't make any sense of it. What went on? Tell me. Tell me!"

Anton staggered with the reply. "Sorry for the upheaval. I was chatting with myself. As you know, sometimes I grill myself about why am I acting so silly. But I was not aware that I was screaming. Are you sure that this..."

Henrietta cut him off. "You were squaring off with somebody at the top of your voice. Whatever you argued about infuriated you. Your face is still purple. And your hands are trembling. What was it? A boxing match with your dad? Your screaming woke me so at least I deserve a truthful explanation. I had a bad dream! I was shaken by it! And yours...."

Aware now of the sharpness of her scorn and how it stunned him, Henrietta reversed her stance.

"Oh, my God, why am I punishing you?" She clasped her hands to her cheeks. "I"ve done it before. It's because I am so scared – for you. What you are doing to yourself makes me so tense. Anger subdues my despair. Oh, my lovely darling, I'm sorry. Forgive me!"

She embraced him, leaning her head on his chest, then whispered, "I promise, I won't do it again. But if I do, remember it's anxiety. I can't control it. As you would say, it is a force that's bigger than I..."

Anton softly replied, “Indeed it is. That’s what I often try to convey. But ....” He stopped, then continued, “ is there anything I can do for you?”

Henrietta answered with a smile. “Yes, you can. Write a poem. An eulogy for your bride. But concentrate not on how she cooks or vacuums the house, but...”

Anton intervened, “How she lifts up the spirits of the abused women, silver-lining their existence by words that are soft spoken and full of compassion. That tell them of a better future gleaming on the horizon. That....”

Henrietta interrupted, “That’s their hope. And mine. But I don’t know how valid it is. Their lives are so tangled....”

Hearing a tremor in her voice, Anton put his arms around her and said quietly, “You are giving them advice about how to straighten out their lives. How to unwind. How to distance themselves in their hearts and minds from their tormentors and how to face a new life that is difficult and puzzling – but better. You say to them, ‘There is a bright light on the horizon. It will shine on you.’ Stick to this view. The world in which we live is in a mess. The best that we can do is....”

Henrietta lifted her head, their eyes met and she completed Anton’s sentence. “To press for less misery. No matter how it hurts. To make people suffer less. And less. And less.”

They embraced tightly then Henrietta stepped aside, curtsied, slightly lifting her nightgown and smiled, “I thank you for your tender reflection on my idea. You are a sweet man. The sweetest I have ever known. As you would say, ‘the motor of my ecstasy.’ The safeguard of my...what? What!” she exclaimed. “Supply the word! You know them better than I. I’ll buy it! For a...”

Anton replied, intoning magisterially: “Madam, your supplication is denied. You are entitled to know that I’m about to put a rigorous clamp on this finagling. I have acquired the necessary resistance. So it is wrong...”

Henrietta cut him off with an outburst of joy. “What? You have quit rhyming? Oh, my God! And I thought...Anton you have made the grade. I’m so happy! You will make a slip or two but so what? Your willpower is in gear. How do we celebrate? Shall we have a drink of champagne? Not now but tonight! Now it's time coffee. You had yours, I assume," she rushed to his desk and checked his cup. "But you made enough for two."

Without waiting for his reply, she raced back to him, gave him a few pecks on his cheeks, then she noticed some dirt on Anton's house robe. She teasingly berated him, "Your robe is filthy. And stinks! How is it that you don't notice it? Must it always be me who draws your attention to it? When you're done with your chat, let me wash it. Today is my laundry day. You'll have it back without delay. Don't worry. I'll do it. I'll do it!"

Again she kissed his cheeks then rushed to the kitchen. She shouted from the bottom of the stairs: "I'll be back in a minute. When I return, make me laugh. I feel giddy this morning. No! Very rough!"

While she was in the kitchen, Anton pondered Henrietta's shenanigans. 'Why is she rhyming so much?' he wondered. 'She seems seduced by that clumsy sing song. Is it to imprint on me how stupid it sounds when I do it? Or to impress me that her aptitude is as high as mine at this game? Or higher?

No! She is so fed up with my failure to get better that it borders on contempt. She comments on all my weaknesses with a silly smirk on her face. Perhaps even with a sense of glee. As my father would have said: Now she's paying you back for all the offenses you committed in the good old days. When you were the law maker and she was the haze. Now its you who is the shadow. And it is she who's ablaze. Because you misused your power, you're being paid back.'

Realizing what had happened, Anton spluttered: "Once again you are putting on your father's mantle! You have never heard him say things like that. So why do you think he would come up with such blabber? Because you are afraid to admit that those are your thoughts? You're a coward. A coward! And it will cost you another 100 bucks, you shmuck! Or more! Anton, detox your brain!"

The rhyming word was about to come out, but Henrietta's reappearance brought his musing to a halt. She entered the room, still in her nightgown, a cup of coffee in her hand. She sat on the sofa opposite Anton's desk and said sharply, "Detox your brain! That's what you must do. Be free of this poisonous stain!"

Anton, who was unaware that he had uttered those words, didn't let her finish the sentence. Leaving his chair and kneeling beside her he blurted out, "No, no! I didn't say anything of the kind. In fact I didn't speak! You were .... bright enough to listen to what was rolling in my mind! "

Henrietta responded harshly. "Don't give me that shit! Your yelling woke me up. That's why I'm here. To find out....."

Anton, shocked by her stance, didn't let her finish the sentence. He embraced her and apologized profusely. "Henriushka, I am sorry! Very, very sorry! I was not aware that I was screaming! I was so involved in my effort to...."

Henrietta once again shut him up. Sharply removing his arms from around her, she stepped aside, then scolded him angrily: "Don't touch me unless you become the man I knew in the past. You have done this baiting many times before! But you have never kept your promises. I have little faith that you will do it now. As I have told you before, you need medical treatment that will be harsh but free you from your illness. Dr. Wright has done nothing to change your condition. You must look for other doctors who could be tougher! And...."

Now it was Anton's turn. Very upset, he stepped aside and barked: "What's the matter with you? Your lashes are hurtful! They increase not diminish my confusion. And my pain. It's not up to you to tell me how to handle my illness. I do the best I can! So...."

Henrietta responded instantly. The way she spoke indicated that she regretted her explosion. "You're right! I should not interfere with your medical treatment. And I should have thanked you for waking me. For smashing my horrible dream. That is the reason why I was nasty with you. It made me feel so tense." She rushed to Anton, embraced him again and whispered, "Would you like to hear my dream? I want to tell you but I should warn you that you will be shocked. Distressed."

Anton responded softly after a moment of silence, "Yes. I want to know what kind of dream you had. But first let's sit down. And speak softly to each other. Once you reveal what haunted your sleep...."

Henrietta finished his sentence. She said gently, "I'll feel better. I'll relax. And then, I will sing you a song. One of those you inherited from your father." With a light smile on her lips she sang: *"Tala tala tala tala."*

Anton joined in. *"Tala tala tala bala."* Then he put his arms around her, took her to the sofa and made her sit down. Sitting beside her and kissing her lips, he said, "It's time for your nightmare."

Henrietta replied, "A nightmare it was. But also a... dross. A stinky, dirty dross!" Then she started her story. "As you know, last night I went early to bed. I was very tired. I needed to rest. I fell asleep quickly and I didn't hear you come to bed and I didn't hear you snore. No," she smiled, "when I woke it was 2 a.m. Your music was loud. But I didn't pay attention to it . For some reason, I was boiling, covered with sweat, so I decided to have a bath. I sneaked out to the bathroom without waking you, let the hot water run and then crept into the tub and relaxed. Then....," she inhaled heavily, "my mental misery started to develop."

She stopped speaking, inhaled and exhaled a deep, audible breath and continued: "The tub was filling up with water and I was comfortably curled up in this wonderfully warm, liquid bed, then suddenly, totally unexpectedly, a thought was born in my brain: You are alone here. Very alone. Who would you like to join you? Instantly and without any warning, the reply resonated in mind. My parents. My parents!"

"What!" Anton exclaimed. "You wanted to be with your parents? Outside of the fact that they have been dead for a long time...."

"I surely know that," Henrietta shushed him. "And you know I was without them for many years before their death. They let me go when I was eighteen, when I barely knew what life was all about. And when they....." She stopped talking but tears were spilling from her eyes. Anton, gently placing the palm of his hand on her neck, spoke softly, "They screamed at you, punched you, locked you in a closet for being disobedient, tormented you. And when they died from some infectious disease during their trip to Latin America where they wanted to live some day, 'under the sun'......"

Henrietta, calmer now, put her finger on Anton's lips and whispered: "Enough, my love. Enough. You know my story well. I've told you too many times how I was treated by my parents.

After the funeral, I tried to understand why they were so cruel. As you know, I lived with my aunt after my parents were gone. Our house had to be sold to cover my father's monstrous debts. Not one uncle, aunt or cousin would deal with the subject. Some would say: 'We don't believe your stories. We mustn't speak of the dead that way.' And they would change the subject. Others would say: 'Forget it! Forget it! If you want to be happy and strong, let go of this ugliness. You must have hated them to tell these horrible lies." She paused, then added: "I must stop this. You know the pain. And I am having trouble reliving it....."

"But what about your dream?"

Henrietta answered, "When I came back to bed, I had more memories of my family. When I fell asleep, I cried, watching my parents who were sitting beside me in the garden and scolding me for not visiting their graves." She was silent now, staring into space.

Then Anton whispered, "Please tell me why you want to see your parents? Is it because I am ill? And quite soon will disappear? That's why you would like them beside you, helping you to set up a .... new life? Is that what haunts you? The misery, no, the mystery of the days to come after I am gone?"

"No! No," Henrietta replied with a stutter. "I do not expect you will be gone soon. The way I feel .... I've never told you .... I think I will go before you. Yes, I will be dead, quite possibly much sooner than you expect. I am not as strong as I used to be. And seeing you suffer so horribly I feel......"

Anton jumped up from his seat and lifting her up from hers, hugged her tightly and spoke, shattered by pain. "No! No! No! I am first! Then..... you will go! But the distance between my departure and yours will be enormous. You'll travel and capture forever the visions and the sounds of the Earth. I will be less lucky. I will lose it all! This will be my curse."

They stayed tied together a touch longer. Then they abandoned the subject. They were yearning for lightness. Henrietta stretched out on the sofa and Anton reached into the liquor cabinet. He poured out two glasses of brandy, their favorite drink, and returned to his wife. Giving her a glass and lifting his, he said, "To our happy life!"

Henrietta responded, "My dream too! But if it doesn't happen, then we sue!"

They smiled at each other, took a sip of the liquor and then Anton, sitting on the rocking chair beside the sofa, remarked, "Changing the subject. Are you aware you're rhyming? You seem to be in the grips of my bygone obsession. Take my advice. Suppress the desire to bring them out. Otherwise..."

Henrietta butted in: "I will lose my glitz! Or as you would say simulating your father, I will turn into a wretched bitch!"

Anton, startled by the intensity of Henrietta's response exploded, "Henrietta, what the hell was that?"

She answered dramatically: "A copy of your bygone performance and the source of my malfeasance! I wanted to serve as your mirror. To make you shocked by it. To force you to abhor it and dump it into your mental garbage bin. And you have done it, so my act was effective. But this damned germ lodged in my brain. So to force it out will take some time. And some pain. But don't worry. Like you, I will succeed. I'd rather..."

She was breathless now, and momentarily overwhelmed by her outburst. She leaned backwards, put her head on the back of the sofa, stretched out her hand to Anton. "Sorry, sorry, for my loose tongue. I should have kept my mouth shut. I..."

"Shh..." Anton whispered to her. "No need to apologize. Your words told me how concerned you were about me. Your..."

Henrietta didn't let him finish. She exclaimed: "Enough of this gloom. It's past. There is another story in my dream. Now comes the farce. At last."

She jumped off the sofa, stepped into the centre of the room, wiggling her hips, her breasts bouncing, and addressed Anton pointing around the room with the index finger of her right hand. "Look! In front of that boat house was a stretch of overgrown lawn. You were sitting on it a few feet away from me, in your white shorts, no shirt, just a naked, hairless chest," she chortled. "Nina and Paul were coming to visit and I was telling you:

'Wise guy, just look around. The view is stunning. And the garden looks nice. You did something proper. The rent was worth the price.' Then I exclaimed: 'Oh, my God! I forgot to cook some rice! Chicken and rice, that's our lunch! A meal to satisfy our unruly bunch!'

"Then I turned around, ready to walk inside and I stopped and screamed: 'Oh my God, I forgot to put a brassiere on my tits! I'm fit to be tied! My brain is for the pits!'

"I ran inside and, a moment later , returned, yelling: 'The oven is a bust! Why didn't you check it to see how long it would last?'

"And you replied: 'Shut up, Henrietta! You're baiting me. Stop it! Fast!'

"You were on your feet. I thought that you were going to give me a smack. Then your mother appeared. She looked at both of us and said: 'The two of you are like my husband and me. We too crossed swords. Often! For real! That's the difference between you, my babes, and us. For you both it's a spiel!"

Henrietta paused for a moment, then added: "That's it. That's what woke me up. What to you think of that farce? That..."

Anton interrupted softly, "I will tell you later. You were again in your crazy spell of rhyming. You must stop it, Henrietta. And though you blame me for your addiction, I'm convinced that some inner force imposes on you that..."

The word 'dereliction' flushed in his mind, but he dismissed it. Instead he said: "that thing".

Henrietta realized what happened. She smiled and said, "Good for you, Anton. You put it in the garbage dump. I must follow your example. What does it rhyme with? Rumple? Crumple?"

They both laughed then Anton said, "When my mother appeared to you, how did she look?"

Henrietta answered, pointing at Rosa's photograph that was hanging on the wall beside Anton's desk. "Like the woman up there. As if she had stepped out of that frame. Ensconced in sweetness. Gentleness. And gentility."

She offered Anton a soft smile. "Now I know why some people call you an Eastern European gentleman. Or Polish-Jewish aristocrat. You got it all from her. As you often said to me, she was your soul former. And a loving frat."

She was on her way back to the sofa and noticed the stamped envelope on Anton's desk. She glanced at it, read the address. She joked, "Are you applying for a job? No, that wouldn't work. It would ruin your naval gazing. So it's a donation. How nice of you!"

Anton responded, "A donation, yes. But also a penalty for rhyming. Each time I come up with clinching words I pay a fine, 20 bucks."

"What?" Henrietta exploded. "This is outrageous! You're throwing our money away. You're..."

Then, as if struck by a new thought, she continued more calmly. "On the other hand, you help disabled kids. The more you 'sing song,' the more they get. And they need it badly. Anton, I approve of your idea. As long as it will not drain our savings to zero. I need to feed you. And you need to feed me. And also you made me a promise that once you're ok, we'll travel to countries we have never seen. So don't waste all that we have."

She returned to the sofa, sat on it, softly caressed Anton's head and whispered: "I love you so much. Though often you're a brat! When I touch you, a torrent of emotion swooshes through me. I think often, without you, where would I be? You're the root of my existence! No," she corrected herself. "My tressle tree!"

Again they laughed, then Anton, a soft grin on his lips, said to Henrietta, "I need you! I need you to mock me! 'Cause I cannot..you rhyme!"

Henrietta responded without the slightest hesitation: "Not true, Mr. Slime! No! Mr. Muck! I do it to please you! ' Cause you're locked in my heart! Though you're rough! Though often, in my mind, I name you Master Tough!"

Anton responded: "As long as we're locked in each other's heart, the bitching we go through doesn't make us smart! No! It's just a fart! An empty fart!"

They howled with laughter and when their mirth subsided, Anton said, seriously this time: "Your dreams are so legible. So connected with what we're going through. With what you are going through," he corrected himself.

"And yours are not?" questioned Henrietta.

Anton shook his head. "No. They come and go so fast that most of the time they elude me. I just can't hold on to them. When I wake up, only a tiny segment of those dreams flickers in my head. And when my recall is better, it happens so rarely. I cannot decipher their meaning. A few days ago, I had such a dream. Would you like me to tell you who I saw? And what I heard?"

"Just let me guess," Henrietta said in a frisky tone. "As you so often see and talk to your father, this time it must have been your grandfather. Or your great grandfather. The rabbinical..."

"Triglodyte," Anton slipped in. "No. None of those. It is quite amazing how divorced I am from them. As I told Dr. Wright, I don't even remember how they looked. I met my great grandfater only a few times when I was a child. Briefly. But surely I've seen his photograph. I can't even revive the face of my grandfather. I knew him so well. I was his pet," he smiled sadly. "I was the only male youngster on the paternal side of the Melenbaum family. Ginia, my father's sister, had a daughter. Fela, the other sister, was still unmarried. I was to be the future Master of that Empire," he chortled again, yet his face was grim. "I sometimes wonder if that disaster hadn't happened, if my family had stayed alive, what would have happened to me? Would I have stayed there and run that land, an idea that I hated, or would I've had the gumption to leave it behind. To make it on my own. To..."

Henrietta interrupted him, "I've heard it before. So forget it! The door to that store must be shut tightly." She giggled lightly and sweetly. "And tell me about your mysterious dream. So who did you see?"

"My father," Anton answered. "And his lawyer. His bosom buddy. They were both in my father's study. I was a teenager. I stood beside the half-opened door and heard them argue. The lawyer, his name was Eisensher, a short, dark-haired, mustachioed fellow with glasses on the tip of his nose, was yelling to my dad. 'My life is in order now! I'm redeemed! I've joined a new faith! I'm a follower of Zoroaster!'

"My father who was sitting behind his desk, his face purple with rage, responded in a similar fashion. 'A new faith? You must be kidding. Five hundred years older than Christianity. Now on the burial ground of all religions. And I didn't know you wanted to embrace a faith. I imaged you as a thoughtful, secular Jew who scorns attachments to religious cults. You're a cabbage! A sack of rotting potatoes! An empty-headed dunce! By joining that group you have besmirched Jewish honor! You have embraced falsehood! So quit talking to me! Faze out! Faze out!'"

While saying this, Anton increased the level of his voice as if emulating that of his father. Then he continued, "That image indeed faded but another emerged. I was asleep in the barracks of a concentration camp. I was snoring heavily and an inmate who occupied the next bunk shook me and said to me that I was snoring so loudly that the walls were trembling. He whispered to me: 'Stop it or you will wake up the guard!'

"At that moment, the guard, a monstrously large fellow, barged in and yelled: 'The snorers – out! You're ruining the building. You will be executed. Heraus! Heraus!'

"And a group of naked inmates was pushing through the door, out of the barracks. Then there were gun shots. And screams. Ahh! And the guard, bursting with laughter kept on: 'Heraus! Heraus!'

Then he left. And I remained in the barracks. Alone. Still hearing the shots. The laughter of the guards. And the..."

Anton raised his voice again: "Heraus! Heraus!

Then I woke up. My head was pounding. I wanted to talk to you but you were soundly asleep. So I slipped out of the bedroom, tip-toed to my study, sat at my desk – it was still very dark, there were a lot of stars in the sky – and I tried to make some sense of those pictures."

Saying that, he smiled lightly and, noticing an anguished expression on Henrietta's face, stretched out his hand to her and said, "That's what I was afraid of. That my story would make you feel grieved. Puzzled. Perhaps even miffed."

Henrietta merged her fingers with his but did not respond to Anton's effort to lighten the mood. Instead of absorbing his demeanor, she said, "Miffed by your suffering? Don't be silly. But puzzled, yes. What's the connection between the first and the second part of your dream? Your father was so angry. In fact..."

She stopped, shocked by the thought that appeared in her mind. "What he said to his friend was in a way quite similar to how the guard shrieked at the snorers and at you!"

She focussed on these words: "Faze out! Faze out! Heraus! Heraus!"

"Oh, my God," Anton whispered. "There's some sense to what you have said. But what's the link? Henrietta, Henrietta, it scares me stiff! Henrietta, I'm losing my mind! I'm going mad!"

"Calm down, my love. Calm down," Henrietta responded to his outburst, softly embracing his torso, yet shaking with tension.

"The link, as you saw it, must only be accidental. Don't torment yourself by it. Did you speak about that dream with Dr. Wright?"

Anton replied: "No. I wanted to but I couldn't. He would have seen my father in such a bad light."

Henrietta shook her head, disappointed with Anton's decision. But she didn't reprimand him for it. Instead she said:

"Yes, you were again on fire about your dad. I haven't heard you say a word about him for years and now he appears in your mind so often. He visits you or you visit him. In your dreams, the two of you meet almost always in his study."

She paused, then continued, "Are you certain those two stories were a part of the same fantasy? Or is it you who subconsciously tied them together? You seem to carry so much anger toward your dad. As if..."

She stopped talking but her eyes were lingering on Anton's face as if testing his capability to endure what she wanted to say. Anton noticed her hesitation and said softly to her, "Please, go on. So often your instinct conquers my dilemmas. Tell me what you think and don't be concerned about my reaction. The subject of my father is my topsy turvy slope. As he would say, my old-age predilection!"

Henrietta responded with a glint of impatience. "You don't know what your father would have said. You quote him often, but these are your phrases, not his. Your imagination takes you astray, that's my opinion. To follow your way of speaking, you're on the skids when it comes to remembering your dad. The way I understand it —forgive my observation —you barely knew him, if at all. You've created an image of him that fits the turmoil that boils in you. An image that is rough and unpleasant and I believe untrue. Which responds to your effort to mask your anger with yourself. Your never-ending sense of guilt, perhaps even shame that you are alive and he is not. That you survived and he didn't! That what you have done to save his life..."

Anton no longer heard her. In his mind, he was transported to the kitchen of an apartment in Warsaw where he and his mother lived after the Second World War. It was a warm spring day, sunlight was storming the small space, they were sitting at the table, and he heard his mother say:

'We didn't do enough, my dearest son. He was a truculent man and stubborn, but that doesn't change the fact that we didn't do enough to save his life. Once I had my false papers, I should have gone back to drag him out of the ghetto in Lwow and bring him to Warsaw. He was unwilling to take such a step. He kidded himself that as the Head of the Pharmaceutical Service of the Judenrat, he would survive, but he would have left that barbed wired jail had I gone to lure him out. He also would have listened to you. We didn't do enough. We thought only of ourselves. We were afraid to risk our lives to...'

And then Anton saw himself interrupting his mother, his voice veiled in anger. 'Mum, what you have said is absurd! That he didn't survive had nothing to do with us. Sophia, the Christian woman who brought you to Warsaw, wanted to go back to Lwow to smuggle him out and then bring him by train to where we were. Her male companion gave him all the details and urged him to take that route but he refused! He told the man that such an escape was too risky. That his features were so obviously Semitic that somebody would rat on him to the guards who were on the train and that would be the end of him. He also said that his conscience didn't allow him to risk Sophia's life. So he decided to leave to Fate what would happen to him while he continued living in the ghetto. He was not prepared to risk his life to save it! That he didn't survive had nothing to do with us. Had he sent us a message that he wanted to flee, I would have gone back to Lwow. But he didn't! So don't blame yourself for his death. And don't blame me!'

Then his mother, her head bent, her eyes focussed on some spot on the table, whispered, 'Some people thought he was a coward but he was not. He was a proud man. Unable to live in hiding. Unwilling to put the lives of other people in danger to secure his. He was stubborn, tough, he followed only his own views. But there was saintliness about him. Yes, son. That's beyond dispute. That's the truth. The truth.'

That image evaporated and a thought of a totally different nature rumbled in Anton's mind. His head was now resting on Henrietta's breast and he silently questioned himself: "Which is worse? The grief caused by abandoning my father to his fate, or the pain that tears me up now that I'm not aroused by Henrietta's body? I'm also abandoned. Betrayed. But by whom? That deprivation is the worst experience of my life. It makes me inept. Cringy! Unable to bloom!'

Revolted by his absurd equation of the two subjects that denigrated his father, he jerked away from Henrietta and she instantly responded, "Have I said too much? Sorry, my love. Sorry. I thought it would help you. Make you less tormented."

Anton answered, "I had similar thoughts before. As I have told you, your instinct often is flawless. Yes, indeed I lost track of my father. Or possibly, I never was on it. I lost him so early in my life. And have never ... outgrown it."

He lifted himself up, stretched, returned to the chair behind his desk and said, "I bet you would want to hear a thing or two about Zoroaster. Should I tell you who he was?"

"I wouldn't mind," Henrietta replied. "I was going to ask you what you know about that saint," she laughed. "Was he in that category? I have never heard of him before. And how did it enter into your mind? Like all dreams, it must have had some beginning."

Anton, more relaxed now, interrupted her. "I don't know how to answer your question. When I woke up, I was quite befuddled by the name. I couldn't make any rational connection. So I did some research. As you know, the top shelves behind me," he pointed at the bookcase with his thumb, "carry volumes dealing with the start of the human race and the development of ancient civilizations. There's also a section about the origin and the incubation of religion across the globe. I looked at some of those books, searched for the name Zoroaster and I found it. He was a religious teacher and a prophet of ancient Persia. Way before the Talmud or the New Testament were born. He was also called Zarathustra. Which possibly meant old camel! And he carried a lot on his hunched back, so it seems. He was a visionary, so the hazy records say, with a soul-stirring skill of speaking. He was fed up with politheism and wrapped up in the belief that a monotheistic regime governs the Universe. And he must have been endowed with the awesome spiritual power of converting the citizens of that part of the world; his God, what was his name?" he stumbled. "I have written it down somewhere." He searched though piles of notes stacked on his desk, pulled out the one he was looking for. "Here it is!" Then he read from it:

"His name was Ahura-Mazda. His body is the light and the sovereign glory. The sun and the moon are his eyes. Zoroaster's words. A poetic phrase, quite potent, don't you think?"

Then he continued: "So Ahura-Mazda was the Master of the Cosmos. But evil spirits hovered in the air all the time, always tempting human beings to commit crime and sin. And their leader, Ahriman, Prince of Darkness and the ruler of the netherworld, stood up to the God of Light, Ahura-Mazda, and the struggle between those two giants for the dominance over humankind and nature was the foundation of that faith. Ah," he added, "the soul of human beings was the battleground of beneficent and maleficent spirits. Every person was a warrior – whether he or she liked it or not – in the army of the Lord or the Devil. And the Prince of Darkness was the prototype of Satan. It appears that the Jews have adopted him from Persia and willed him to Christianity. So, on one side were the People of Righteousness, on the other the People of the Lie. After death, each person crossed a bridge to the hereafter. If that person was reprobate, the bridge narrowed and that being tumbled to Hell. But if that creature was worthy of salvation, the bridge widened – a path that led to the shaft of light."

The last words made him shiver. He stopped speaking and a thought reverberated in his mind: ' The shaft of light! The ship that I will be taking on my way out of the Earth. Will I travel alone or will I be surrounded by a crowd of peace-seeking souls like me? And those companions, who will they be? Only males? Or females too? And that congregation, will they come from different corners of the world or will they all belong to the same crop? Embellished by a maple leaf, like me! And those who master the ship, do they know our names? Or do they address us: 'Welcome aboard Mr. and Mrs. Bee!'

Those crazy thoughts made him titter and catch Henrietta's eye. She was focussed on him and her face carried, unmistakably, a signal of puzzlement and concern.

She said, "Did something happen to you? Are you still with me?"

Anton answered, "Of course I am. For a moment, I was distracted by some silly thoughts. Who does one go with on a flight to... Heaven? And does it really happen? Or is it..."

He froze for a moment, his arms up in the air, his eyes bulging and riveted to something in space, then he roared, "Oh, my God, it hit me! It hit me!"

"Anton!" Henrietta responded fearfully again. "What's wrong?"

Anton replied, his face now beaming with excitement, "I remember! I remember when I've heard the name Zoroaster! Why didn't I think of it sooner? Why wasn't I hit by it faster?!"

Now listen to this," he spoke with increasing animation. "In my school days, I had a teacher of religious history, a devout Christian. For whom Catholicism was the cornerstone of the civilized world. He was a dilettante, a turret of mediocrity, but had many followers in the school because he talked about the power of his religion all the time and scorned all those who didn't cross themselves before the figure of Jesus Christ. To be a decent human being, he sermonized, you must be his disciple. All those who are not, are faithless animals. Spiritually disemboweled. They must be saved. Made to kneel in front of His altar. Bow to His wisdom and His power.

And that teacher had a fight with my father. He once demanded that my dad come to learn from him what an anti-religious maniac I was. Why? At the beginning of his class he wanted his students to pray. To elicit God's support for our work. Most students followed his instruction, but some refused and I was one of them. First, I told him that I'm a Jew. And therefore I did not intend to raise my hands in prayer to Jesus Christ. Then I said that my father had told me that he doubted that God existed. So, as a loyal son, I stuck to my dad's view. And I said that I didn't know if the Almighty was real. And, if He was, whether He cared enough for me to pay attention to my prayers. So I declined to listen to his command. And he yelled at me: 'You do what I order you to do or you'll be dismissed from my class! Only a soft-brained person would behave the way you do! So raise your hands and pray or get out, you son of a cretin. You silly ass! I don't want to look at people like you! I don't want them in my class!'

Once again, I refused to obey him and, in return, I was kicked out of school that day. And a letter was delivered to my dad asking him to appear before the Principal to face the charge. Yes, the charge," Anton bared his teeth in a bitter smile, "that his ungodly stance was detrimental to the school system and to his son's learning!

So my father had a verbal battle with that teacher. I was there. So was the school boss. My dad cooly presented his view that religion was a private matter and that it was improper to make students believe that only imbeciles, stupid asses and cretins would question God's existence. When his argument was dismissed by the teacher's contemptible statement that Christ's sacred revelations came straight from God and were the only laws for human beings that separated righteousness from malfeasance, good from evil, and that only a malevolent Jew, a progeny of Judas would deny those gospels, my father erupted with fury.

'What about the Talmudic Tradition?' he yelled. 'And before it, what about Zoroaster? Have you heard of him? Centuries before Christ, he preached in Persia that there's God in the sky and the Demon of Evil who rules the netherworld! And they compete with each other for the dominance of the human soul. Was that a part of your curriculum? No! For you only Jesus Christ was the messenger of God! You're faith blind! An antisemite! So I will sue you! You'll have my lawyer at your back! Unless I get an apology, I will call you Mr. Dreck! I bet you know what that means! If you don't..."

"You are impersonating your father again," Henrietta intervened. "It's just impossible to discern whether what you're saying is a real recall of your father's words or the way you hear it."

She changed the subject. "How did he know so much about Zarathustra? According to your picture of your dad, for him, religion was taboo. Why would he...?"

Anton cut her off, "In the journal he published, he would write about the ascent of the world religions. Of that I'm certain.

What he was trying to say to his readers was that the fear of life – its mystery, its danger-filled path – and the fear of death are the premordial reasons for the creation of God in the human mind. And for the subservience to the rituals that followed that invention. I have no doubt that he was familiar with the teaching of Zoroaster who possibly was the first man on Earth who brought to the surface monotheistic ideas. My father spent so much time studying..."

"And the lawyer? How do you explain his appearance in your dream?" Henrietta asked.

Anton shook his head. "Can't make any sense of it. That lawyer was as crazy as a coot. He would come to our house late in the evening, drunk, and he would coerce my father to play cards with him. Or he would sing, accompanied by my dad. He was a lonely man, taking care of his legal business and his daughter who was my age. Her mother, his wife, died early in their lives. And she, I mean Ivanka, was the first girl I ... touched...under her dress. I was sixteen. It was an experience I still remember. And will never forget. There was such serenity to it."

"Serenity?" Henrietta asked with surprise, "I would have thought..."

"Yes, serenity," Anton continued. "It was summer, a late afternoon, we went for a walk in a small forest by the river. We sat down beside a tree, an oak tree I think, then we stretched out on the grass. We were kissing each other, then I opened her blouse and touched her breasts. It shook her a bit but she let me hold on to her. And she unbuttoned my shirt and stroked my chest. Then, I lifted up her skirt and explored the lower part of her body. I removed her underwear, she helped me do it and I touched her, gently caressing her thighs, the lower part of her belly and her pubic hair. And she did the same to me. We were beside each other for quite a while. The softness of her body, the taste of her lips...that is what sometimes awakens in my mind. I was so at ease then. So full of optimism about the future. And so young."

When he stopped describing the scene, baffled by the outpouring of the confession, Henrietta asked softly, "Didn't you make love to her?"

"Yes, I did," Anton replied, a light smile on his face. "The way I described it. For some reason we didn't go any further. We were overwhelmed by the joyous discovery of the erotic mystery. What we achieved, I called it the first level, was totally satisfying. We didn't pursue it any further. The second level was an experience we never explored."

Henrietta responded, "A very touching story. It's the first time that you've told it to me. You're full of secrets, my old fellow. Why don't you share them more often? But be mellow when you do it. As you are now. Be mellow! My sweet soul! Don't bellow! Don't bellow!"

An outburst of mirthful laughter was the follow-up of her words. Anton jumped up from the floor, went on his knees before Henrietta, she was still on the soft cushioned chair, lifted his arms in her direction as if in a Muslim supplication and exclaimed: "Did I hear right? You compared me with Saul Bellow! I'll be mellow! I promise! I'll be mellow! But I want a kiss! And a massage of my penis! To heighten my bliss!"

Henrietta, pretending to be offended, responded with a shrill, "Not now! That's the fun I'd rather miss! In any case, you must go to the bathroom first! To get rid of your piss!"

Anton replied in mock fury: "Don't tell me what to do! Remember, I'm your groom! You're my bride!"

Henrietta, instantly barked back: "But the vow was that the two will never collide! Never collide!"

"Never?" Anton acted out his derision. "The human species must bicker! Or they'll be strapped by silence! Not a flicker of sound! Not a flicker!"

Henrietta replied in a similar vein:

> "Bicker, flicker,
> Who gives a banana!
> As long as you're my babe.
> And I'm your mamma!"

Anton replied in the same tone:

> "Mamma and babe?
> You and me?!
> That's a barmy statement!
> I'm leaving! Here's the key!"

He made a gesture as if throwing a key at her, leaped towards the door but stopped and exclaimed:

"No! I am staying! Where would I go?
To Sodom and Gomorah?
That would be a blow!
Besides, on the scale of my testing
there's no one better than you!
So whatever it costs
I'm staying in this zoo!
Shall we dance?
We're two lonely people who prance
and prance and prance
'cause we're scared that the end is looming
and what's before us
has so little sense!
So we boo each other often
to stay afloat!
Our verbal bombast, that's what
makes us gloat!"

At that moment Henrietta, on her feet now, intervened:

"You are damn right, my hubby!
Finally we agree! So boo me!
And when I'm in a mood for it,
I will boo thee!'

Then she changed her tone, there was nothing but pure joy in it:

"And now let's dance!
Hurray to our wisdom!
We have managed to smash
the fence!"

The hugging and dancing that followed looked as if they were on stage and on the brink of madness. Holding hands, their cheeks pressed against each other, they moved forward and changed direction with the rapid rhythm of a tango melody that they hummed, replacing the lyrics with:

Tatatata, tatatata
Tah! Tah!
Balalala, balala fatah!

Zoom!
Taloota, pala boom!
Boom boom!

When they stopped, gazing at each other with adoration yet also conveying that they considered themselves to be 'crazy coots,' Henrietta collaped on her chair saying, "We have danced like this throughout all our married life. Not only in bars, but at home. In the living room. In our kitchen. Our record player was humming all the time. Music, dancing, made us so happy. So lets keep doing it. Let us continue teasing each other. But not bitching. Not bitching."

Anton murmured, "As I said before, I buy that advice." Then he turned his head towards the clock and blurted out, "My God, its quarter to ten!"

Then Henrietta exclaimed with amazement, "Ten o'clock? My God, how time flies! I'm still undressed!" She winked at Anton, "Without my brassiere!"

Anton responded, his index finger directed at her: "You"re damn right! And you are still showing me your rear!"

Henrietta stood the test. She left the chair and recited:

"Rear, gear, who gives a tango?
As long as I have my good coffee
For breakfast!
And a ripe...mango!"
"Mango?", Anton whistled with scorn.
"Don't be so crude!
Mangos are for soubrettes! Or dudes!
We eat eggs and jam!
Which reminds me, I'm hungry!
I want a piece of bread. And ham!"

He giggled then continued, "Then I will sit at my desk and write my memoirs. My life as seen through the eyes of a...Tzar! That's how I see myself writing that study for Dr. Wright. About the stud called Anton Thomas, Anton Melenbaum, Anton Lubecki, seen through the eyes of a dispassionate critic whose name is...who cares? And who will shape the facts of my life according to his poetic vision. Instead of a tearful report, there will be a lot of humbug in it. Pages full of derision!

"And then my doctor will say" – now he spoke as if he were the old vaudevillian – "you see, you have examined yourself. You're at bay! Your problems are imaginary! Which is customary for persons of your age. So accept your own judgement and live with it as long as you will. Now, there is one more thing that matters. Your bill. According to OHIP...He...He...He...!"

Henrietta who was listening with increasing intensity to Anton's barrage of words, interrupted him gently. "Enough, my battered man. Enough. Your spirit is low again. You're hurting. That writing will be rough. But once you're done with it, I so much hope you will be over the hill. As I said to you before, it's up to you to beat the torment that you're going through. It's up to your willpower. No one else who can help you but yourself. Accept life as it is. And be well. Relax! Relax!"

She approached Anton, tears in her eyes, embraced him, and speedily left the room. But she called to him once again from the bottom of the staircase: "I'm off to the bathroom and, when I get dressed, I'm going to work. But I will be thinking of you. I love you! I love you!"

Then she was gone. Anton, surrounded now by silence, pondered what he had heard and whispered to himself, "In spite of her grumping, she is a star of sanity in the sky of madness. But am I really a will-devoid nerd? A paradigm of badness? She dreams of dolce in our vita. But am I fit to take it? Time will tell! And my willpower, it better be stronger than it is now. It better flower. It better be well."

He pulled out the pad of paper which was to contain his 'novella.' On the first page, there was the note that he had scribbled for Dr. Wright. Looking at it, he again reflected how to shape Anton's past.

'He tried to bury his Jewish roots for many years of his life,' he thought. 'During his young days, he was a non-Jewish Jew. During the Second World War, he was a non-Jew. When the war ended and he started to live and work, not to be endangered by his ancestry, he again was a non-Jew.

For different reasons. Not to save his skin but, nevertheless, his Jewishness was in hiding. Practically non-existent.

Only in Canada did his Jewish affiliation begin to emerge, making a growing impact on his life.

So, in fact, his inner reality for many, many years was disguised. Strongly suppressed!

That was the source of his self-questioning Who am I?

And this is what I must deal with. This enigma has surely affected Anton's way of thinking. And feeling! This is what I need to concentrate on. Reveal it. Reveal it!'

He started to write. The images, the phrases came out of his mind with greater ease than he had expected. Optimism seeped into his heart. He whispered to himself: "I may be able to come up with my story. I might! I might be able to get rid of the toxicity of my blight. Of the fear of my earthly carousel ride..."

CHAPTER SIX

Two weeks after he started to write his story, Anton called Dr. Wright. He wanted to tell the psychiatrist that he was progressing surprisingly well with the assignment. Toward the end of the following week, he would bring him the finished text.

Dr. Wright was not in his office but the receptionist informed Anton that he was out of the country for the next ten days and that she had been instructed to make appointments with his patients. Anton chose the date: Tuesday, October 29 at 3 p.m.

On the day he made the appointment, Anton was half way into the 'novella.' He was convinced that he would accomplish his task within a week. Though he recognized there were serious gaps in the story – in spite of his effort he had been unable to shed enough light on the early days – he was quite satisfied with what he had written. He showed it to Henrietta, asked her to read it and enter it into the computer.

She went through the text and voiced her opinion. "It is not only informative but riveting. The style of some passages should be modified a bit. Some of your phrases sing/ring. But the story should please your doctor ... and your publisher."

The remarks about Anton's writing style were characteristic of Henrietta. She often pointed out that his creative process carried the features of "Polish physiognomy," and that it required some transformation to be easily absorbed by "Anglo readers."

Her observations were often astute but, nonetheless, Anton vehemently defended his mode of writing.

"I am what I am," he would retort. "I can't control my soul! It has foreign roots! In my dreams I see and smell the shores of the Vistula River. Not those of Georgian Bay! My style reflects that collision that I cannot change. I'm not Joseph Conrad, but his prose also reflected his upbringing. He wrote in a language that was rich in images, colorful, flamboyant, not rigid, impassive or phlegmatic. Whether you like it or not, it rang polonaise. And I am following the same pattern. I am a prisoner of my past. That's my curse and my virtue."

This time, however, he refrained from verbal battle with his wife. Encouraged by the upbeat reception of what she had read, he suggested that while typing the text she introduce the required changes. "As long as you make me aware of them and I give you the nod". A week later, working on it non-stop and often late into the night, Anton came up with another part of the story and gave the hand-scribbled pages to Henrietta.

She went through it, her comments about the stylistic awkwardness of some passages were unusually restrained and, once again, she expressed her conviction that Harold Topper should look at it.

Anton was thrilled by Henrietta's praise and by her commitment to be helpful. By this time, the first section of the 'novella' was on the disc of the word processor, but Anton decided his psychiatrist should see the story first and then, perhaps, he would let the publisher read it. He carefully explained what made him resistent to her suggestion.

"Tempting as it is, at this stage of the game, such a step would only augment my confusion. I am in a state of psychological recession. To put a stop to its progress, I am trying to define the source of my malaise. Who am I? What am I? What forces shaped my being? Those are the questions I need to find answers for. But what concerns me most are the black holes in my life. And to what degree am I responsible for my mental and emotional shape? Was it chiefly the external world that formed and re-formed my needs and my desires, or were they injected into my veins by the experiences of my youth? And would I be happier now if in my earlier life I were less...crescendo! Uninspired by creative ego! Drier! I'm hoping that once I have the truthful answers to those questions, I will regain my composure. And no matter how rewarding it could be, I don't want to be deflected from this track. And such a turn would be inevitable if Topper were to be involved.

He would say: 'Change this, change that. Your piece, exciting as it is, tumbles. It is short on logic. Be more rational about your observations. You're so phantasmagoric! Or he could say just the very opposite! Be more fantastic! You're too commonsensical! There are no labyrinths in the life of your hero. All that you have written is so dry. Embellish it with some fancy. Be more dramatic! More drastic! And that's what I wouldn't want to happen. Once his words would ring in my ear, I would be uncertain of the accuracy of my story. I would question its integrity! I would torment myself: Was I trying unconsciously to conceal some elements of Anton's life? Was the missing light my perverse invention? I must be fair to myself. Do you see what I mean?"

Then he added with a wink, "In my now forgotten days I would have finished this speech with a line: 'Did I make myself clean? But no more! The floor is yours! Only don't be ignoble! You see, I didn't use the word mean!"

Henrietta was ruffled by Anton's position but, to his surprise, she did not contest him. She typed and printed the second part of the story and encouraged him to continue with the writing. "Once you've finished you will decide its future. I will not bribe you to do it my way. You must listen to your own voice." She paused and then continued with pleading in her voice. "And once you deliver the text to Dr. Wright and get his opinion, can we please go to California? I so much want to travel. To see Amanda in L.A. and Ludmila in San Francisco. Say yes," she laughed. "Don't be a devil! Don't be a devil!"

Ludmila, who now lived in San Francisco, entered Henrietta's life when she was sixteen. Ludmila was nineteen. She and her two younger sisters came to Canada from Europe in 1947 on a ship that moored in Halifax. They were part of a group of Jewish orphans, redeemed children who survived the Nazi days in hiding and, under the sponsorship of the Canadian Jewish Congress, were given shelter by Jewish families in various cities. Henrietta's father was one of the participants.

He and his wife brought Ludmila to their house; her sisters were taken care of by his brother. Ludmila lived with Henrietta's family for five years, was well taken care of and given all that she needed in material terms to shake off the trauma of her terrifying past. Then, she started to correspond with an Austrian Jew. She helped him in his effort to leave his bloodstained homeland, welcomed him to Canada, married him and, soon afterwards, they left for a "better life" in San Francisco.

Henrietta's contact with Ludmila, even during the days when they had lived under the same roof, was of a minor nature. Her sudden appearance in that house was unexpected; Henrietta's parents had not told their children that they would be sharing their home with a stranger who was to be treated as their sister.

Ludmila, re-living the suffering – the loss of her parents who were killed in a concentration camp, the daily terror of living in disguise as a Christian teenager – was in constant need to be tied to her sisters. She did not pay too much attention to her new family.

After she moved to San Francisco where her husband started a successful import business, he purchased pearls in China, turned them into necklaces, sold them to local jewelers and eventually made pots of money, she connected with the Dobins, writing a few letters thanking them for their help and inviting them to visit.

The letters were politely answered but face-to-face contact occurred only once or twice when Ludmila returned to Montreal to spend a few days with her sisters.

Then, after a number of years, those ties ceased to exist. After the death of Noreen and Lou, the Dobin family consisted of Henrietta, Carole and Peter, their spouses and their children. None of them felt obliged to continue that relationship. But one day, after years of unperturbed silence, Henrietta was awakened by a persistent inner voice that told her she should check up on Ludmila and re-bind old ties.

What was the reason? It's difficult to say. Possibly a sense of guilt. Older now and married to a Holocaust survivor, Henrietta had a deeper comprehension of Ludmilla's torturous life during the war and afterward. She understood now that, once in Canada, Ludmila had to find a way to subdue, if not squash, her haunting memories.

'I should have been more observant, more caring,' she thought. 'More supportive. More aware of how injured she was. My parents should have told me. But they never did. So now I feel that I was unfair to Ludmila. That I increased her pain.'

She shared her thoughts with Anton whose view of the situation added to her discomfort.

"She was distant, I'm sure of that," he made his point gently, holding her tightly in his arms. "But there was a reason for it. You were in different shells. Yours was luxurious, exorbitantly large, and seemingly free of restraint. Hers was tiny, bleak and stifling beyond relief. In your dreams – we know the reality was different – you were a part of a world that was safe, cushy, comfy. The world she saw in her dreams was harsh, filled with murderers who shot Jews on the streets, or raped them, and robbed them and shoved them into cages ringed with barbed wire. Barbed wire was the symbol of Ludmila's existence. In her dreams, she was wrapped in it. She walked on it. Rested on it. Do you follow what I'm trying to say? She ached all the time. What she needed most was the chance to reveal the gruesome details of her suffering. She needed badly to share the torment of her experiences. By not being invited to talk to you and your family about the scenes that were blazing in her mind, she felt deserted. I have gone through it myself. Enjoying the safety and the glamour of my Canadian existence, yet being drawn to those old days, always thinking of those who were left behind, resting not in their graves but in dumps, their bodies crushed and turned into ashes. I think that Ludmila, in her early days in Canada, went through an upheaval like mine. Had she been induced to break her silence, to talk about where she came from, who her parents were, how they died, and how she and her sisters survived, the relationshionship between the two of you wouldn't have been encased in mist. It would have been warm and fine."

Henrietta agreed. "I wish I had been more aware of those circumstances when Ludmila was around. I wish my parents had awakened me. But they didn't. Or couldn't. They were narrow-minded, grasping for quick recognition and money. Had I confronted my father, he would have replied: 'I brought her here. I paid my dues. How to cope with life is up to her. We all have our problems! We all have to deal on our own with our woes!'"

A few days later, Henrietta connected with her aunt who had taken care of Ludmila's sisters. She got their telephone numbers from her and contacted them. They were married with adult children and living in financial comfort. She obtained Ludmila's address and mailed her a long, rambling letter. She told her what had made her silent for such a long time, how unable she had been to grasp the reason for the "wall between us from the very beginning," how much she had thought about it and regretted her misjudgement of the situation.

The letter of response, concise but very warm, arrived three weeks later. Ludmila was happy to meet and to talk about their present lives without rehashing the memories of the past. "Those harsh, bitter days are so far away. And filled with so much sadness that, to return to them, would only do us harm. My life is peaceful now and without trouble. I want it to stay that way."

She inquired about Henrietta's life. She wanted to know more about her "new companion and about all the children" and she gently proposed that Henrietta and Anton visit her in San Francisco.

Further correspondence followed. Then some phone calls that made them teary eyed and keen to meet. Each time they engaged in a telephone conversation, Ludmila extended her invitation and Henrietta responded that she would "take her up on the offer." And that "one of these days, soon" she and Anton would arrive in San Francisco.

Henrietta wanted first to fly to L.A. and to descend on Amanda, an old friend. When they met, Amanda had just arrived in Montreal from New Zealand and was madly in love with a world-renowned poet whom she thought she would marry. When he dumped her, she moved to Toronto with a new lover, an actor. She told her friends, he was "A Jewish Brit who is hungry for fame and entranced with my tits!" She also often called him "My nomad!" Or "My Tartar!"

When asked why he merited such a title, her reply was delivered with a giggle. "He floats. In his mind, he floats across the world. That's what makes him a nomad. And in bed he's seductively aggressive. There's no way to stop his drive. That's why he's a Tartar! A hard-working, horny guy!"

They didn't last long in Toronto. She did some writing – stories for children – but failed to find a publisher. The fame-hungry nomad couldn't find work so they made the shift to Los Angeles. Amanda and her "amato" had been there for the last five years, consuming the upside and downside of L.A. living.

Henrietta was fond of Amanda. She loved her insightfulness, her loquacious, funny chatter, her unshakable energy. Her departure from Toronto made Henrietta suffer intensely.

"I'm so pained that she's not around," she would say to Anton. "I miss her so much. She was the best friend I ever had. I could listen to her talk to her, for hours. She would reveal her holy secrets to me, I would share mine. When I talk to her or receive a letter from her, I get misty. I want to see her. Get the sense of her life. Is she still happy with her Tartar? She says yes, but is it true? He is so busy now, working like a demon, so how does she cope? Anton do me that favor and let's go! Once you feel better and you will, you will let's take off for a month and visit, as you call her, your Amandushka! You like her, and her man. So why shouldn't we go? It would make us happy! And once we're there, we'll drive to San Francisco and visit Ludmila. And make a detour to Santa Fe. To fulfill my dream to walk in the desert. With you beside me. Musing about stone-age people. Anton, once you're on your feet again, we must go! Otherwise, as you would say, there will be a cleavage between us. A deep crack! So let's not abandon this trek!"

She finished her ebullient speech, rushed to the bathroom to pee, leaving Anton alone in his study. He was startled by Henrietta's mental switch from the discussion about his pseudo-documentary to the sojourn in California and his instant response to her proposal was stained by negativity and irritability. What whizzed in his mind was: 'Is she berserk? I am a sick man! Destined to die, soon! I cannot crouch in a car for days. I cannot fly! I must live without stress until...' But then, unexpectedly, the images of their vacations in Europe during his teaching days flashed in his mind. He recalled how those weeks of traveling not only lifted his spirits which were often subdued by the humdrum of his working routine, but also how they brightened his mind. Artistic endeavours in countries like France, Holland, Italy, Denmark and Sweden – in theatres, art galleries, museums – were so revelatory, so filled with sociopolitical examination, so unorthodox, so challenging and upbeat, that, in comparison, what was taking place in Canada was inconspicuous. Moronic. Anton dealt with this subject at the University and wrote about it in theatrical journals. For him and Henrietta, their European jaunts were experiences of valour and value and, for several years, their regular routine.

Soon after Anton withdrew from the teaching 'underworld,' – his scornful observation of the gap between teaching moguls and the common world – he was overcome by Meniere's disease and travels abroad came to an abrupt halt. Anton was not affected by it. Physically and emotionally in the dumps, he had bowed to his illness.

What for him was an unpleasant but inevitable reality was a huge blow for Henrietta. Fascinated by the beauty and cultural riches of Europe, she wanted to continue the yearly excursions.

Then, aware how hard it would be for Anton to travel so far, she changed her direction. It was California not Europe that buzzed in her head. Anton would say to her: "You're riding that horse with passion! At least twice a week, you plead with me for that concession!"

Moved now to give Henrietta some respite from his "shoddy state," he decided to go along with her wishes.

'I will promise her to do my best not to hinder her plans but, at the same time, I will warn her again that I am, health-wise, a creep. And it is beyond me to control what might happen. But if I am well, we shall travel. We will dance on a Pacific beach. We will...'

At this moment, Henrietta returned. Anton did not finish his monologue. He jumped up from his chair, kissed her, then said with a giggle, "When we talk, you should go to the loo more often. It gives me time to think. And...."

Henrietta interrupted him, "I know what's on your mind! Our trip to California..."

Anton cut her off. "Is on! As long as I can stay on my feet. As long as I don't slide into a murky pit."

Henrietta instantly replied, "You won't! I guarantee! I will inject you with my fighting spirit! I love thee! You love me!"

They ended their conversation with a hug. Henrietta left the house to do some of her business errands and Anton, in his usual fashion, let her out and locked the front door before returning to his study to continue his writing. He was pleased that the mood floating in the house was "fragrant not malodorous, mephitic."

He muttered to himself, "I so much hope that fetid stench will not pollute our relationship. That we will talk freely, unfettered by the imagery that haunts us; the vicissitude of the aging process, the ever-presence of the finality of our lives, the existence or non-existence of post-mortal salvation. Henrietta is aging. She is sixty and is as anxious about it as I am. She watches my torment and does all she can to be un-subdued by it, unaffected by that scene. Her involvement with the stream of battered women carries the mark of that inner battle. She is compassionate, truly in need to be helpful to people at loose ends. But it also does her good. It improves, stiffens her mettle!

Staying so close to me, she can't help but think of herself. 'Will I soon face the same horror?' That question lingers in her mind. 'Will I suffer like him day after day? Will I crawl through the rest of my life without a moment of respite? Without ease?'"

Seeing her troubled face in his mind, his elbows on his desk, the palms of his hands covering his cheeks and his eyes, he mused silently: 'I must find a way to relieve her of this scare. I must help her to extirpate this worry from her heart. And her brain. I must force her to bury it in the darkest corner of her mental train. Oh God!'

He chuckled, unable to stop the rhyming cadenza. He made a note to write a cheque the next day for the due amount to the Foundation of Disabled Children. Then, as if pulled by some inner force, he turned his head toward the photograph of his mother that was pinned to the wall behind his desk. As usual, he was captivated by her face. Her eyes were focused on him. There was a gentle, affectionate smile on her slightly parted lips. The way she looked at him was the reason Anton loved that picture.

Then it occurred to him that what he saw carried a new message: she warmly approved his stance concerning Henrietta. Rosa listened and understood the problem. She wanted him to know it and to find a resolution.

"Oh," he uttered a sigh of relief. "My sweet mom understands my worry. She encourages me to be strong and to remove the burden of concern that overwhelms Henrietta. She says to me, don't blow it! She does not say: you blew it!"

He chortled again and stated firmly, "We are going to California!" Then he kissed his mother's photograph, picked up a pad of paper, a pen and went back to the final stages of his story.

He worked late into the night, untroubled by Henrietta who, after returning from her errants, appeared a few times at his desk. She looked for a moment at his "scrabble," kissed his temple then quietly left to do her work. When the sun was about to set – the red glow between two high-rise buildings captured Anton's attention for a moment – she again entered his study, carrying a tray with his supper, a few chicken wings, a sweet potato and a glass of red wine. She placed it on his desk, kissed him, then gently stepped away.

Soon after midnight, Anton finished his task. He re-read what he had written , made some final corrections and, with a sigh of relief, placed the pages on the table beside the word processor. "The story is completed," he muttered to himself. "How revealing it is we will soon see. Dr. Wright will tell me how open I was describing my bygone life. How truthful I was. How what I have described has affected my instinct to survive. I was intimating that it had pushed me to the brink. But also, I was aiming to say that I was trying, and still am trying, to resist that pressure. This is the main factor of my struggle. The resistance to the inner notion that questions the meaningfulness, the validity of my present existence. The resistance exists, yes, but it's on a down slide. It is getting weaker. And weaker!

I hope Dr. Wright will strengthen my resilience. That he will boost my spirit. Make my passion shine. Not barely flicker!"

He was about to turn off the lights and leave the room but his concern for Henrietta made him stay a little longer.

'I want to tell her how much I love her,' he nodded to himself. 'I want to put it on paper. So that she can look at it whenever she wants. That will make her life... richer,' he smiled. 'And safer!'

He quickly returned to his desk and, within a few minutes, composed a poem. Then he read it softly to himself:

> To my Jewish Princess.
> No! To my Queen!
> From a man who loves you
> and who is getting thin...
> ner! And thinner!
> Who often thinks – am I soon to see
> the Redeemer?
> But who does not trust that spirit!
> who even questions whether He/She/It
> really exists!
> So you see the dilemma I'm in?
> That's what makes me wobbly! Confused!

And on a level of response, sometimes a...
beast!
I bully those around me 'cause I am
in fear!
So please steer me to become less stringent!
Yes, I want your steering gear!
Which you possess!
The soft drill, the soft words, it is
the best way to clean up my mess!
Or at least to keep it on a
low level!
What I need most is
a caress!
So make me cling to you!
No more bruising! No more bitching!
Or as my Father would have said:
no more thunder storms!
Softness in your eyes, softness of
your touch
that's all that I need to cease to
be a grouch! And a slouch!
Your need is just the same!
So let's live up to that commandment!
Let's not maim one another!
Let's be the winners!
Not the losers!
Let's skip forever this
mindless meander!
And if this would help let's become
...boozers!
A bottle of rum once or twice a week
that would do the trick, don't you think?
Yes! For sure it would make us click!
And would make us hug each other, peaceable then
snooze!
Yes, I'm for it! Once or twice a week
a lot of tasty booze!
These are the thoughts that rumble in my mind!
Let me hear yours! Though I know that

they are most kind!
And filled with heart-breaking stress
about my well-being!
Look, I'm kneeling before you!
I'm kneeling!
So be certain, there is nothing more important for me
than our fest!
I love you. I adore you.
And that feeling is my main link to life.
My crest.
Written by Anton, your hubby
who tries to play a role of a sage.
Would you say it's his custom?
Or it has to do with his
age?
Who cares? What we need now is
unity!
Not the reverse!
So let's make it happen!
Let us be done with this malaise!
Let us live in peace till the
end of our days!
Oh, my lovely darling,
let us enter, let us sustain
this new, no, the very old phase!

When he finished, he thought of the text and decided that he had poured out his feelings just as he wanted – simply and directly.

He put the pages in an envelope, addressed it to "My sweet wife, Henrietta," sealed it and left it beside the computer.

Then he switched off the lights, took off his clothes, left them on a soft-cushioned chair close to his desk, went down to the kitchen to have a drink of soda water, then went to the bedroom. He put on his pyjamas, Henrietta had put them on his side of the bed and quietly slid under the duvet. Hearing her soft snores, he was pleased that he had managed not to wake her up. He fell asleep almost immediately.

Henrietta knew he had come to bed. She was on the edge of sleep, thinking of him and awaiting his arrival. She had heard him tip-toe into the room, and was aware of him lying down. Yet, though awake, she didn't budge. In fact, she did a small performance: she snored a touch to show that she was peacefully asleep. And she thought: 'He is such a sufferer! Such a pain-ridden fellow. Yet, he is the person I love most. And his body has such a nice smell. Anton, I will dance for you. Just give me some music. Just ...'

She wanted to move close to him, to snuggle, but she resisted the temptation.

'I'm not going to stir him up. A good sleep is what he needs most. It diffuses the pain that comes when he connects with his past. So sleep well, my love. And have a nice dream. I know, it doesn't happen often. But when it does, you're like a bluebird. You chirp happily. You don't scream!'

Hearing herself imitating Anton's rhyming pattern, she chortled slightly then decided to get up and check whether he had completed his task. She wanted to type and print out the remaining pages as soon as possible; she hoped that once it was daylight she would finish her assignment. She sneaked out of bed, walked on her toes to his study, closed the door, turned on the desk lamp and instantly noticed the letter that Anton had left for her.

She opened the envelope, read the poem and was deeply affected by it. Pressing the pages to her heart, she thought: 'His fear of dying is so rampant. I must help him stop it. I must keep consoling him. Joy, not grief! He must breathe the fun of living! I must make him do it. Even at the cost of... weaving!'

She put the poem on the table, quickly scanned the pages of Anton's story, then turned off the light and tip-toed back to the bedroom. When she snuck back into bed, looking at her husband, she repeated to herself: 'He suffers so much! He is in so much pain. Anton, my love, I will do all I can to lift your spirit. Or as you would say, to drain that sewage. Just drain it!'

Anton was snoring loudly. She was used to that sound. It was a part of their nightly experience. She changed her position – now her face was turned away from him – and a few minutes later she was also asleep.

Her last thought before she dozed off was: 'California, we soon will be there. Amanda, Ludmila, get ready! Make me and Anton happy during that phase. He needs it more than I do. To get out of his maze!'

CHAPTER SEVEN

The next day, without warning Anton was hit by the sharp pain of his illness. It was Thursday, October 24. He was awakened at 5 a.m. by a surge of nausea that rocked his body. He was severely dizzy and pulsating pressure was crushing the left part of his chest.

He lifted himself up, determined not to wake Henrietta. He tiptoed in darkness to the bathroom. To maintain his balance, he clutched a chest of drawers, then the door frame and the wall in the hall that led to the bathroom. When he entered, he closed the door, turned on the light and stepped toward the toilet.

His control was gone. He needed to throw up, instantly. To his luck, the lid of the toilet was up. He bent over and started to vomit. He threw up again and again, choking out all that was clustered in his stomach. When he was rid of that burden, he pressed the lever to flush the toilet. The level of his discharge was so high that, with the water running, some of the mess went over the top and spilled on the tiled floor. Then, the motion in his head still rampant, he sat on the tiles beside the tub. That move was instinctive: he was exhausted. He needed to rest; the thinking process had nothing to do with this motion. But, because of that, what he so desperately tried to avoid took place. When he was sliding down to put his buttocks on the ground, the wrist of his left hand hit the edge of the low marble construct which separated the bathtub from the toilet. The pain was sharp. He screamed loudly. Henrietta awakened by this noise, jumped out of bed and raced to the bathroom. She pushed the door open, saw Anton sitting on the floor, his head leaning on the curved edge of the tub, the fingers of his right hand squeezing the wrist of his other hand. His face was torn by suffering. She shrieked, "Oh, my God! What happened?"

Then, noticing the splatter of vomit on the tiles in front of the toilet, she exclaimed: "You threw up! You had an attack! Are you still in pain?"

Anton, now in a state of slight recovery yet physically exhausted, gave her a thin, encouraging smile and responded softly, "Yes, I had a dizzy spell. I threw up. But the discomfort is gone. I feel better now."

After a brief pause, he added: "I'm quite weak. Please, help me stand up. And guide me to bed. I'll be alright. Don't be shocked. Or sad. Don't be sad."

With Henrietta's help, he struggled to his feet, took off his pyjamas that were badly stained. He let her cleanse his body with a warm, wet towel and, assisted by her, limped to the bedroom. Henrietta switched on the lamp on the night table, took out a fresh pair of pyjamas from the closet, helped Anton put them on and, a few moments later, he was under the duvet .

The activity made him more tired. He wondered fearfully, 'Will the dizziness come back? Will I need to vomit again? No,' he convinced himself. 'There's not a trace of food in my stomach. So throwing up is over and done with. But the hum in my ear and the revolving motion in my head...'

Henrietta watched him closely and noticed the increase of stress reflected on his face. "Should I call your doctor? Should I ask him to come?"

Anton, pointing his finger at the clock, replied in a whisper, "So early in the morning? It's only twenty-five past six. No, there's no need to wake him up. Besides, there's nothing he can do. As you well know, this damnation comes and goes. How to stop it, no one knows."

Henrietta didn't agree and observed, softly, "But he could give you some medication. Some pills that could lessen your discomfort."

Anton replied soothingly, "Don't worry, my angel. Don't worry. I will rest. I will be fine. But one Xenox would help. I'm quite anxious. Not dizzy anymore, but scared. This bloody nuisance hit me so strongly. And so abruptly."

"Scared about what?" Henrietta asked, taking out a pill from the container that was on the night table.

"But don't rush with the answer. First, let me first bring you a glass of juice. What would you prefer, orange, grapefruit, apple?"

Anton's response was "Soda water. I have a bad taste in my mouth. Soda water would tackle it better."

Henrietta rushed to the kitchen and while she was away, question after question raced through Anton's head.

'Should I tell her what scary thoughts inhabit my mind? That one of these days, soon, I will be overcome by these attacks? That the pounding in my chest may mean that my heart needs a rest? The vertigo and nausea, why does it happen mostly in the fall? Is it the gray sky that makes me go through this? Is there some hidden message to it? A signal that tells me; Be prepared! Grayness is the main element of post-life existence! That's what's ahead of you! The set-up of the final departure is well planned. There is consistence to it. A sharply defined, well-controlled consistence. So I will be gone. But paying my visit to...where? Should I let Henrietta know that I so often ponder whether Heaven or Hell exists? And if the answer is yes, who will greet me before I enter one of those spaces? Will it be a sweet looking angel extending his welcome to celestial bliss or will it be a humongous monster...'

Before he completed this thought, his father's voice rang softly in his ear. He was saying with sarcastic condescension: 'Do you still smell the joy of paradise? Do you still tremble at the thought of Hell? If your mind is so corroded by this Christian belief, what about purgatory? How will you reach Heaven if your soul is not cleansed by the brush of suffering? You are a sinful being! That's what any priest would tell you. God will not talk to you unless you purge yourself. So be ready to receive the clobbering. Enjoy the heavy doubts. If paradise is your destination. If you are not assigned to go to the Netherworld!'

As if summoned by those words, a strange, grotesque image blazoned Anton's mind. He saw a cave-like structure – encased in marble, surrounded by a large spread of white sand and hanging high in the air. Then a person, clothed in riding boots, jodhpurs, red jacket and velvet hat, stepped out of it. He was huge, his belly bulging, thin, long hair touched his shoulders, round glasses covered his eyes. There was a censorious expression on his face.

Lifting the riding crop that he held in his hand, the man addressed Anton.

'Welcome to Purgatory. I'm the top guardian, Prince Messiah Celestos. Prince, the title was a reward for bringing to life a mineral called asbestos.

'Obviously you know why you are here. According to the rules you are to suffer punishment for the sins you committed while on Earth. They were; pride, covetousness, lust, anger, gluttony, envy and sloth! Lust and anger were your main slips. You were a lascivious womanizer and a first-class screamer. But, compared to all other sinners, you were rated as median. Mediocrity was your minus and your plus. When you functioned down there – the man pointed at the empty space beneath him – you were a ... so-so ... achiever, a condition that made you despise yourself and made you extraneous, irrelevant.

But being here gives you a chance to step upwards, be admitted to Heaven, with thousands of others, providing that you live up,' he smiled again, 'to what's expected of you.

To make it happen, the load is heavy, on me that is. I must train you to crawl! And to cry! For a period of time this will be your daily reality. You will be chained and whipped with precision and harshness that are the marks of my prowess. There will be an even rhythm to it, and steady, most steady, consistence.

But to sustain your ability to cope with pain,' he chortled, 'to keep on the upswing your instinctive climb upward, you will also be one of my advisors and my servants. Your task will be to offer me your opinion on the literati on a world scale. When and where should they go. You know what I mean. Our radiographic files are well geared to handle this task. But this is a studious job, it requires not an automaton but a sharply constructed brain that could attest and assess the revelations. A brain that belongs to a male. It is always he. The female gender is not up to this assignment.

As a servant, you will take care of my nourishment. I don't eat too much. Mostly meat, vegetables and fruits. So you will serve me steaks, salads, grapes, bananas, whatever I demand. And keep me clean. Ah,...' he lifted up his rod again, 'I almost forgot! Your new name will be Maven. We rename our patients,' he grinned. 'We have our own system of keeping them on our list. And we like to connect them with their racial origin and antiquity.

As a celestial being who is to tackle the when and where, you'd better live up to what I am expecting of you. Particularly when you wash my feet. And my buttocks! I like that job done well. Not a crumb of you know what, left lingering. And no smell!' After a moment of silence, his eyes focussed sharply on Anton's face. The man continued, pointing at the structure behind him: ' So, are you ready to step in? Your eyes tell me you are not too eager. You seem to be revulsed by what I have told you. Remember, you are on the lowest level of Heaven. That's how I view Purgatory.

Would you prefer to go to the Netherworld? To be burned by fire? Roasted for eternal steak? Is this what you are after? A huge, dark cave cramped by sinners who burn and burn and burn? There's no return! Am I not offering you a more comfortable option? Once your treatment here is over and done with, wouldn't you prefer to linger under the blue sky? To float on a white soft cloud? You seem so ready to go to Hell! Are you so median? So ignorant that you don't know what you are about to lose? Eternal happiness instead of what you will gain – eternal pain and grief!

So what will it be? Will you serve the servant of the Master of Heaven or will you end up in the netherworld? I am charitably minded! It is up to you to choose your fate. What will it be? Burning coal or...'

The image dissolved as abruptly as it appeared, leaving Anton in a state of shock. He jumped out of the bed, ran to the top of the staircase, yelled, "Henrietta! Come back, quickly! I have gone berserk! Henrietta, save me! Save me!"

Then, he turned around, returned to the bedroom and collapsed on the wooden bench at the foot of the bed. And he grieved silently, 'What was the meaning of that rampage? Who was that holy creep? My brain is so often invaded by notions, images that are inane. That totally deny that I am a rational human being. This is what makes me sick! Scared shitless! What's the meaning of it all? I grappled with it before. What does it signal? That my exit is about to happen? That the messenger of death is already sitting at my desk?'

Another image blocked his view. This time he saw his mother standing close to the familiar fir tree against the red glow of a rising sun on the pale blue sky. She was wearing a silky white nightgown and shaking her head with disbelief and anxiety. She was saying in a stern, disgruntled fashion:

'What shocked you was a scene from a play your father wrote and put on stage when you were nine years old. He also performed the main part of Prince Celestos. You saw it. He insisted. He told the audience that Heaven or Hell do not exist. That was a subject that gripped him as long as I knew him. He rejected and ridiculed that sacred belief. When the play ended, there was heavy booing. And cursing. That production in a small town called Zydaczow cost him his business. The people who had seen the play were mostly Christian. They were offended and turned their backs on your father, boycotting his pharmacy. A rich landlord even challenged him to a duel! Your father dismissed the demand as ridiculous bombast. He informed the man in a letter which he later published, that he didn't intend to offend anybody. He had only expressed, in a comic fashion, his views of the world. And he was as privileged to do that as all those who were critical of him, the righteous protectors of religious faith. He also told him that to act as a defender of the honor of the community, he should have proposed to do so with words not with a pistol or a sword, and challenged the man to face him on the podium of the local library before an audience to spar about the issue. The landlord refused and kept abusing your father, calling him a coward and a Jewish bug who despised Christianity and, with ardor, stood for the Judaic faith. But that was not the case. First of all he was anything but a coward. He risked his safety to express his views. And he was an atheist, not a faithful Jew...'

At this moment, Anton's father appeared from behind the tree. He was wearing white pajamas with black squares on them and exclaimed with happy agitation:

'That's true! That's true! I also poked fun at Talmudic precepts. In my play, I made Moses deaf in one ear. Listening to the Big Voice and not hearing the lines well enough, he conjectured what he had missed and memorized it in the way he saw fit. That's the reason why the Talmud was – and still is – such a book of quarrel! Each rabbinical wizard interpreted the commandments differently. The throne speech was unclear. So the rabbi I presented in the play was befuddled about his religious duty. And he found a solution. Instead of preaching, he started to give music lessons. And cook! It turned him into a person loved by the community! They called him...'

Rosa stopped him by stepping on his foot. 'Your palaver is not frugal,' she said. 'It is you, not him who is the gook!'

They burst out laughing, holding each other's hands, then the background of that image dissolved abruptly, replaced by another.

Anton's parents were again a part of it. Still in their night-clothes, they were in their living room in the capital city of Eastern Poland. The sun was setting and, through the window, the turret of a monastery across the street was defined against the purple glaze of the sky.

Rosa was sitting in a rocking chair, drinking tea. Emil stood nearby and was adddressing her with the speed and emphasis of an accomplished actor:

'I know, philosophical banter is not your favorite game. We have tangled about it before but I must give it another try. To convince you that you are stuck to a fable. Rosa, Heaven and Hell do not exist! Monotheism, the phenomenon of immortality,' he laughed, 'then Paradise and the Netherworld emerged when human minds made a jump forward. When they ceased to be as primitive and instinctive as those of wild animals. When so-called intellect started to play a role in human life. When humanoids began to really think and, bedazzled now by the magnificence of Nature, transfixed by its mode of operation and its beauty – the sunrises, the sunsets, the moon and the stars on the dark sky, the thunderstorms, the heat, the stone-covered mountains, the azure-like waters of the sea, the swishing rivers, the trees bearing fruits, birds and animals that were turned into food, and the reproductive process of all living creatures – they tried to unravel that mystery.

How did it all begin? What forces made it happen? Once the genesis of the Universe was a subject that bothered human minds, more and more the demand for some explanation was pressing. The same applies to the awareness of the blight of human existence on Earth. Humankind struggled horribly to survive. Their life span was short, packed with inexhaustible pain, frustration and triviality. This accepted reality required justification. And sanctification! This is when spiritual sages of those very early days of civilization, the most soul-searching, imaginative beings in human history – Moses was one of them – appeared on the horizon. They were sensing and witnessing the terror that was seeping through the veins of their people, the members of their clan. Deeply concerned about their fate and solemnly examining those two gigantic issues, those wise men came up with emotional relief. They found a poetic solution to their dilemma. They conceived God, the Supreme Judge of human behavior. They envisaged Heaven, His residence and the net of happiness for those who were prepared to worship the Master and resist the temptation to slaughter, exploit other members of the tribe. And brought to life Hell, the cavern for ever-lasting revenge aimed at those who refused to follow the credo that honesty and love were the pillars of daily existence on Earth. The condemnatory lodgings for all those who chose, while alive, to benefit from being evil.

This magnetic brainchild of those sages spread like fire. It couldn't have been more timely. It subdued the torment that ravaged the minds and hearts of many people. But it did more harm than good!

It made human beings less responsible for themselves. Not driven enough to accept that life is hard and that they, only they – or should I have said us – can improve it.

Without waiting and relying on the Super Power to determine what to do! Without depending on the award of immortality for honest life on Earth. Or living under a threat of being burned for being a bad person.

Decency has nothing to do with post mortem remuneration. The best proof is that millions of people lost their lives in religious wars.

Love and mercy cannot be induced by well-sounding paragraphs supposedly coming from the External Force. Neither by the bribe of reaching Heaven!

The same applies to badness. The thought of after-death mutilation of the human body doesn't make us better. Just the opposite! It increases our ferocity! It turns us into cowards! It skyrockets our fears! Our feelings of hate! We don't need to be fused to Heaven to love our neighbors, to have respect for life. We must be alert to it on our own! That's what I stand by. And I want my children to follow that credo. And you too!' Emil's finger was now sternly pointed at Rosa. Then he continued:

Please say that I made my point. That I convinced you that my view is correct. If not...'

Rosa responded turgidly, 'I do not buy that trumpery. But you are free to believe whatever you desire. You are so absolutely certain that you are right. And I happen to believe that you could be wrong. I am more perplexed by the mystery of the Universe than you are. I would like to accept...'

Emil returned the salvo, 'That there's life after death? You are filling the minds of our children with this crap! After you stop breathing and you're dumped into the grave, there's nothing else! Only darkness! No sound that you can hear. No smell that you can inhale. You are a corpse that enriches the soil. That's all! To follow your way of thinking, where are you now? What space do you inhabit?'

Rosa replied, 'The one that you routinely blaspheme! The middle level of Heaven! We are both gone, but we are addressing our son. Could we do that if we were nothing but gravel? Could we make him listen to us? Could we...'

Emil cut her off, now screaming with fury, 'Shit! Shit! Your eschatological findings are inane. We are skeletons! Empty shells! Buried in the ground – no, I was gassed, burned and my ashes were dumped into a river – and hidden in the crevices of our son's memory. When he needs to, he drags us out. To resolve his doubts. To put the blame on his parents for his clumsy track through life. What misdeeds he committed were started by one of us, mostly by me. I tortured him! I tormented him! Don't you agree? Don't you agree?'

Rosa jumped up and answered in kind: 'No! I don't! You offended him and me! What you have said about us both was an affrontery! Yes, affrontery! So vanish! Disappear!'

Emil instantly changed his tune. He grabbed his wife's hand and exclaimed, 'Sorry!'

The storm raging in Anton's head came to an abrupt end. Torn by laughter, he didn't hear Henrietta. She was at the bottom of the staircase and was saying loudly: "I'm coming! I'm coming!

Sorry that it took me so long but I had to pee! And get rid of that other stuff. My stomach was so upset. Are you ok?"

She was now in the doorway to the bedroom and noticed how Anton's mood had changed. Mirth was etched on his face. She cried out, "Good gracious! You've changed. Aren't you sick any more?"

Anton jumped from the bench and, still guffawing, replied: "You bet! I had a...dream! No! I was in a long trance! The craziest I ever had in my life. In my mind, I was talking to a servant of God, no, he was addressing me. His name was Celestos, he was a prince who was the inventor of asbestos. He invited me to spend some time with him – listen to this – in purgatory. He assessed me as a being of median caliber and assured me that if I let him beat me on a daily basis, for awhile, and if I wash his ass, I will have a free access to Heaven.

Then I saw my parents who quarreled violently about the existence or non-existence of Heaven and Hell! And about me! What I saw and heard was a mixture of a truthful recollection of my early days – my parents often argued or bantered about religion, I remember that distinctly – and of my own dramatic transfiguration of it. When they speared each other, in my trance that is, they used language and gestures that were replicas of how you and I speak when we are involved in a controversy. We punch each other, then we laugh. They did just the same. We are the carbon copies of them. Or they are the carbon copies of us!"

He burst out laughing, then spurted out, "That contact with my parents, absurd as it was, made me feel better. Recharged my energy. Expelled my dizziness. You see the shape I am in? But I am still going to take my pill. Just in case...Henrietta, my love, don't look so bewildered. I am not ill anymore. I have the will to cope with it! No! To beat it! I have the will!"

He snatched the glass from Henrietta's hand, rushed to the night table, picked up the pill and swallowed it, gulping his drink. Then he exclaimed, pretending to be upset, "It was water! From the tap! I wanted soda water! Not this tasteless slop!"

Henrietta instantly responded in a similar manner. "There was no soda water. The bottle was empty. Which means you drank it. Last night! And you left the fridge door open! There's a hell of a mess. Anton, sometimes you are so inattentive to what you are doing. So thoughtless! It makes me angry. As you would say, I'd rather be on the moon. Where somebody takes care of me. I need some attention too. And to be free of stress. I am tired of this routine. Overwhelmed..."

Seeing how stunned he was by this pummelling she abruptly reversed her tune. "Oh, my love," she uttered, tears shining in her eyes, "I'm ruining your recovery. I am tense, that's all. When I saw you on the bathroom floor, a black hole opened in my heart. I am so scared that one day you might lose the will to stand up to your enemy. The one who drugs you and drags you down. Whoever it is. There's nothing I want more than to see you strong and happy. Ready to challenge whatever you want to challenge. Whatever lifts up your spirit. On your own terms. You have heard me say that before, so..."

She caught her breath and then went on, "I also want you to know that during the night when you were asleep I read the poem you wrote for me. It made me teary-eyed and happy. And I bow my head to your suggestion. I want love and peace, nothing else. I will do all I can to stop quarreling. I want it banned forever. Banned.

"I have also read the last few pages of your story. I was riveted by it, but there were a few gram..."

She stopped speaking, covering her mouth with her hand, frightened that what she was going to say would make Anton angry.

But Anton responded with equanimity. He gently removed her fingers from her lips and asked her to continue. And when Henrietta once again repeated that the ending of the piece was most moving but that it required some "grammatical changes," Anton said softly: "I bow to your suggestion. When you type it, please do what you consider right. I trust you implicitly. As I said to you many times, you are my grace. Without you..."

He lifted his hands in a gesture that indicated how empty his life would have been without Henrietta. Then pointing at her watery eyes, he continued, "For me, you are Princess Teary-iana. That's how my father would have called you. Or Queen Teasle-drizzle. If you like those names. If you don't, forget it. Please, don't sizzle. Don't sizzle."

He paused then his face brightened with a joyous smile. He said, "One more thing. What I am going to tell you now, might amuse you. So here it is. I was struck by a thought: perhaps I am not to be blamed for not shutting the door of the fridge! That it was instigated by, what's his name, Prince Celestos, the messenger of Deity who wanted to put us both to a test. For our own good. To make us rediscover how we feel about each other. To see clearly that love is all that matters. That, without it, there is nothing but silence, violence and darkness. The program set for human souls by some cruel, highwinded Satan. But, as we belong to each other, that rule does not apply to us. We should not be fearful of the days ahead. There is nothing but...warm weather," he smiled. "And lots of light. No thunderstorms. No blight."

They were looking at each other with nothing but the deepest affection. They embraced silently. The grip was tight and it lasted long.

When they let go of each other, they noticed it was past 7 a.m. and bright daylight was invading the bedroom. They opened the blinds and, for a moment, enjoyed the sunny and cloudy horizon, then put their robes on and decided to go down to the kitchen to have coffee and some kind of breakfast.

Henrietta preceded Anton. He walked first to the bathroom, peed, then seeing the badly soiled floor, went down on his knees and wiped it up as best as he could with a towel that he took from the laundry basket. When he finished, he was fatigued. He would have preferred to return to bed than handle the crappy day – these were the words that flickered in his mind – but he didn't want Henrietta to be aware of it.

'She is in an upbeat mood now and I am not going to spoil it,' he thought. 'She has suffered enough. I wonder how I would have behaved had it been she who was rocked by illness and depression? Would I have suffered it gladly?' He giggled internally, 'Or would I have been short-changing her? Treating her with impatience and diminishing compassion? Protecting myself, not her? In short, would I have been able to stand up to the task? Or, like an ox, would I have performed poorly? I don't know. But I am glad I am not put to that test. She is ok! So, Anton, be of help to her. And put your fatigue, your anxiety to rest. So breakfast it is! And ham and eggs, no, only eggs, soft boiled, and a chunk of bread will make me feel better. And yogurt mixed with jam! We'll talk and laugh! The kind of a jolt that we need badly!'

He washed his hands, dumped the filthy towel into the laundry basket and went down. Once in the kitchen he realized how much food had been wasted because he hadn't shut the fridge door. The kitchen counters were covered with containers, boxes filled with partly used jars, perishable goods demanding refrigeration; milk, yogurt, eggs, creamy cheese, spicy herrings, slices of ham, salmon, all the good things that a while ago would have tasted splendid, but now looked rotten and exuded an unpleasant, acidy smell.

Henrietta was concentrating on shoving it all into a black garbage bag and Anton uttered with self-contempt, "I have surely put a lot of good food to rot. I'm sorry for it. Very sorry. And I will punish myself for what I have done. For being a fool. Absent-minded bum!"

"Punish yourself? How?" Henrietta inquired with a smile.

"By rhyming! Of course! It will cost me money. Rot, what's the rhyming companion of that word? Trot! No! That applies only to elderly women! Not to greyhounds like me! Sot! There it is! It'll cost me forty dollars, so I am a klutzy sot!"

"I wish you were," Henrietta responded pretending to be serious. "As you have said in your poem, drinking would make our days less dark. So let's do it. A bottle of champagne for breakfast? Do you like the idea?"

"I love it," Anton exclaimed, clapping with his hands. "As Woody Allen would have said to his mate: Oh, you are so bright! Oh, Mia, Mia!"

They burst out laughing. Then Anton offered to get dressed quickly to go to the corner store to buy some food.

"I will buy muffins. And cheese and some fruit. Will that be alright? What about coffee. Do we need it, or..."

Henrietta, done with the clean-up, had made coffee and was on her way to the basement. She kissed him, cutting him off. Then said:

"No need. No need. There's a lot to eat in the small fridge downstairs. There's milk,bagels and muffins. And jars of jam. Some cheese and a few eggs. And lots of sparkly or not sparkly wine."

The basement larder was a holdover from the days when she and Anton entertained frequently and lavishly. Stocking it was a habit, she could not – would not – break.

She kissed him again, asked him to set the table and ran downstairs. While she was away, Anton muttering to himself, set out the mats, plates, champagne glasses, coffee cups, knives and forks on the kitchen table:

"Food-wise this breakfast it's going to be fun. Talk-wise, I don't know. What if she recalls what I said to her in the bedroom? That I was scared. Will she ask me, as intensely as usual, to elaborate? If she does, what do I say? Why did I tell her that I was scared in the first place? How inconsistent can I be? I made a promise to myself that I would protect her from the terror that she is a victim of, then, I increase it by revealing that I am ravaged by fear!

She assumes what makes me tremble has something to do with my expectancy of dying, but that's not true. Death is not what scares me. Just the opposite. I am curious about it and ready for that trip. What frightens me is the torment of waiting for the final blow. The undefined duration of it. And the suffering it imposes on those who I love, my wife and my kids. Their faces are already clouded with grief. That is what scares me! What if the pain they go through does some damage to them? Makes them ill?

It applies much more to Henrietta than to Adrian, Nina, Paul or Greg. Her blood pressure is high. Doesn't it shatter her life to see me disolve? Tear her to bits?"

His whispered contemplation was broken by Henrietta's return. She was carrying a tray of food. "No eggs, but dark bread, bagels, smoked salmon, boursin cheese, honey, orange marmalade, orange juice. I hope that's enough. Were you saying something to me when I was downstairs?" She smiled, "It sounded as if you mumbled..."

"No! No!" Anton responded quickly. "I wasn't addressing you. I muttered to myself that this breakfast is the grace of God! If I believed in Him! What better treat for an empty stomach than a warm, brown bagel smeared with cheese? I am going to cut mine into two halves and put it in the broiler! Your bagel, would you like me to put a knife to it too? I will gladly do it! I will..."

"Into the broiler?" Henrietta querried with a frown. "You mean the toaster! What's the matter with you? Why did you call it a broiler?"

Anton responded, "The right word escaped my mind. It's not the first time that that's happened! But it is most kind of you to put it back where it belongs," he knocked his temple with one of his fingers.

"Most kind. But where's the champagne? You forgot to bring it? Or is it gone?" He giggled, "Shall I fly to Spain to get it? Or to France?"

Henrietta stared at him for a moment then replied softly, "No. We have a few bottles. But I decided that it shouldn't be a part of our breakfast. After what you went through this morning, liquor might do you no good. Don't be upset. I don't want you to think that..."

Anton cut her off, "Don't be silly! I appreciate your concern! This is a quality I lack to quite a degree! I wish I were you! I wish you were me!"

Henrietta took his hand, made him sit down at the table and said, "Anton, please cool it. I haven't seen you so agitated for quite a while. I'm not certain you know what you're saying. And you are rhyming. Now stop. Are you perturbed by something I'm not aware of? The quarrel between your parents? Is that the problem? I am afraid to say it, but the way you act borders on insanity."

It took Anton a while to respond. He looked at Henrietta with dullness in his eyes. He rubbed his fingers, his body was in a slump, a troublesome pinch was squeezing his chest. And before he spoke to her he thought:

'Some weeks ago, at the same table, we had a similar encounter. When I try to hide my disgust for the kind of life I am tied to, I go bonkers. I freeze all rational thoughts and feelings that I believed would stay with me till the last day of my life. But this is not the case. I am not the man I once was. My mind fades. Instead of being aware of the sound of reason, I often hear only...the whistle of the wind. Or the crackle of the fire that is burning my body and my soul. I am the dumbest old man on the roll!'

This time he absorbed the fact that he was rhyming, smirked with self-contempt and in a low voice addressed Henrietta.

"I tried to keep your upbeat mood going. I overdid it. I must confess this to you, I was unaware that I was rhyming. Next time, please let me know right away that I am doing it. Force me to stop. I can't tell you how much I hate myself for speaking in that fashion. Instinctively, I feel this humbug is funny. Engrossing! But when sensibility takes over..."

He stopped, was silent for a few seconds, then offered another twist.

"What scares me is that I seem to have no inner power to put an end to it. It comes and goes. The way I recall my father's style of speaking. This is what keeps my head burning. Why had he so... raped my mind? Imposed on me his way of thinking and feeling? Why can't I manage to resist it? Was I so weak then? So ready to accept his dictum? Or am I using him as a shield of my own stupidity? I would like to know! Maybe that would help me..."

He didn't finish. With his head raised and his eyes focused on the door that led to the garden, he saw his mother.

She was standing beside her grave at the Jewish cemetery in Montreal and whispered to him: ' My son, my son, stop being bothered by this conundrum. Your father loved to lampoon. So, yes, you got it from him. He introduced you to it. It was terra nova for you, when you were a child. It was terra alta for him. Yes, he was your model. But in many more ways than one. He was a wonderful man but, sometimes, a tyrant. Like many people whose brain power is high. He fed you good and bad. So accept it. And suppress the whizz that is whirring through your head. It makes you sick. It sends you to bed. You don't need it. So quit it! Stop being so dour! '

The image was gone and Anton, brushing his eyes and his face with his hand, said slowly to Henrietta, "Once again, I have seen my mother. This time, she was defending my father. She was saying that my destiny was created by him. That he inbred me with weakness and with strength."

He paused, then questioned himself. "Why do I see them so often? It's not good for my health."

Henrietta held his trembling hand and uttered, "Anton, my love, your thoughts relating to your parents, their appearance, have nothing to do with how you were formed when you were little.

You see them because you believe that ... you will not be with us too long. And you seek an answer to a question, will you meet them? Will you share your afterlife with them? Or will you be alone? In darkness... Enough of this! Anton, if you need to rhyme, do it! And stop being troubled by it! I will not comment on it anymore. That door is shut! No more of my... smut!"

A soft tingle of laughter reverberated in the kitchen and it slightly changed the gray atmosphere.

Henrietta ruffled her husband's hair, a familiar gesture that indicated her appreciation of his improved mood, put two bagels into the toaster, filled their large cups with strong coffee and carried them to the table. She unwrapped plastic containers that held cheeses, smoked salmon – their smells were fresh and fragrant – and pushed them toward Anton. Then she took a radio from the cabinet above the counter and placed it on the table. She brought the hot bagels. While spreading the herb-filled cheese on his bagel, Anton turned on the radio. It was 8 a.m. The CBC news broadcast had just began. The spate of events was dismal as usual. Blood-soaked fighting was continuing between Serbs and Croatians, Tamil insurgents were slaughtered in Sri Lanka, the former Soviet Union was in shambles, Parizeunians in Quebec screamed for the dismantling of Canada, Palestinian terrorists killed a Jewish bus driver, Jewish settlers in Gaza gunned down a few Palestinians, Sikh separatists slaughtered Hindus on a train in Punjab, death from hunger was to be the Christmas present for the people of Ethiopia.

Listening to the announcements and biting his bagel, Anton began sinking into depression. His face showed it; his cheeks were pale, the blueness of his eyes was overtaken by a gray mist, and he stopped eating. Henrietta noticed what was happening and turned off the radio. She was also affected by the grimness of the news but was able to shake it off. Anton's perturbed, contemplative response was still etched on his face when the broadcast ended. At that moment, the telephone rang. She rushed to it, talked with the person on the other end for a short while, then hung up.

"It was Joanna," she told Anton. "She'll be here in fifteen minutes to pick me up. I'm going to take a shower, get dressed, then I'll be gone. When I get back, I'll type the last pages of your story. Call Dr. Wright's office. We could deliver it this afternoon if you want. Alright?"

She rushed to the staircase leading to the basement, then she stopped and once again faced Anton.

"I hope you're ok," she said. "If you are not, I won't go. You were upset by the news. So was I. But there's nothing we can do about it. So forget it! Have a shower, go to your desk and write. And stop fretting! Instead clean up the kitchen table! And wash the few dishes! Stop fretting!"

Reading from his face that he would be alright without her, she ran down to the bathroom, took a quick shower, put on her work clothes – blue jeans, white sweater, running shoes – and a few minutes later, was outside waiting for Joanna.

Before she left the house, she said, "After I'm gone, please lock the door. And if you need me, call. The phone number for Joanna's car is on my desk downstairs. I'll be back, the moment..."

A gray Subaru stopped in front of the house and two soft honks followed. It was Joanna. As usual, she was on time and in a hurry. Henrietta blew a kiss to Anton, went out, and a few moments later they were gone. Anton shut and locked the front door, watched the traffic on the street for a couple of minutes muttering to himself: "My wife, she's just incredible! So full of concern for unlucky people! So filled with passion! And vigour! I so much wish this kind of spirit would invade me. It would help me to keep going. And maybe it would relieve the pain that is rutledging my chest."

"Rutledging? What does it mean? I wanted to say, the pain that's racking or ruffling my chest. Why does such a non-existent expression enter my head? Anton, your brain is dead! You're mad! Mad!"

Now, hit by the rhyme, he burst out laughing then slapped his face harshly and marched to the kitchen to fulfill Henrietta's instructions. While clearing the table, he turned his mind to the news broadcast. He was troubled by it more than ever and decided it would be useful to prepare a note for Dr. Wright. It would capture his observations and his feelings.

'What I read in the Globe and in the Star each day increases my fear,' he thought. 'I should punctiliously describe it to him. And ask him how to deal with it.'

Once his kitchen job was done, he went to the bathroom, took a shower, shaved, returned to the bedroom, made the bed, put on his clothes, corduroy pants and a turtle neck sweater, then sat by his desk and carefully wrote a long memorandum. It read:

Dear Dr. Wright,

The story you want is in your hands. Whether and how will it change my life, time will tell. I have told you a lot about fears that haunt me. And hound me! That waiting for the last day is torture beyond belief. But another issue that I have not shared with you torments me as well. Here it is.

The world we live in is in a state of disintegration! The caring, careful handling on a political level of the condition of life of millions and millions of people across the globe is gone. If it ever existed. Brutal exploitation, oppression and starvation are the climaxes of the day.

The origin of those calamities? The unfettered capitalism that rules over and ruins our lives. This is the brutal fact!

Egotism is deeply embedded in our psyche. But greed for power, cupidity for wealth, do not improve the condition of human existence. On the contrary, they squeeze our track through life with the most fatal consistence. They suppress our humanity, bring our sensitivity to the lowest level, they make us deaf, blind to the horrendous suffering of billions of people, they deny the words of the Gospel and compel many to absorb, accept the woeing of the Devil!

During our days on earth we are entitled to search for comfort, for joyous careening, yes! But not by subjecting masses of people to falsehood, to pain by forcing them to believe that each human being possesses their inner resources to climb to the top and therefore he or she are totally responsible for their well-being!

This voodoo philosophy as broadly spread as it is – is empty brained Disgracefully untrue! Many, many people who inhabit the earth, no matter how hard they struggle, for reasons outside of their control, cannot stand on their feet. They are shattered by poverty, suffer hunger, lack the roots of education, are deprived of basic medical care; unfettered torment is the destiny of their lives. Their daily nightmarish fare. Sharing power equitably, sharing/dividing the abundance of wealth, caring for those who are impoverished, dispossessed – this should be the standard devotion of those who are free of that curse!

Fettered egomania, fettered expansion of riches, those should be the tenants of our existence. No more the rotten subsistence of the masses! No more the super luxurious grandeur of life of the bloody/lucky few! Those who are at the top of the hill must see the squalor, the despair of those who are under! To alter this calamity, they must consciously, willingly pay their dues!

Will it ever happen?

I don't know! But if it doesn't, the world we have known and loved will...vamouse! That's the bitter fact! Without an action on the global scale we are doomed to oblivion. The signs of it are clearly marked already. The name of it? The nationalistic binge! That is growing rapidly. Masterminded by power-hungry demagogues, the oncoming despots, it is the compost and combustion of the manipulation of the hungry, confused, desperate masses of the ordinary people! The underdogs! It is the rope that ties them together! The lubricant that smoothes the tension that hounds them!

The outcome?

Ethnic, racial, religious conflicts raise their ugly heads. They lead to local bloodshed, then they spread out, involve other localities, regions, states. The flare of exploding bombs, rockets, the gunning down of armed or unarmed people is the common occurrence in our world!

With the prevalence of this condition, I desperately fear for the future of my children. In spite of the horror I went through in my young days, I stayed alive, counting on, trusting that the lesson of the Second World War would squelch the malignant ethnic, racial stress. And that it would forever remove the use of slaughter, manpowered by the politicians and the military, as the model of resolving controversial problems that beleaguer our kind! But that's not the case! The world is aflame with hatred, anger, frustration! And the danger that a cataclysmic devastation brought about by some inane, insane monsters who, after gaining control over nuclear weapons, will be keen to teach their enemy a lesson – *is real!*

Most possibly I will be gone by then, followed by Henrietta. But our children, struggling to fit into this dilapidating cosmos, will be alive and, with millions of others, will be the target of that deluded act!

Their bodies will be torn apart by that blast. Yes, those thoughts beleaguer my mind and they devour me!

I am convinced that hatred, not mercy, is the caterpillar of mankind. And I dread that doom which hangs over the heads of the next generation. That we who preceded them and brought them to life, had no wisdom, no compulsion to put a stop to that evolution.

The guilty are those who are silent, and I was one of them!

Silence in matters of life and death equals complicity!

That's what destroys me now. The feeling of guilt that, in my life, I was so self-involved that I didn't pay enough attention to the serpent that was creeping into our world.

I wouldn't have been able to halt it's sleazy slide on my own, that's for sure, but at least the effort of screaming about its ascent would possibly have made me feel less responsible for its presence!

Yes, the awareness that our children are in danger makes me suffer badly. That's one of the reasons for my shaky state. I detest myself for blindly becoming a partner in that shameful collusion. For living the way I did. Thinking mostly of myself. Pursuing my career with vigour but rarely raising my voice to protect people in distress. I violated principles established by my father. In short, in my life, I was an egocentric bum! If I were to write a book about it, I would entitle it...

Triggered by those thoughts, a sudden recall from his young days rang with impeccable clarity in his mind. He was in a small theatre with his mother watching Ibsen's *An Enemy of the People*. It was the second amateur production that his father, who also played the main role of Dr. Stockmann, had directed. When the play ended and the applause abated, Emil Melenbaum still in his stage costume, addressed the audience. He said: "Brothers and sisters, I want to express our thanks for your warm reception of our work. And as Christmas and Chanukka are soon on our doorstep, as is the New Year, 1935, I would like to share a few thoughts with you.

We heard today that Adolf Hitler, Chancellor of the German Republic, delivered a speech announcing the introduction of new laws in his country. They are based on the following precepts:

> Thou shalt keep thy blood pure.
> Thou shalt have no social intercourse with the Jew.
> Blood and the desecration of the race are the original sins in this world and the end of humanity that surrenders to it.

This land which gave birth to poets, composers like Goethe, Schiller, Bach, Beethoven and Brahms, men who made everlasting imprints on the world, is now in a state of political and social disintegration. Hatred, not compassion, is the main factor of Nazi rule, equality among people is considered to be the most hideous offence in human existence. Many people whose names are like ours, Singers, Cohens, Tenenbaums, Melenbaums are killed or shoved into concentration camps, a place for punishment or re-education, established by the Aryan Master race.

The crime of those people? Their origin, their racial stamp. If you are a Semite, you are a human being who is crass, crude and mentally crippled! To make life on our planet more secure, better, that enemy of the Aryan people must be removed from the villages, from the cities into compounds surrounded by barbed wire, then killed by bullets or by fire.

In the country of its origin, this disease is spreading with vehement intensity and it is already blazing on our own territory! And unless the wicked Master is stopped by powers that have the power to disarrange his progress, to make him suffer mercilessly for what he is doing and for what he has done, his conquests will widen. The Master race will break all barriers, will cross all borders to annihilate the opponents, to stampede its supremacy, to turn the conquered countries into labor camps.

What we can do to reverse this trend?

We must all speak as loudly as we can about how inhuman, insane those ideas are!

We must oppose the suppression of rights of all people, whoever they are!

We must reject nationalistic, religious credo of supremacy!

We must ask for – demand – that the highest standard of equality will be a part and parcel of life of all people, not the privilege of a lucky few!

Brotherhood and sisterhood are the only basic ingredients of a peaceful existence on Earth!

So please stand up and show your approval for what I have just said.

Please call out: Equality! Equality! Equality! That's our sacred principle! Our first! Our first!"

The audience's reaction was divided. Some spectators, mostly Jews , stood and loudly followed Emil's plea. Others sat in their seats, silent. Some screamed offensive words and stormed out of the auditorium.

Anton was deeply moved by this memory, dug from his past. He was also astounded by the resounding echo of this recollection. And he muttered to himself:

"I have done just the same! I have talked about political issues endlessly. I have lectured my students on that subject. I have tried, in a similar way, to sharpen the political awareness of my colleagues on the campus. They didn't like it. They called me a pessimistic bore."

He chortled then toyed with that revelation.

'When I saw my father giving the speech, I was fourteen. What he said hit me hard but it didn't stay in my mind for too long. I was busy, studying Greek and Roman history, their languages, literature, flirting with girls, playing soccer and hockey...

I did not grasp well enough how insightful and deeply concerned he was about the oncoming years. And how much courage it required to deal with that subject, to dispute it with such condemnation. He had the intuitive awareness of what lay ahead of us once a racist, fascistic philosophy had become a coveted, widely accepted solution to the economic and social ills that beleaguered the impoverished masses of German people. The same applied to other countries like Italy. Or Spain.

The image of my father speaking to that crowd returned often when I fought with the Underground, belly down behind a barricade during the Warsaw Uprising, gunning down the advancing SS men and soldiers of the German Army.

I was saying to him, Dad, I wish you were beside me instead of lying somewhere, ripped apart by the Nazi Jew-hunters who murdered millions of our people, our family.

We would have heard each other's heartbeat while we were aiming our rifles at the German military. We would have felt a vengeful pride while pulling the triggers and seeing the oppressors collapse on the ground.

We would have sobbed together, watching many of our companions falling down dead, pierced by artillery shrapnel, grenades or machine gun bullets. Someone on our side would have been whimpering or crying out: God Almighty! Why do you allow all this to happen? Be merciful! Arrange a miracle that would allow us to win this battle! And survive!

My father would have said:

God Almighty? Who is that?

And I would have uttered:

My mother taught me that our brains are too feeble to know whether He really exists. And as long as we are not certain about it, one way or the other, we must not deny His heavenly presence. We must speak of Him or to Him, gently, softly. And, if one needs to, one should bend his or her head and kiss this invisible wrist!'

Hearing those words echoing in his mind, Anton turned toward the picture of his mother. As always, her loving smile brought a touch of pain into his heart. Then he focussed his eyes on the photographs of his sister and his father.

As usual, he was instantly struck by the quizzicality of their stare, but this time he was not bothered by it. He said to them: "It is such a joy to see your faces every day.
I may join you soon. It will be a most special event for me. The crescendo of my life. The biggest boom."

He sent them a kiss, then grabbed hold of the last page of his notes for Dr. Wright and scribbled one more paragraph on it.

It read:

I would like very much to converse with you about my father. When I described my relationship with him I called him pest. Or piss! That was crude, stupid and untrue. I think of him a lot recently. And have decided that he was an unusual man. Not a Prince of Darkness but the vanguard of the good part of my life. The maker of my bliss. Please examine me. And please wipe that ugly word, pest from your notes. Or piss!

Once he was done, Anton placed his notes in a file, then went down to the kitchen, drank a glass of orange juice and walked back to the bedroom. He was quite tired now and he decided that a little rest would do him good.

'Henrietta needs to see that I'm fine,' he thought. 'That I am not Master Deficient! No! Prince Anthony Passover! On his way to...'

He shook his head in disbelief, realizing what was rumbling in his brain, but it didn't make him angry or upset. He shrugged it off as a literary flop, took out a blanket and a pillow from the closet, removed his pants and sweater and lay down. Suddenly, he jumped up, jolted by a thought that exploded in his mind.

'Life on Earth, for elderly people like me, stands for Purgatory! The hoary things that we go through are what Prince Celestos called the preparatory steps to enter Heaven. Why no religious sage has thought that way before? Did it need a wizard like me to come up with this revelation? Anton, you have a mind that is sharp as hell! The Judaic folks would call you, Maven! Maven!'

He burst out laughing, recalling that Prince Celestos clamped that name on him. Then he returned to his previous position and a few minutes later was solidly asleep.

He was snoring loudly; Henrietta heard him the moment she entered the house. She was exhausted. The manager of the shelter had received a phone call from a clothing manufacturer who said that new garments, all in perfect condition, were his gift to the shelter. Henrietta and Joanna drove to the warehouse and loaded several plastic wrapped boxes into the car. They returned to the hostel and were quickly surrounded by excited residents who helped unload and unpack the treasure. For years, these women were the victims of ruthless physical and financial hardship; possessing a piece of new clothing was beyond their wildest expectation. Then the shock came. Some of the garments were in good shape but many were filthy or badly torn. The women were distraught. And Henrietta was furious.

Saying she would "give shit to the owner of the factory for his dishonesty and insults to battered women," she was prepared to return the unfit stuff. But the manager of the shelter stopped her. She said: "Some of it is not too good, that's true. But we need a lot of clothing. Most of that stuff can be repaired. We will do it and then we will give it away. So go home and relax. Next time will be better. Thank you for your help. Go. Go."

Henrietta left the agency and was soon home. She took off her coat, softly walked upstairs, stopped at the bedroom door, her eyes drawn to her husband. He was soundly asleep, though his breathing and snoring was heavy.

She went downstairs, had a light lunch in the kitchen, returned to the upper level of the house, slipped into Anton's study, closed the door, turned on the computer and, half an hour later, had finished typing his story. She wanted to print it but changed her mind. She decided the noise would wake him up .

When she turned off the Mac, she again tiptoed downstairs to the kitchen, made herself another cup of coffee and drinking it, she thought, 'There's so much going on outside of this house. The streets are filled with happy and unhappy people. But when I'm among them I feel so strongly that I am alive. Here I am overcome by anxiety. And sadness. The morbidity of each day under this roof is overbearing. It seeps into every nook and cranny of my existence. Will it ever change? Or is it what I must be prepared for, until...'

She wept softly, then finished her coffee, wiped the tears and went down to her working space to weave. She turned on the lamps and, sitting on the bench in front of the loom, she relaxed. 'Once I'm here, I feel better. No doubt about it. Work distracts me. In a good way. It makes me play with moral and esthetic values. Makes me forget, at least for awhile, what drains me. His pain.'

She concentrated on her weaving and stayed with it for hours; the sun and the daylight were gone and that the sky was now dark and sprinkled with glimmering stars.

Anton broke her concentration when he woke up in darkness, then walked down to the lower level of the house which was also very dim. Seeing the light gleaming in the basement, he tiptoed downstairs.

He stopped at the bottom of the stairs, quite close to where Henrietta was sitting. The space was blazing with light, but she was unaware of his presence. She was bent over the loom which was warped with blue, green and white mohair yarn, throwing the shuttle from right to left then from left to right. Her whole attention was fiercely focussed on what she was doing. Nothing else occupied her mind.

Anton, on his toes, sneaked behind her, softly put the palms of his hands on her shoulders and whispered, "I love you so much. I so much cherish your help. And your strength."

Henrietta exclaimed, "Ah!" Then placing the back of her head on his chest said gently, "You love me. And I love you. At our age, that's all that matters. Anything else is..."

Anton cut her off and spoke in the same fragile manner as before, "The avoidance of facing death. I have absorbed the lesson and I want you to be free of that suffering for as long as it is possible I don't want you to be the mirror of my pain. I will do whatever I can to help you to ban that... bane."

They laughed lightly, then stayed silent, frozen in the position that made them in touch with each other. They felt that what took place was the highest level of emotional linkage they had ever experienced.

A short while later, Henrietta resumed her weaving and Anton went back to the bedroom, put his clothes on and returned to his study. Once at his desk, he switched on the lamp, pulled out the few pages of the unfinished novel about Adam and, leafing through it, he wondered, 'If he were alive, would he be faced with problems like mine? Would he be struggling to keep on living? Or would he lack the mettle to go on battling the physical and mental disease? Would he kvetch non-stop about his poor, unjust condition? The way I do it? Kvetch and kvetch and kvetch! I must put a stop to it! Or otherwise I will call Prince Celestos and tell him:

Change my name! Whether you like it or not I am not Maven! Do call me...Blewit! Yes! Mr. Blew it! And don't argue about it! That's all there is to it!'

Hearing himself, Anton took two more Xenox pills and went to bed without telling Henrietta. An hour or so later, she left the basement to prepare supper. When she found he was not in the living room watching the TV set – "his daily fanaticism" was her phrase for this preoccupation – she went to his study. The light was on but Anton wasn't there, so she knew the had gone to bed. She peeked into their bedroom and noticed that the container of

Anton's pills was left open. She knew that he had taken another dose.

She was alarmed but managed to choke down the fear. 'As impetuous as he is, he must do what he wants. What he needs to do. I must help him. Give him courage. Make him convinced that he will beat this illness. That, hard as it is, he will get through it.'

She turned off the light in his study, stepped down to the kitchen, had supper then watched the television in the living room. At midnight, she went to bed. Anton was still soundly asleep.

And he had a dream.

He and Henrietta were standing on a high cliff by a turbulant lake. Holding hands, they were whispering to each other, "Before we fall down, shall we dance? Shall we dance?"

Then a beaver crawled out of the lake. He faced them and uttered: "It makes sense! It makes sense!"

CHAPTER EIGHT

Early the next day, the complete text of Anton's story was in his hands. Henrietta printed the final pages as soon as he woke up. She was already in her street clothes, prepared to go to the shelter. Seeing Anton on his way to the bathroom, she delayed her exit. She rushed to his study, set the printer in motion and, fifteen minutes later, handed him the remainder of his work. While he drank his coffee and ate a muffin, she also told him she would be back soon, then after lunch, she would be gone again doing shopping chores. She was full of energy, her face was brimming with smiles and she didn't make any reference to his silent retreat to his bed

The awareness of this evolution made him very happy. He observed that Henrietta was prepared to accept, without rancor, the unpredictability of his behavior and just because of this startling change, he too must improve the quality of his comportment.

At some point after she had left, Anton, as usual for this early hour of the day, was sitting behind his desk. He issued an order to himself: 'From now on, you will marginalize your suffering! You will coax yourself to believe that those echoes from your past will become the renaissance of your creativity. That those pictures and verbal punches that subvert your mind, as sordid as they often are, will serve as a theme for your novel. Or a play! Those shenanigans, convoluted as they are, carry a message that has mixed feelings to it. Some of it is mind-blowing, revolting! Some of it is mind-opening, exciting! And surely that's what intelligent readers want. Or bright-minded theatre goers! Fresh smells and poisonous vapors, well mixed together. That's the art form in demand and you have the material to put it in shape. So do it! Just do it!

And you will take care of your humdrum tasks that are handled by Henrietta. Like the delivery of the story to Dr. Wright. Henrietta doesn't need to drive you there. You go by subway!

Today! Anton, your thoughts reveal your stamina has returned. So put it to a good use! No rhyming! What you have come up with has nothing to do with muse! Or booze!'

He quickly decided that he would bring the stack of pages to Dr. Wright's office today, assuming that the doctor was back from his European trip and that this early delivery would give him enough time to go over the material before they were to meet. The appointment was scheduled for the following week.

Anton also made up his mind that he would not tell Henrietta what he was planning to do and that he would be on his way while she was doing the shopping at Loblaws.

'That purchase spree,' he thought gleefully. 'She will select bags of goodies. It will take a long while and will give me time to do my errand without her being aware of it.. I don't want her to be nervous about my journey. If she know about it, she would insist that she drive me to the Institute.. And that's what I want to avoid!'

He was stirred up by what reverberated in his mind and decided to get dressed. But instead of sliding into his usual grubby outfit – worn-out corduroy pants and a sweater – he mused, 'Once Henrietta is gone, I will sneak out and be back in before she returns! So every minute counts. Therefore I will choose what I want to wear now and put it on, anon! And I will be set up to go! Good thought, Prince Anton! No! Prince Solomon!'

He rushed to the bathroom, took a shower, marched jauntily to the closet in the bedroom where he kept his suits, took one of them off the rack and was ready to put it on, then hit by another thought, he nixed the idea.

He muttered to himself, "The moment Henrietta sees me so dressed up she will say to me: What's up? What's your jaunt? And if I pretend that I don't follow her query, she will persist in her brusque fashion: The nifty garb you are wearing tells the story! You're up to go somewhere or you're ready to receive somebody! So don't give me this charade! What are you up to? And your plan, it is horny or hoary?"

Amused by the biting comments he implanted on Henrietta, he chortled. Then for a few minutes, he circled the house cursing himself:

"What the fuck are you doing? You invent lines for you father, and now you pseudo imitate Henrietta! Your jibberish is insane! Get rid of this schlock! Put a vacuum cleaner to your brain!"

Once the tension subsided, he put on his daily garb, sat down again behind his desk and crunched a few raisin cookies which he kept in his study. Their sweetness often helped to regain his calm. Henrietta, aware of this effect, supplied them to him on a weekly basis.

While eating, he absently scribbled on a sheet of paper:

Lucky people, those who eat
Fallafel!
Lucky people, those who do not
Suffer!
Lucky people, those who sing
a song!
Lucky people, those who do no
wrong!
Lucky people, those who do not
lie!
Lucky people, those who do not
die!
Lucky people, those who go
abroad!
Lucky people, those who witness
God!
Lucky people, those who know
His name!
I don't. Which perhaps is a
shame!
But one of these days I will discover
the truth!
And if I do, I will do my best to send
a message to my family passing on
to them the precise information.
And if He or She exists,
I will tell them,
don't be like me!

Establish your trust in that dreamlike Power!
And be prepared that one day, at one
hour...

Anton stopped and went through the lines. He was jolted by the sensitivity of his poetic statement and amused by it. But more, he was perplexed by the fact that while he was composing it, he was utterly unaware of what he was putting down on paper.

'How is it possible,' he thought, 'that while I was writing this blurb, I didn't follow what it conveyed? Why was I so distant from it? Was I so concentrated on the verbal ploy that it obfuscated the inner meaning of those observations?

Or perhaps, it was a discreet hint from the Other World? A message that It and He exist? That it is Anton Melenbaum Thomas who is wrong! That he is a mortal ravaged by distrust! That's why he is ceaselessly stomping the soil of the earth, enveiled by heavy, blinding mist! And deafness inducing dust!'

Dismayed by this deadly musing but still short tempered, he decided to go for a walk.

'Once I am on the street, I will relinquish that garbage! I will cease thinking about me! That's my problem when I am alone! Anton, you better get drunk, swallowing the gulps of the city life that you will witness. In the cloister of your room you are a...'

He caught the disapproving stare of his father and sister emanating from the photographs on his desk and stopped fuming. He slipped the poem into the file of "odd texts" he kept at the bottom of a small, wooden box which sat beside the chair. He put on a leather jacket and was ready to go out when he caught sight of the material destined for Dr. Wright.

He was looking at the printed pages, the stack was high and, unexpectedly, he was hit by another mentally depressive sensation.

'One hundred pages! The text I prepared for him is too long! He is a busy man, he won't have the time to study it thoroughly. So he will only leaf through it! And if that happens, how would he be able to figure out the driblet-like items that possibly were the grains of my present condition? Each incident, big or small, each description of it, each phrase requires the most careful evaluation. So, if he only rushes through it, I will be no less indecipherable than I was when he examined me before! So I wasted my time working on my story! Unless...'

A fresh thought flashed in his mind. Stirred by it, Anton quickly plunked into his chair, pulled the 'novella' in front of him and started to go through it, carefully, page after page. He was searching for sections of his work that had a revelatory quality; he was going to bring them to the attention of his doctor, but more than that! He decided that he would make an attempt to convince the psychiatrist to allow him to read those pages aloud during the next session.

'My way of painting a picture from my life is not always easy to grasp. I often speak of it so mutely, as if my experience was a common one, not exceptional. Unique! But it isn't so! There is a lot of distinctiveness to my existential circuity. To my brutally imposed or sheepishly self-imposed fluctuation!. And to absorb it, define it with logical clarity is not that easy! But if I would read the important parts of what I wrote, expressed it simply yet allowed the emotional tinge to come through, it could reveal roots of my emotional disorder. As my father would have said: Who or what initiated it? And what compelled you to hoard it for so long? Who was your enforcer? Your hostile boarder?'

His eyes fell on the most painful passage of his story. He had fought with himself to avoid committing the terrifying memory to paper. He had buried it at the very bottom of his mind. 'There is no need to excavate it now. I cannot do it,' he told himself. Then he argued, 'But my story is incomplete – shot through with a hole – if I do not face it.' In the end, he had written it with tears in his eyes. Now, he was drawn to those paragraphs. They read:

Soon after we were enclosed in the ghetto, the Nazis started to "cleanse" that barbed-wired space of those who were not working. So with the help of our Christian friend, I and Hanka, my beloved sister, acquired a job. We were assigned by a German industrial company to collect used metal from the non-Jewish inhabitants of the city. In return, we were given a document stating that we were "wirtschaflich wichtig" – workwise valuable. With such an evaluation, we were not the targets of the S.S. police.

We would leave the ghetto early in the morning, walk the streets of Lwow and knock at the doors of the inhabitants. We would tell them what we were searching for, receive the broken cutlery and other objects, and pay for them with our own money. Then we would drop what we collected at the yard of those who employed us and who were speedily sending all that metalic garbage to the weapon-producing companies in Nazi Germany.

We would be on our feet for six hours and upon our return to the ghetto, we would eat our early supper and go to bed.

I and Hanna handled his labor for three months. Then, one day, an incident took place which tore my mind and heart apart.

It was a sunny afternoon. We were on the outskirts of the city, knocking on doors, when we were stopped by German S.S. men. They demanded to know why we "Jewish creeps" were in this area and what we were begging for. When we explained our task to them and showed them our cards, they laughed. They kicked me in the ass and ordered me to disappear. I walked away a bit then hid behind some trees. I watched as they pulled Hanka away and dragged her to a truck. I ran to my parent's house and told my father what had happened. He rushed to the Judenratt and informed the top people what had taken place. But they couldn't do a thing.

Hanka never returned to us. As we learned some time later, she was sent to the Bergen Belsen concentration camp where she died.

This tragic incident lives with me forever. Why was I to witness her kidnapping? Why was there nothing I could do to save her? Why did I survive and she had to die?

When Anton finished reading, he was overwhelmed by sadness but felt oddly lighter as if a terrible burden had been removed. He sat silent, staring into space for a few moments, then focused his thoughts. Within half an hour, he chose what he wanted to act out for Dr. Wright. He put all the print-outs into a briefcase and impatiently awaited Henrietta's return and her next errand to the supermarket which would allow him to make his trip downtown. Anton walked around the house for a short while, drank another cup of coffee to suppress his irritability – where is she? Why is she staying downtown for so long? He returned to his desk to make some notes relating to the novel he was writing. Suddenly, without warning, he was hit by a ferocious attack of vertigo. He experienced a strong, circular motion in his head, loud humming in his ears, sharply diminished vision and nausea. He got up from the chair, took one step forward, collapsed on the floor and threw up a bucketful of stomach garbage. He was completely incapacitated for half an hour. Then, feeling a touch better, he slowly shuffled to the bathroom, washed his face, dried it, then soaking the towel he shuffled back to his study. He got down on his knees and did his best to clean the carpet that was stained with vomit. Once he had completed this job and feeling very weak again, he crawled to the bedroom and climbed onto his bed. When some strength returned to his body, he tried to examine the puzzle of the terror that hit him.

The first inner question was : 'Should I call the doctor? This attack was vicious. During my illness, something of similar proportions rarely happened; maybe only three or four times!'

For a short while, the thought of calling Dr. Hopkins, his family physician, lingered in his mind but eventually he abandoned this notion.

"'What could he do?" he snickered. 'In past days, he didn't have a clue how to handle this ....atrocity! Meuniere's Disease is not life-threatening so we don't know much about it! Those were his words! A program of salt restriction, diuretic therapy and potassium supplements is advised. As well as a low-caffeine diet! That's all that he said! No advice on how to cope with the vehemence of the attacks! No medication to make them go away! This misery will pass, be assured. He told me to subdue my inner anger and stay quiet! When you experience an attack, remember it does not last forever! Only for a couple of hours! So supress your fury! Your emotional havoc only increases your pain! So....'

Anton now feeling a touch more relaxed, murmured to himself: "He was right about my emotional uprisings. Henrietta has the same thoughts. But it doesn't mean that Dr. Hopkins is bright! Doesn't the suffering I go through deserve some treatment? Till the end of my days, am I to be exposed and accept this rite?"

He giggled but his discomfort increased. There was again a visceral motion in his head, his stomach seemed bloated and suddenly he felt a nerve-racking disorder in the upper part of his body as if an edged drill was slowly piercing the bones close to his heart.

"Fuck!" he uttered softly. 'This rot... does it carry a message that what I go through now is what I am faced with at the end of my days? If this is so I want to go soon! I can't keep going like this any longer! I'd rather go to Hell than to stay on Earth! My daily life is a disaster! I dream, I crave for a hole in the ground and I'm carried to it in a hearse. Or better, I desire to be cremated. Yes! So that the members of my family do not feel it is their duty to visit my grave. They have enough troubles on their plates. So I will nix another one. Once I equal dust..." He took a deep breath, exhaled, then continued: "Why am I torn by such volcanic pain? Why am I deprived of the normal function of my brain? No matter how hard I try, I cannot focus on the most crucial events of my past. My past that goes way, way back but also on events that took place only a few days ago. A few days! I cannot write! I cannot capture the correct word when I am speaking or thinking! I am an old man whose vision and hearing are irreparably stained! In brief, I am the subject of a most maliciously imposed drain! And I ask myself: Am I a convict of a malady for which there is no cure! And why is it that the only help carrying words that I hear are: Stay strong! Relax! Endure! Endure! As if a human being had the power to stem the torment that tears his body apart! As if his brain and heart were the masters and the wicked serpent that crawls inside of him was a weakling! Or a toady! But what drills me the most is why, why am I given the taste of this rape for so long? My mother would have said: 'There's no answer to this question. But many people believe that the penal code of the Supreme Power....."

Shaken by those thoughts, he sat up and screamed: "Fuck! Fuck! I am again in the mood of the old days. And I am rhyming to boot! If that Super Power has such an impact on my life..."

His father's image appeared. He stood beside him and said: 'Son, don't be silly. Your illness has nothing to do with God. You are in a dangerous state due to some chemical mishmash in your body, squirted by some collisions in your cells. Or, to put it in other terms, you are captured by some bacterial creeps, created by nature that have invaded your organism. And they are the particles of your ruination. That's what life is all about. You are brave to die. So accept this rule and as your mother would have said, do not cry, do not cry! And do not hope that when you are gone you will be given a chance to approach God who sits on his throne. Such a sing-song of a religious magician is a sad joke! But if it helps you now to be strong do not sash out those thoughts! To believe in the existence of the Supreme Judge, this safety net....

You and all others are tied to it by your own volition!
What matters most it to have the stamina to stay alive
So make it happen! Whatever the price!'

The image of Emil Mellenbaum evaporated and Anton, his face still drawn to the corner of the room where he saw his father, was in a grip of terror. With tears in his eyes, he mumbled: "I have seen him again! Does this mean that he knows exactly how I feel? That I am fading? Or that he hears my whisper: Come here! Come here! I am on a fast downhill slide! What's next? I need a guide! I need a guide!"

The response to this query came from his mother. He saw her bending over him, wiping his sweating body with a soft cloth and saying with vigour : 'Mordant sadness is verbotten! You surely know that! So instead of shedding tears .... giggle! Have a happy grin on your face! To make that happen, put your hands on your rump and make it ....wiggle! Such a comedic ploy is fun-producing, life-saving and legal! So do your job right now! Do it fast! Your daily morbid tremor makes me unwell! If it goes on, and on I will follow your route. I will be a target of a sickly blast! Do you absorb what I am saying? Please answer and release, release this mind-blowing, numbing clasp!'

Rosa was gone but Anton instantly recalled an incident that happened when he was still a little boy. It involved his father and compelled his mother to come up with this romp. The Mellenbaum family was living in a small town in Poland – it was called Zydaczow – where Emil owned a pharmacy. One day, in the early fall after a long working day, Emil went for a walk in a nearby park. This was his daily routine. He did it to relax and to say goodbye to the sun, as he would explain the reason for his lonely walk to his children. When he sat down for a moment on a bench to smoke a cigarette – he was a heavy smoker – he was suddenly attacked by a drunken man who appeared from behind a tree, yelling: 'Get out of here you dirty Jew! Give me your wallet!' He was kicking Anton's father and hitting him with his fists, trying to rob him. But Emil did not give in. He fought back. The fight ended when a man appeared and the robber ran off. But Emil's left arm was broken in the struggle. He returned home assisted by the stranger who, as he later learned, was the local baker. Rosa took him to the hospital. He stayed there for a couple of days and, after his arm was put in order, returned home. He tried to expunge the incident from his mind. But he couldn't. The state of shock stayed with him. The emotional upheaval was induced not only by injury and the act of robbery but by their antisemitic viciousness. Though his arm was in order, he despaired constantly, reflecting on what had happened to him and on the centuries of long-suffering Jewish people who were torn to pieces not only by some Christian robbers but by wicked rulers of the civilized world who prayed to God for His blessing to rid us of the Jewish race! He was unable to subdue this inner tension and, one day, was confronted by Rosa who couldn't cope any longer. They argued with anger and tears then, when the emotional evolution subsided and the feeling of love that tied them, took over, Rosa, in a warm-hearted mood, came up with the poetic, comedic statement that Anton recalled. "When I heard it, I was a kid! Six or seven years old!" he murmured to himself. "I heard them argue! I saw them dance! Why is this incident so strongly embedded in my memory and so many others have flown away? No matter how hard I wanted them to stay!"

Feeling a sharp pain, he stretched out on his bed. He closed his eyes and hoped he would fall asleep but, when it didn't happen, he once again stumbled into the bathroom. He took out a container of sleeping pills, removed the lid and poured a batch of them into the palm of his hand. He shoved them into his mouth, drank a glass of water, then shuffled back to bed. The pain was excruciating. A few hours of sleep will do me good, he thought. Then he was hit by what he had done and exclaimed, "I have swallowed a cluster of sleeping pills. My mind went to sleep before I wanted it to! I will not crawl out of this bed ever again! But I am not really surprised. For a long time, I have been in the clutches of a wicked, viscous snake! So what do I do now? Call a doctor? Force myself to vomit or," he stopped breathing for a moment, "leave it as it is? Possibly my sleep will last forever. Am I ready to accept this choice?" After a brief pause, "I think I am. I will miss a lot. But the hardship I go through ... and the harshness of suffering I impose on those who love me .... So what's next? This is beyond my understanding. But I'd better say goodbye to my most beloved wife. And to my beloved children. I will write them a note. This will be the end of my work behind my desk. The final, final task before I take my rest."

Saying this, Anton stared at a large photograph of Henrietta that was framed and hanging on the wall and then at another photograph of her, surrounded by the children. He slowly got up from his bed and, more relaxed now, sauntered to his study. He sat at his desk, pulled out some sheets of paper, lifted a pen and wrote two long notes, one to Henrietta, the other to his offspring. This is what he scribbled:

My sweetest soul, my dearest Henrietta, I am gone to .... rest. As you were aware, I expected this would happen though I didn't talk about it. But I want you to know that I am comfortably snuggled in my nest! But I have a last request. Do not surrender to pain that is tied to my .... sleep! Dislodge the stress! Do not plunge into brain and heart-damaging distress! Enjoy for a long time your very fine skill of living! And keep on weaving all your happy segments of life. I postulate once again, yes, keep on weaving. And one more thing: Do not be abrasive to yourself! You are a most unusual person, almost saintly, that's for sure! I wish that all people of this world were like you. Then the barriers between them would vanish. They would have a peaceful, happy trip through life. No endless bickering, quarrels! No menace! Life as you know is a journey to death. So to cope with it, one needs nothing else but a long lasting caress! This is what you gave me! I thank you for that! And I love thee! Forever I love thee!

Signed by - Anton Mellenbaum - Anton Lubecki - Anton Thomas - your hubby! My new title is Prince of Darkness. Stony.....

That is what Anton said on paper to his wife. The note to his children was quite different. He wrote:

My lovely children, I am gone on a never-ending trip. I wish I could give you a description of it. But this is beyond the capability of my mind. So please accept my message and, once I am gone, be loving and kind to your Mum. As I said in my note to her, life is a journey to death. To cope with it, one needs nothing else but a life-long caress! For people of my age, life without loving care is like walking through a dark tunnel filled with ice. Each step is slippery. Lack of light makes all movements very shaky! One spreads both arms searching for the supporting wall. One thinks: any moment now I will fall....

But when loving care is a part of those days, the tunnel vanishes and the light burns brightly! One is walking on a ground shining with snow or on a field covered with green grass. One is holding the hand of a person one loves; one is comfortable. Happy, free of internal fuss! Your mum and I were like this and I often thought: How lucky I am! She and I sharing the view of the panorama of nature! Enjoying what we see, we smile to each other, jibber jabber and, when we are downtown, we look at streets, stores, go to movies, visit friends who also visit us! Nothing that we do together is mindless. Heartless! Or crass! It would be nice if, in general terms, our existence and that of all human beings was somewhat different. Less trouble-filled! Less stressful! More munificent! If people truly cared for each other then stress would not command our existence. We would maneuver our daily march without anxiety. Without fear. Without begging on our knees for assistance. Our journey through life is so brief. Wouldn't it be better if we navigated on less stormy waters to make it safe and happy? If we could clamp down our sorrows. Expunge our grief. We claim that individuality is the most unique human trait. And that we must protect this quality at all cost. But in my opinion, this view is imbecilic. Egocentricity is the main cause of the misery that so often tears us apart. No matter how we differ from each other. No matter that some of us are silly and others are smart. In basic terms we are all structured in the same fashion! We are all subjected to similar shocks! We all observe intently the daily motion of the clock! And for these reasons, we must stay together. Support each other! This is my advice to you, my warning, that when you reach my age – don't be alone! Share your final days with other people, with those who you love or respect. And who love or respect you. When you develop this trait, you will benefit from it. So start roping those ties, it is never too late!

Please, remember my vision. I am thinking of you all. Until I am ordered to pay my....toll!

That's all! Your father.

P.S. Please keep it in mind when I am gone, pay special attention to your Mum. She needs it badly. So share your free time with her. Do it often and gladly!

When he finished, he re-read both notes. Satisfied with what he had said, he put each of them into a properly addressed envelope and placed them at the very centre of his desk. 'Henrietta will spot them right away,' he thought. 'Oh, how I wish I knew what her reaction will be to what I scribbled to her!'

The rotating motion in his head and the hum in his ear, barely noticeable while he was writing, returned. Anton got up, ready to return to bed, but was struck by another thought. He pulled out a drawer of his cabinet where he kept his "precious documents" and took out a copy of a long article he had written and had been published by *Frontline Magazine*. The subject was the Uprising in the Warsaw Ghetto. He tore off a part of it and attached it to the envelope that contained the note to his children.

The document read:

Adolph Hitler is dead.

But his satanic gospel that Aryan men blessed by the SuperPower are destined to top/govern all other terrestrial human beings is still alive! And kicking! So is his outcry that Jewish people deserve to be despised and slaughtered! For our children to absorb happiness, to live in peace, those scumbag views must die! They must be expunged forever from our existence! Forbidden! Verbotten! And fast! Or the world our loved ones will inherit, doped by this racial crap and torn by ethnic strife, will not last! Yes, unless we learn quickly how to combat this despicable preaching, unless we make sure that those who inhabit our planet know and never forget how monstrous was the damage inflicted by the carriers of this insane dogma – the terra nostra will be exposed to a horrendous fire. Yes, that explosion is imminent! Yes, unless we remove the most poisonous gas from our brains and hearts – it is called SUPREMACY of one band of folk upon all others – the earth as we know it will vanish. Inevitably it will be ruined by man – *madmen* —powered to concoct a cosmic blast!

This horror-packed forecast, crazy as it may sound, due to my Holocaust experience, I am forced to trust. When hate is the motivating power of human life, earth-shaking disaster is a MUST!

For many short-sighted people, this cantankerous conclusion might seem dubious or outside of their concerns. Perhaps even beyond their grasp! Nonetheless the awareness of this impending calamity must be taken seriously by those who care! We must spread this message cogently, passionately on a global scale! We must treat it as a warning, a dreadful foreboding dominated by facts. Not as a grim yet fantastic, fictitious tale! As I said before, the happy future for our children is in jeopardy, to put it meekly. So with all the conviction we can muster, we must influence the inhabitants of our planet very quickly! If we want them to have a future! If we don't want the planet to be reduced into DUST! So we broadcast: racism is a game of gangsters! Of bloody fools! Love, tolerance, help fostering endeavours, those are our life and joyous pride-sustaining tools! We make sure this convenant clings tightly to the daily surface of our existence! WIN WE MUST! WE MUST NOT BECOME SLAVES OF XENOPHOBIC, MENDACIOUS LUST!

Looking at the article, Anton thought: 'I wish this subject was forever imbedded in their minds! Racial feuds are on the upswing. So they must rebel against it, one must be tied to the remembrance of the Holocaust! One must speak about it! Retain this link!'

He looked at the photographs of his father and his sister that were on his desk and, staring at their faces, he whispered to them: "Am I right? I am imposing on my children the horror and the pain that those memories bring about. To push them in that direction. Does it make sense? Am I silly? Or am I ..... bright?"

"Please answer. He stopped then uttered: There is such a quizzical expression on your faces. As if you can't comprehend what is rotating in my mind. You of all people should know! Your lives were shortened because of this racist glow. I was deprived of your presence because the counteraction to the preaching and wicked nobility of the Aryan Sage, his name was Hitler, was so empty-minded! So fuckingly slow! "

Shocked by the recollection of those horrible days and perplexed by the intensity and speed of his work – he had been at his desk for no more than twenty minutes – Anton stood up. He looked around the room that reflected the joyous part of his life then slowly went to the bedroom. While walking he thought: 'I have a loud hum in my ear. And a squeeze in my chest and in my stomach. But there's nothing new to that and I am not frightened by it. Does that mean those sleeping pills have not done me any harm? Have I really let them slip into my pharynx and glide into my esophagus,' he chortled. Or was this act a figment of my sickly imagination? To make me experience fear, I....'

By then he was in bed, stretched out, his head comfortably resting on a soft pillow. Closing his eyes, he whispered: "I am going to have a nice nap. And then...."

He heard his father's voice. He spoke gently : 'You will be going on your trip. No more flow of blood in your veins. No more terror in your brain. A quiet departure. Anton responded in a whisper: "Thank you, Dad. I am relieved. From now on I will be sane. Am I right? No more madness in my brain."

Those were the last thoughts and words that crossed Anton's mind. A few moments later, he was asleep. And soon afterwards, he stopped breathing.

Upon her return, Henrietta announced: "Hi, my beloved fellow! I'm back. I'm back!"

This was her usual loud message to Anton to make him aware that he was no longer alone and he most frequently responded: "I am glad you're in! But you were out for a hell of a long time! So come up and kiss me! This will invalidate your sin!" When silence answered her, Henrietta assumed Anton was asleep but, just to be sure, she climbed the stairs and entered the bedroom. She saw him comfortably stretched out on his bed, his eyes shut, his head turned up toward the ceiling. His arms across his chest.

'He's asleep,' Henrietta thought. 'But why can't I hear him breathing?' She stepped closer to his bed, touched his chest and then was struck by what had happened. "My love, you're gone! You're gone," she cried then gasped. "Maybe not!"

She lifted the upper part of his body and tried to resuscitate him by blowing into his mouth. But soon she realized he was really gone. She gently put him down, kissed his lips and, deeply shaken, walked away from him into his study to phone the children.

Passing by his desk, she noticed the envelope with her name on it, grabbed it and opened it, then read the note Anton had written. She was so moved by what he had written that she began to sob. A few moments later, composing herself, she returned to the bedroom, embraced Anton's body, then again walked into his workroom to phone their offspring.

She then saw the envelope addressed to the children. She wanted to open it, but suppressed this desire. 'It is his message to them,' she convinced herself, 'and it's their right to read it first. She sat down in his chair and dialed the phone numbers of their children. She didn't speak to any of them. Paul and Nina, both in Toronto, were out of their offices. Greg was away from Montreal working in Florida. Adrian was in New York but his voice mail informed the caller that, for the next few days, he was out of the city doing research.

Henrietta, her voice reflecting her grief, left messages for each of them, saying their father had passed away and she was in despair and alone. And that the feeling of loneliness would stay with her to the end of her life. "The depth of love that your father gave me and his non-wavering, thoughtful attention to my needs, was unmatched by anyone. As he would have said, the flag of my happy life is gone. From now on I will be in chains of sadness. Pain-filled and alone."

After she was done with those messages, she called Dr. Hopkins, informed him that Anton had died and asked if he would arrange an autopsy. She wanted to know the cause of his sudden departure. A short time later, an ambulance arrived and Anton's body was taken to Mt. Sinai Hospital. An autopsy was performed. It showed the cause of death was abrupt failure of the heart. Dr. Hopkins told Henrietta that Anton's discomfort prior to his death was mild. He had "departed swiftly." In his view, he was "lucky. He hadn't gone through a period of turbulence and misery because of pain."

Then Henrietta arranged Anton's cremation. This had been an agreement made years ago between them. Neither of them wanted to be buried and have a flag on a cemetery, Anton's phrase. They had stated in their wills that the surviving spouse had to arrange the cremation of whoever died first. This took place three days after Anton's death. His ashes were spread over the shore and water of Georgian Bay, close to their cottage.

This sacrificial act was done with the assistance of Adrian, Paul and Nina. They had rushed to be with her the moment they heard the message on their phones. When they arrived two days after Anton's death, they shared her grief and tried to comfort her.

They drank wine and offered each other succor. This was exactly what Henrietta badly needed. Without the mix of them and alcohol her emotional balance would have been non-existent.

At some point, she took them to Anton's study and gave them the envelope with their names on it. Adrian opened it and read the note aloud, softly. Anton's concern for them evoked tears and more drinks. This was the shape of their sojourn in Henrietta's house.

Now, they stood behind a huge rock facing the lake. A tall maple tree was nearby and, a few steps beside it, was their elegant white cottage. For a couple of minutes, they absorbed the magnificence of the landscape: the cloudless blue sky brightened by the gold rays of the sun, the dark blue, almost motionless expanse of water, the mountainous range on the opposite shore adorned by trees with their leaves red, yellow, dark brown or green. Some of the leaves were clinging to their branches while others, in a cluster or alone, were sliding, gliding through the air into the lake.

Henrietta, holding the casket with Anton's ashes, whispered to her companions: "My husband, your father, would have been moved by this view. He would have said: 'What you see is a sign of Nature's glory. It fades away but it comes back in a different shape. And it tells you: unravel my mystery if you so desire. But do not destroy me! Do not set me ablaze by the power of your conceit and the devastating growth of your tribal, industrial fire!"

A few seconds later she uttered, " His rhyming....it was part of his instinct for survival. It drew his mind away from the scary effect of his disease. I should have let him do it. Instead of scolding him for it.. I would have....made him feel at ease!"

After a few sobs she said: " Now, do your job. And be careful when you climb on the boulder." She pointed at the massive rock that was before them. "This is the one he used to sit on in the morning and watch the horizon. This is where he gathered his creative thoughts. He once said to me: This is where I would like to be buried. No! My ashes....to be spilled from this rock. So that what's left of me feeds the birds. Or helps some bushes grow.'"

Handing the casket to Adrian, she whispered to all of them: "Go, go."

Adrian was the first. He climbed carefully to the wide, flat top. Paul and Nina followed and, once the three of them stood on the rocky giant, Adrian took the lid off the container, turned it over, shook it, dropping some ashes at the edge of the sandy beach and into the water. Paul and Nina followed this ritual.

Then Adrian said:

"Dad, we did what you wanted. So rest in peace. And be sure that I regret that sometimes I defied you, boldly. It was due to my lack of brain power to grasp and grapple with the high quality of your good sense. I was too short-sighted, often disoriented. That is why I balked, obstinately refusing to accept your guidance. The value of your high level stance.

So, I repeat, you are in my heart and mind forever! Oh....," now tears were moistening his cheeks, "you were so ... decent. So clever...." He wiped his eyes and whispered to his brother, "It's your turn."

Paul lifted his head and said, "Dad, I thank you for ... bringing me to life. You shaped me, my mind and my heart. Your interventions in my silly stands improved my daily steps. And therefore," he began crying, "I so deeply regret that you ... collapsed." Weeping, he uttered to Nina: "Now you..."

She said: "Be well, my beloved Dad. Your body was turned into ashes. But your soul is alive and protects us. Yes, your soul lives within us. It is not dead."

When she had finished, they all turned their faces to Henrietta, who, with tears dripping from her eyes, said to them: "Thank you for your ... recitation. The words – the rhyming – were so much in Anton's fashion. He would have ...."

Adrian interrupted her: "Each of us was given a thought what to say. We wanted to ..."

Paul interjected: "Spread his ashes near the lake and would celebrate his death!"

Nina intervened with anger, "Celebrate his death? You celebrate life not death! You..."

Now Adrian upstaged both of them. He said calmly: "We talked to each other on the phone and decided how we would say goodbye to him. What we have said ..."

Paul again butted in: "Had the right tone! We replicated his mode of thinking and speaking!"

Henrietta smiled and shouted: "Enough of this jabber! Your verbal gymnastics are boring. He did it all the time. But instead of scolding him, I should have..."

Adrian and Paul didn't let her finish the sentence. They jumped off the boulder, ran towards her, embraced her. Soon afterwards, they climbed into the car, Paul at the wheel, and drove back to Toronto. Once there, they spent another few hours in Henrietta's house talking about trivialities of their daily lives and drinking several glasses of vodka and orange juice, Anton's favorite drink. Then, with sunset approaching, they told Henrietta they would be leaving soon. They hugged her and were about to leave when she stopped them at the front door. She asked them to wait for a few seconds and rushed to her workroom. She pulled out three sheets of paper from her filing cabinet . She handed the pages to them and said, " This is a note your father wrote to all of you. I discovered it in the drawer of his desk after...."

Adrian, Nina and Paul, perturbed by her stumbling way of speaking, stopped her saying almost in unison: "May we read it now? We're in a hurry!" Henrietta nodded and they quickly glanced at the printed text. It said:

My dear, sweet children. All of you, Greg, Adrian, Nina and Paul. I have been thinking of you whenever I thought that I am about to...depart. I know how tormented you will be once I am gone. You are thoughtful, tender, sensitive human beings and the love that ties us together will be the source of your pain.

Yes, Sensitivity is a blessing.
It is also a curse!
The emotional fire it provides,
the long lasting wounds it procures,
there's nothing else that is so
non-mundane! So turbulent! So
stained by pain!
Also there is nothing more
adverse!
When you receive bad news, you
often can't cope with it!
You are most often tormented by fear!
Clogged by despair!
And your self-protective

armour isn't there!
You visualize, smell
disaster!
And you can't tame
this inner voice!
Your struggle is in vain!
This is the penalty you pay
For possessing this
Gift of Nature
that makes you superior
to many, many people, but
that also forces you to
suffer more sharply than they do!
So no matter what, make
good use of this condition.
And do not diminish youself
by the squeeze of suffering!
To subdue this inner
calamity!
Keep working!
And Laughing!
And Laughing!

When they finished reading, they stared at Henrietta. She said softly: "As he would have said, 'I've gone down the drain. But without abhorrent suffering. Without torturous pain.'" She paused then opened the front door and whispered: "Go. Go."

That was the start of Henrietta's lonely existence. Anton visited her frequently; she saw his face and his naked body. Listened to his creed: "You're my Goddess! I love you so deeply! And forever! I will not abandon you! Never! Never!

She smiled sadly when those words rang in her ear but, from time to time, she was overridden by the broken link— the days that were gone. She sometimes thought: 'I wish I could erase the memory of my ties with Anton. What I see and hear tears me apart.' Then she reprimanded herself: 'Don't succumb to this falsehood! He knows that! That is why he comes to tease you! To make you stay alive! To make you breathe!'

With this in mind, she managed to cope with those dreams. She established fresh bonds with some of her old female friends, got involved with some worthwhile social activities. She kept going. As Anton would have said: "Her resilience to pain was a paradigm of her duress! She was a Goddess of Goodness! And a victorious warrior in the battle with stress!" But forever shaken by Anton's departure, nontheless. By the loathsome silence that lingered in her home after his death.

This
is
the end
of
the story of
The Battered Man
A reflective compendium
of his Holocaust past.
And a MONUMENT to all
those who were not
chosen to last!